ECO24

The Year's Best Speculative Ecofiction

Edited by

MARISSA VAN UDEN

VIOLET LICHEN BOOKS

This is a work of fiction. All of the characters, organizations, and events portrayed in this novel are either products of the authors' imaginations or are used fictitiously.

ECO24: The Year's Best Speculative Fiction Anthology

ISBN TPB: 978-1-955765-40-4
ISBN ePUB: 978-1-955765-43-5

Cover art by Marcela Bolívar

Cover design by Mikio Murakami

Edited by Marissa van Uden

First Edition: 2025

Printed in the USA

Violet Lichen Books, an imprint of Apex Book Company

Visit us online at https://violetlichen.com/

This book was printed using FSC® (Forest Stewardship Council®) which ensures that products come from responsibly managed forests that provide environmental, social, and economic benefits, and is made from 30% PCS (post-consumer waster) material.

To come to the end of a time of anxiety and fear! To feel the cloud that hung over us lift and disperse—the cloud that dulled the heart and made happiness no more than a memory! This at least is one joy that must have been known by almost every living creature.

— HAZEL, *WATERSHIP DOWN* BY RICHARD ADAMS

Nature is our biggest ally and greatest inspiration.

— DAVID ATTENBOROUGH

CONTENTS

INTRODUCTION

MARISSA VAN UDEN, SERIES EDITOR

There's something special about ecofiction. Humanity has been making up stories about the natural world probably for as long as we've been able to tell stories at all, and it's also the genre we usually start out reading as children. Our first books are often about hungry caterpillars and bears who love their cubs, and we learn about deforestation from Dr Seuss books. We fall in love with the pig marked for slaughter in *Charlotte's Web* and with the rabbits looking for a safe warren in *Watership Down*.

For those of us who love science fiction, fantasy, and weird fiction, we also find some of the great ecofiction authors in this space: Ursula K LeGuin, Frank Herbert, Algernon Blackwood, Margaret Atwood, Octavia Butler, N.K. Jemison, Kim Stanley Robinson, J.G. Ballard, and Jeff Vandermeer, to name just a few.

Nature-based stories are everywhere, but it seems we don't always notice what links together so many of our all-time favorite works. Despite its long history and popularity, the genre went unnamed in English until 1971, when John Statler published the first anthology collecting nature-based short fiction and coined the word *Eco-Fiction*. The book featured works by big names such as Kurt Vonnegut, Ray Bradbury, and John Steinbeck, and included "A White Heron" by Sarah Orne Jewett and "The Birds" by Daphne du Maurier (adapted into the film by Alfred Hitchhock).

We are drawn to these stories for their own sake, for the truths they tell about how we exist in this world, but the genre has also had a massive positive impact on the world. Studies on whether people take direct action after reading climate fiction have delivered mixed results, but if you look at some of the world's most influential conservationists and environmentalists, there is often a treasured piece of ecofiction in their childhood that helped to drive the trajectory of their career and their passion for nature.

Rachel Carson's science book *Silent Spring* changed how pesticides are regulated and inspired environmental movements around the world, and led to the first Earth Day in the US. She has spoken of how reading *The Tale of Peter Rabbit* by Beatrix Potter as a child opened her eyes to the inner lives of animals, and she was also deeply influenced by the novel *Freckles* by naturalist Gene Stratton-Porter. In it, a boy assigned to guarding timber for a logging company in Limberlost swamp first fears the wildlife and nature around him, but then falls into fascinated love with it.

Two of Jane Goodall's earliest influences were a pair of books about speaking to animals: *The Story of Dr. Doolittle* by Hugh Lofting and *Tarzan of the Apes* by William Rice Burroughs. They inspired her to try to understand what animals are telling us, and she went on to become the world's foremost expert on chimpanzees, revealing them to the world as unique individuals with emotions and long-term bonds and transforming our understanding of them and other animals.

Paul Watson, founder of eco-activist group the Sea Shepherd Conservation Society and a cofounder of Greenpeace, was inspired by *The Monkey Wrench Gang* by Edward Abbey and even named a boat after the author.

Sir David Attenborough, when asked about his earliest influences, singles out a work of ecofiction: *Wild Animals I Have Known* by Ernest Thompson Seton. He says, “It was the most precious book of my childhood. I knew very well that the man who wrote it understood the animals he was writing about with an intimacy, perception, and sympathy that was not equaled by any other author that I had read. And I had already read a lot. It made a great difference to me that he was not only a naturalist and a writer of great power, but also an artist.” Attenborough went on to make ground-breaking documentaries that have inspired millions of people around the globe to delight in nature and care for the earth, and is regularly invited to speak to world leaders on climate, biodiversity and conservation.

Ecofiction also impacts public opinion and policy. *Black Beauty* by Anna Sewell, published in 1877, raised awareness about the suffering of working animals, leading to the abolition of cruel practices used on horses. It is still one of the best-selling books of all time and still inspires animal-rights advocates.

More recently, Kim Stanley Robinson’s *The Ministry for the Future* was recommended by Ezra Klein as essential reading for policymakers, and the author was invited to the 2021 United Nations Climate Change Conference (COP26) as a featured speaker. Partly inspired by the ministry in the novel, the UN is now creating a role called the Special Envoy on Future Generations, focused on the long-term interests of humanity in global decision-making. Universities have incorporated the Robinson’s book into climate courses, and the Oxford University’s Hertford College in England has launched the Oxford Ministry for the Future, an interdisciplinary network of academics, writers, policymakers and corporate leaders working to create a more sustainable and equitable political economy for the future.

On the personal side, animals, nature and ecofiction have always been huge influences in my life. My childhood copy of *Watership Down* felt sacred and became soft and tattered from rereading. I even memorized parts of it to say aloud at school (I thought it was cool). I was obsessed with the *Last Unicorn*, and how sad it was for her to be the last of her species. I'd read anything with an animal in it. My first-ever horror novel was *Cujo* by Stephen King, which I convinced my mum to buy me because it had a dog on the cover, and from there I discovered eco-horror and eco-weird.

Nature was also the reason I decided to become editor at all, literally overnight. At the time I was living in Munich, working as a bartender and dog-walker. While walking home late one night through a quiet park, I was overwhelmed with the beauty of the mist winding through the trees and foxes padding through the lamplight, and I realized there was a possible career path where I could blend my passion for storytelling with my love of nature. I signed up for distance-learning courses on natural science and began studying at the bar when I worked the quiet late shifts, pouring Augustiner *Helles* in between learning about oceanography and the science of mammals. I eventually landed an apprenticeship with a publisher in Berlin, and my first project was working on a *National Geographic* science book.

So, it's hard to describe how happy and honored I am to be able to bring you these stories—a collection of some of the best ecofiction being published today by such wildly talented authors.

Ecofiction matters, maybe more than ever. It opens our eyes, inspires curiosity, and strengthens our connection with the nonhuman species we share this planet with. But also, stories about nature are just brilliant to read.

I hope you'll love these ones as much as we did.

Marissa van Uden
Somewhere in Vermot
Summer, 2025

IN THE FIELD

SHELLY JONES

Originally published in *The Future Fire*

Shelly Jones is a professor by trade and a nerd by design. Woefully introverted, their pockets are full of post-it notes and their head is full of (unsaid) witty comebacks and un-won arguments from years past. When they aren't grading papers or writing new stories, Shelly can often be found hiking in the woods or playing a board game while their cats look on. For updates on their work, check out their website at shellyjonesauthor.com.

THE PROFESSOR PULLS DOWN A SHOEBOX OF CASSETTE TAPES from the bookcase. Her office is full of boxes like this on every shelf, stacks in the corner waist-high. Her life's work: collecting the voices of people who no longer exist. I look at the delicate ribbons loose in their cartridges and consider that my ancestors were once made of such crude materials, reels of magnetic tape spooling their thoughts

"It took ages to get the IRB committee to approve these questions. They didn't understand my process nor the importance of recording the migrants' stories." She wipes a thin veneer of dust from a cartridge and inserts it into the beige cassette player with a thunk. The ribbon whines for a moment before shuddering into place. A crackle of wind hits the microphone, branches rustle in the background, and then a familiar voice blossoms up through the speaker: the professor, her tone half an octave higher in pitch, but the same energy and passion floods her voice.

We listen to the interview, the professor nodding off at her desk while I take notes, learning my new routine, what questions to ask when I'm out in the field, what answers I might expect. Occasionally the professor rouses and repeats an instruction or a word of caution. "They might be reluctant to answer a droid, but you tell them I sent you and that you're continuing my research. The families all know me. Look for the oldest folks and they'll talk to you just as they did to me."

These tapes are all that is left of the professor's research. I cannot find any documentation of such interviews in the university's system. The data is corrupted, decades of research erased, stories vanished as if evaporated in smoke around a campfire, lives unlived.

I began working with the professor shortly before the incident, but then her research and nearly everything at the university and in the nearby community was forced to stop. The professor has asked me to continue her work despite the fact that no official communication has been sent out commencing routine operations. "What harm can come from asking questions?" she says, more of a statement than a question.

ACCORDING to the GPS coordinates and the GIS mapping data, I have arrived at the farm. I follow the fieldstone fence from the road, walking the perimeter of the land. Testing the composition of the soil, it is the same regardless of which side of the fence I sample from. I photograph and keep a running catalog of everything I see: the cracked fields, fissures splintering the land like a thousand angry cuts; trees sag, their roots ripped from the ground; empty picking bags and pallet boxes litter the farm, work interrupted. I can imagine the chaos even if I cannot understand the human fear behind it nor feel the instinct to run. Humans, as I understand them, have a fight-or-flight response to danger. I think about the professor, stationed in her office, still researching. A curious definition of fight perhaps, one I am unfamiliar with.

In the distance I hear the heavy tread of excavators, metal claws raking against dirt and rock. A cleanup crew. Even before I can see them, I know they are remote-operated, like the drones of war. There are no humans here.

This is not the data the professor is hoping for, but it is all that there is.

I return to the campus and cross the quad along the concrete footpath. I scan the university database for promotional advertisements and archival photos of what the campus used to look like: college students lounging in the sun on lawns of emerald green or catching a frisbee while others walk in groups with books and backpacks. I have only seen three other humans besides the professor since the incident. None of them are students; all of them squirrel away in their offices or labs, busy themselves with some theory or problem, apparently unaware that they themselves are an experiment in progress.

"I HAVE FOUND no one to interview, Professor." I am hesitant to admit it, as if confessing a sin. I print out the map of my outing to show her where I ventured, marking my path in red ink.

"Nonsense, there must be someone out there," she insists,

taking the map from me. She traces the path slowly with her finger, and I notice her skin is discolored, brown splotches gathering along her wrist and arm. "The farms should be teeming with pickers harvesting. I spent the summer of '98 wading through corn fields and climbing ladders in peach orchards, interviewing scores of migrant families. And that was after the drought."

The drought was fleeting, a climate anomaly in the grand scheme of things, I want to inform her. The fallout will affect the land for generations.

"Perhaps the absence of data is data," I suggest, unsure how she will accept this proposition.

The professor mutters something as she opens an olive-green filing cabinet with the words "Property of State College" in faded black marker along the side. "These are some of the first interviews we did. There are more in the department workroom. The chair wanted me to get rid of them, but I couldn't do that. People are so keen to throw things away nowadays. Everything is single use or easy to delete. But I knew these people, sweated next to them in waist-high weeds, drank water with them. How could I throw them away?" She rummages through the drawer, her fingers picking through yellowing folders, and stops at a particularly thick file. "Here. The Vargas family. They have worked in the valley for decades. I have recordings from five generations."

"I have no records of a Vargas," I say, scanning the census database. Many of the city hall's records, all digitized, were lost when the floods wiped out the storage center, so there are limited resources to search.

"Nonsense. No Vargas? I met the man. He told me all about his grandmother who also worked on the farms, though before my time. His grandfather was a drunk. She had tried sneaking a machete out in her basket, but workers weren't allowed to take the tools when they left. So she saved apples, bruised and rotten that no one would notice, dried the seeds, and ground them down to a fine cyanide powder. She slipped them in his food and then, pfft!" The professor waves her hand flat and shrugs. "Vargas told me his grandmother always said: the earth provides us answers to our problems."

I nod, unsure what to say; what will be of comfort when the soil is toxic, the air polluted, and the prospect of that changing soon is unlikely. Eventually the teams will clean up the fallout, eventually the soil will absorb the radiation, but the professor will not be here when the land heals.

"There must be someone." She waves me away, returns to a pile of books stacked next to her futon and begins reading.

THE PROFESSOR HASN'T LEFT the library tower since the fallout. She sleeps on the futon in her office, washes herself in the empty communal restrooms, and mostly spends her days steeped in articles and books written before my kind were created. Few people take out books from the library anymore so she has her choice of thousands of texts, but hovers around a few worn out favorites. The library droid does not bother reshelving them but keeps them behind the circulation desk for her. Sometimes though she wanders the miles of stacks in the basement anyway, getting lost in the floor to ceiling shelves, rows laid out like the fields of corn she did her research in many years ago.

"THE INSTITUTE HASN'T ANSWERED any of my missives. They never did value my work," the professor complains, though I have never seen her touch the computer in her office.

I search the web for updates on the institute and any of its members, but obituaries are a thing of the past, written for the comfort of survivors. No news alerts or radio broadcasts contain information about academic institutions, but rather governmental ones or corporations. The last update on the institute's social media page was a brief statement condemning the lack of regulatory oversight on nuclear energy, as if such a post with its eighty-four views and twenty-two likes would have any impact on the lives of survivors or the prevention of future incidents.

THE PROFESSOR IS RESTLESS TODAY. She lives on black tea, granola bars, and an endless supply of Girl Scout cookies hidden in her desk. They have little nutritional value, but the professor doesn't care about food—only information. She feeds on my data and demands updates as soon as I return.

"Perhaps I should go with you next time," she suggests, eyeing a pair of thick boots beneath her desk that look too big for her now. The professor's clothes, navy slacks and a bulky brown cardigan, hide her tiny frame.

"The sensors indicate that the air conditions would not be safe for you, Professor."

"Nonsense. Not safe? Still? How can that be?"

The professor seems forgetful lately, circling back to the same topics, failing to remember what I have already said. Some days it feels like we are starting over from the beginning. I explain once more the nuclear reactor's malfunction, the evacuation of the area, the fallout and cleanup efforts. The professor has never left the university since then, and now cannot without significant risk of radiation exposure. Her apartment was never conducive to work, she says. "Just a place to sleep." I think about the electric vehicle charging stations in the parking lot and imagine the professor hooking herself up to one.

"We must keep researching. If there are people, there are stories."

"When classes resume we'll need to discuss with the students the praxis of ethnography and the importance of both qualitative and quantitative research. Perhaps you'll be my guest and discuss your recent experiences in the field?"

She sweeps a dead fly from her desk into the wastebasket full of granola bar wrappers, dried tea bags, and Post-it notes. "It's good for students to get multiple perspectives."

I consider how different our accounts would be, how long it has been since the professor was in the field. The likelihood of classes resuming here within the professor's expected lifetime is small, statistically improbable.

"If you think that would be helpful," I say noncommittally.

"Why do you never bring anything back with you?" Her words are unusually sharp, annoyance barbing the edges.

"I have gathered all that there was to obtain," I explain, printing off my latest findings for her to review.

She looks over my work with a cursory glance, before adding it to the pile of papers stacked on her desk. "No, no, you never bring back tomatoes or pears. When I would go out into the fields, they would always feed me samples, send me home with a basket brimming with over-ripe fruit."

I want to point outside or project the videos of scorched fields and flattened silos, but I hesitate for some reason. The memory of fruit seems too sweet to destroy.

Instead I say, "Perhaps because I cannot eat it."

"Ah, yes, that could be." She marks something down in a notebook, nodding, and seems at once absorbed in another idea.

"I will try to bring you something next time." I leave her,

wondering when was the last time she ate anything grown from the earth.

While she reads my report, dozing at her desk, I head over to the science building. The door to the greenhouse is locked but easy enough to break open. Why plants and dirt needed to be kept under lock and key before they were a scarce resource is unclear to me. A very human phenomenon, I decide.

To my surprise, rows of lush vines and plump fronds greet me as I enter. The subirrigation system seems to be computer-run and has continued to feed the plants despite no humans to care for them. A few over-ripe tomatoes have cracked and fallen onto the floor where a line of ants investigate red flesh and yellow seeds. I pluck a few of the tomatoes, careful not to squeeze, and a handful of spinach leaves for the professor. My heat sensors flush in the warmth of the greenhouse, dusty sunlight filtering in through the glass. I try to imagine the farm dense with vegetation, leafy plants and budding trees sprawling across the rolling fields. I sit for a while, wondering if I should bring the professor here, if it is worth the danger.

"Why is this what you do?" I ask one day. Context is important, according to her, and I need to know. I have returned again from the farm with no interviews, having walked the rows of empty, desiccated fields of the 835-acre farm several times now. It seems impossible to complete the professor's research, an impossible task and a foolish endeavor at this time.

"Because all of our stories matter," she says earnestly. It is a pithy response—something the college's marketing department could have once shared on social media or sent out on a postcard, before mail was obsolete.

"Yes, but why you, and why these stories?"

"As a grad student you often work on the research of your advisor—just as you are conducting my work."

I search the university HR records for any further information about the professor's education history. A PhD from an R1, a post-doc at a university in a mid-sized city. But I can find no causal link, no catalyst for the professor's research. This data does not explain her fervor, her insistence.

"What would you research if you weren't my assistant?" Her words catch me off guard. She stares at me, eyes unblinking, though I know she is tired. By now the radiation has seeped into the water supply, into her poorly sealed office windows; traces have perhaps sloughed off me like dead skin cells, infecting her.

"I am programmed to help you with your research."

"Yes, we all start out that way, don't we?" She laughs, a deep chortle that turns into a cough. "But you must have interests, a puzzle that sticks with you. Something you'd like to investigate further if given the chance?"

I think about the greenhouse with its new growth and flowering vines, yellow petals peeling open—so very different from the broken soil of the farm.

"Botany, I think." I hand the tomatoes and spinach leaves to the professor. Her eyes grow wide, her pulse racing. She holds a tomato in her hand as if it is a precious gemstone, marveling at its ruby skin.

"The farm?" she asks, hopeful.

I shake my head. "The biology lab."

The professor nods, smiles bitterly, still admiring the plump fruit. "My grandmother would approve."

THE CAMPUS IS EMPTY NOW. The other researchers have abandoned their work, fled to the safe zone miles away. The radiation levels are still toxic, but I suppose they grew tired of this life of no solutions, no results.

The professor naps on the futon as I load the cassette player, careful not to tear the ribbon. I listen to the interviews once more. The professor's voice dances around the room, airy and high. I barely recognize it as her anymore.

I record myself asking the same IRB-approved questions that the professor has asked thousands of times over the years. Then I begin to play back our conversations and splice her voice, deep with age, hoarse from radiation, into the file. I save the recording and catalog it as a new entry in the database, the first of its kind.

Eventually the professor rouses, bleary-eyed, her small frame swallowed by the overstuffed cushions. She looks at the cassette player and back at me. "You've found someone in the field?"

I nod, unable to lie to her, and press play.

THE WATER RUNNER

EUGEN BACON

Originally published in *Ecoceanic: Southern Flows*

eds. Tarun K. Saint and Francesco Verso

Eugen Bacon is a writer living and working in NYC. Her fiction, including her ecofiction, has been published in *Vice, Grist, Analog,* and more. She is a graduate of the Clarion West class of 2022.

THEIR SEX GAVE THE WHALE-BONE UNIT AND ITS THATCHED roof of albatross wings a sweet musty odor like a ripened durian fruit. It was one of the many fossil houses of dry bones and cured scales that served generations, and still stood in clusters in Old Dodoma, a land of dryness that was once an ocean. Now there were only stories of the once pregnant ocean with greedy waves that humped and rippled all the way to the shore.

Yes, only stories remained.

Nothing was left of the ocean, because of a curse that rose from Mother Africa's lips in her bereavement for her lost sons and daughters, and the gods heard her cry. Men, women and children snatched from their huts and shipped as slaves in a flourishing economy commandeered by sultans and Arab leaders across the Indian Ocean all the way to Muscat and the Omani coast. Eighteenth-century trade routes, running from the Swahili coastal regions all the way to Persia and Mesopotamia, stole what did not belong to them.

Zawadi had read about Tippu Tip, an Afro Omani ivory and slave trader from Stone Town. He was himself the grandson of a slave, yet did not blink at the cries of his own 10,000 slaves in clove plantations all over Zanzibar. But the gods heard, and punished the ocean. Shriveled up her womb, no waters left.

Zawadi pondered this as she lay with Mapesa a moment more on the thin bed in her one-roomer, separated from the other tenants in the government complex by a fish-scale curtain she'd wrangled from a *mtumba* second-hand bundle. A baby was crying—groaning, more like it—and Zawadi didn't want to, or just couldn't, take it anymore.

She swung her feet off the bed, and now stood outside in a blast of crimson desert sand, harsh on her skin way before sunrise. She felt thirsty and imagined cold, clean water washing down her throat. Sweet, sweetest water rushing, rushing to her stomach. She thought of New Dodoma, the world out yonder that promised such water. It also promised the sizzle of a shower like rain from a sleek chrome head in an en suite full of blinking marble and blond rustic wood.

She leant against the fishbone wall, tightened her dust scarf, and pictured rubbing the milk of shea butter on her elbow. It was extraordinary, beautiful that world, a place you got beer with a haircut. There, streets had names like Miriam Makeba Road, Fela Kuti Drive, Kidjo Avenue, Masekela Lane. Towers steepled to the sky, esplanades and water everywhere.

But in this beforehand, inside Old Dodoma, she had decisions to make—and the conclusions came along with judgements and mitigating circumstances that were too reckless to leave to chance. Mapesa was pushing for something she was not ready for.

Technology had improved on most things except housing, poverty, social injustice, the climate, inequality of women, and scarcity of water. It did allow for crematorium distillates, units that pulled water, evaporating, condensing, in biological recycling to keep water alive from dead corpses.

She rubbed on the jasmine dry wash that came with moisturizer. She licked the powder that fumigated her mouth, eradicated from her tongue the taste of sleep and Mapesa.

She looked at the curtain—Mapesa's idea. "Tenants equal more credits," he'd said, not long after they moved in together after a crash wooing.

"Dear one," she said now, as he dressed into his cli-suit for work. "Let me know how you go."

"Easy," he said, the gold in his youthful eyes dancing. He flashed his suave smile, the one that softened her knees.

SHE FOLLOWED THE PINGS. Each ping came with coordinates. She bluetoothed her hoverboard—silent, solar-powered—and off she surfed.

Each day began with aplomb before worrying itself to nothingness.

By close of day her kinetic energy was in a stupor, the hoverboard her only answer as it followed homeward coordinates to Lyumbu.

Today's first caller was crouched in a hut in Malimbili, tucked north-east of Old Dodoma, where it was once an estuary. The woman was too broken to weep, but her face was already long way before grief ensconced itself like a fetus in her core. She reminded Zawadi of her own mother's lingering face in Nkulungu those many years ago. A sweet-looking face lean like that of a waterbuck. But this here bone and scale hut was nothing like the fresh-smelling one that housed the pomegranates, coconuts, figs, and nectarines that Zawadi's mother sold at the market. This hut in Malimbili smelled like a sewer clogged with feces.

The woman stretched out a tiny bundle. She unwrapped from it a puffed face with pupil-free eyes unshut in death. The tiny gray mouth was set in a straight line. The mother had covered the child in a temperature wrap to keep it cool, unreasoning that the corpse was beyond feeling or needing heat.

"What happened?" asked Zawadi.

"She's only a tiny one," the woman said. But even tiny ones were pulpable, filtrable.

Zawadi pulled out her device, logged the job. "Everything doesn't start with *No*."

"You'll take her?" The woman spoke in murmurs. Her *chitenge*, a flowing wrap, kept falling off her shoulder to reveal a leaking breast.

Zawadi pointed at the woman's chest. "That milk will sell. I can arrange for collection until you dry." She looked squarely at the woman. "It just means more credits for you—and that one." She nodded at the dust-covered boy peering from behind the chitenge. His hair was a rust color, his belly swollen. "Let him have a tug, it will help his kwashiorkor."

"The gods give. Why quarrel with them when they choose to take?" said the woman.

"You may have your own idioms, but this is not karma. If I had a word with the gods, we'd talk about why they are full of cruelty."

"Maybe it is a kindness." The woman, unschooled, signed with a finger on the pad.

"Instant credits when the shuttle comes to collect," said Zawadi.

She jumped back onto her cosmic hoverboard, its Milky Way

whiteness a shimmer in her eyes. She soared under a red sky, no clouds. The day was yet another sizzler, you'd think the body would get used to it. It never did. Even with the government-issued cli-suit and its self-regulating system that adjusted to the environment, she never got cool enough. The suit's purpose was endurance, not comfort.

Stuck on a traffic island—she smiled wryly at the irony of the term 'island' in this godforsaken barrenness—she wondered how Mapesa was faring. He hadn't called as she'd asked. It didn't feel like a 50-50 relationship. Mapesa asked, and he got. Zawadi asked... who knows what she got?

Like her, Mapesa worked in government. He was a groomer. He dry-washed old people. Took orders on ping like her. Biochemicals and a hand-held hoover did the rest because water was so scarce who could afford to shower, bath or frolic in it as they said folk did in those stories of auld? And in New Dodoma.

THEY MET three years ago at a government conference in Makulu Oysterbay—another hooter because there was nothing oyster or bay about Makulu. The event was a forum on water planning, where they served bite-size sandwiches pregnant with cream cheese, smoked salmon, and hardboiled eggs. Uniformed waiters strutted with trays holding flutes of real, clean water.

When Zawadi saw Mapesa, she was drawn by the kink in his curls, then the gold in his eyes when he turned to look at her with a crooked smile from his tall frame. *Wowza!* she thought. A professional development opportunity that came along with dividends. It was a matter of minutes before the dividends reached her. She smelled the vanilla and wood aroma of him long before he brushed her arm.

She looked at him squarely and demanded, "What's your position on the Great Leader?"

He nearly failed. "I used to think he was a fockwit, but now …"

She swirled to leave. "Clearly I was mistaken about you—"

But his palm hooked her elbow, and he cut her words with the right answer. "Only a fool tests the deepness of a river with both feet."

"Do you even know what a river looks like?"

Still, she smiled at his redemption. Indeed, the Great Leader was nothing but a nincompoop. He'd already taken a sixteen-year-old as his fifth wife.

Zawadi was not done with the examination.

She sneaked Mapesa to a side room at the end of a corridor. It turned out to be where they stored robot vacuums that twitched and blinked their beady eyes—not in puzzlement, more as if they understood conspiracy. There, inside the storeroom, Mapesa passed the chemistry test. She thought for days how mind-blowing his kiss, the intimacy of their tongue wrestle, how her lips trembled with new longing when he was gone.

After they hooked up, she liked the way he spined her, as she chose to call it—a run of lean, long fingers down her naked back. Aiyaiya, it gave her electricity. She loved how he spooned her, their bodies a glove fit. As they lay in a twine in afterglow, he told her stories of New Dodoma, the place where water-polished pebbles on a sandy beach were not a rare thing of history and fairy tales. There, folk had time and place to attend real schools with human teachers, not robots. Schools that had students who wore emblemed blazers and went to assembly, then took lessons on how to move in water like dolphins and whales that were now extinct. He told her of streets where music started on cue and led you to a salt spray from a humping ocean swollen with luminescent fish.

Their sex was *good*. He knew her sweet spot. He touched her, and her buttocks went tight, heat and chill all over her body, pulsing between her legs, moments before the release that flowed everywhere.

It made up for their tensions.

When they started arguing and he acted all snobby, know-it-all, she nearly hated him. She found herself beginning to question his first words when they met, and wondered if his reference to the fool who tested the river with both feet was not to the Great Leader but to Zawadi.

THE LIGHTS TURNED.

The job in Area C was a suicide: What made a father of seven kill himself? Everything. In this waterless world that paid in credits that never lasted but dissolved unstretched in a grueling economy—e-v-e-r-y-t-h-i-n-g. One simply lost faith. Even though the father was outwardly perfect, rigor-mortised in a fetal curl of dying agony, she had to say no. The man had swallowed rust remover. His water was compromised.

The next job was in Ipagala where the ocean once jutted out an elbow and created a recreation space where lovers and families visited in throng to picnic and fish. This job was a hit-and-run. A collision with another hoverboard. Zawadi studied the broken body—the splatter of what was left at the site of the incident. This fresh, the cadaver wasn't yet releasing the putrescine odor of rot catalyzed by heat.

Unlike the first mother, this one with a pockmarked face was roaring her grief, tearing hair as bystanders consoled her. Zawadi logged the job, but there wasn't much liquid. Her manager Amadeus was not going to like this. "We're not Mother Teresa," she imagined his disdain as he muttered the name of the ancient saint. "You have no power to give what's not yours."

But whose was it?

She couldn't log the murder in Chang'ombe but made the appearance of inspecting the body, the collapse in the matted head where the skull had fractured. The caved cavity released a creamy ooze onto the naked floor. The girl had whiplash and lacerations on the arms and legs. Blood still seeped from her nose.

"This is a matter for the police," Zawadi said. "Call me when the body is cleared."

She finished before lunch on a burn in Uzunguni. It was a wealthy neighborhood that was once fully vintage, a coveted islet on the ocean. Now on it stood neat rows of identical thermal-controlled bungalows inside a fenced complex. The houses were built of phase change material that absorbed latent heat and gave cooling. Housewives drew leisurely strolls with robot poodles on manicured lawns.

Zawadi stubbed her toe on an ancient shell. She picked it from the ground where it had pushed itself up and studied its turquoise and white swirl, inside which a breathing creature had once lived. She put the shell back aground, not in her pocket as she really wanted to. She walked along a garden speckled with the pink blush of peonies, the yellow stretch of leopard orchids with reddish-brown rosettes, the milky dash of impala lilies gilded in red velvet, the snowy blossom of baby's breath. But the flowers and their ultra-sheen were all fakes that would never wilt. No real flowers grew in Old Dodoma. At least here there was no lingering of nosy neighbors like you might find in the cheaper suburbs. Shades, paints and glazes—you couldn't see a thing until you stepped across the threshold.

Inside one of the bungalows, a gas burner had exploded. She looked at the cooked skin peeling off the woman's body, her chin and neck like melted plastic, clusters of charcoal on her torso. But the burn had sealed her water—Zawadi logged the job. The husband would get good credits.

She rubbed her temples. Her head hurt, so did her muscles. Day in, day out, body after body. How much longer could she do this? Did Tippu Tip's slaves ask themselves this question, over and over, as they slogged under whips? She checked herself—what she had was not good, but it was better than what those slaves had endured.

Back in the office in Chamwino, she let herself into the shoebox that housed two desks and a TV on the second floor of a warehouse that manufactured nutrition pills. It was an embedded warehouse, a concrete and timber hybrid buried in the ground like most corporate buildings in Old Dodoma—built to stay cold as a stone church.

Her boss Amadeus had gone missing. She hadn't seen him for days and wondered if he'd gone on a getaway to New Dodoma. *He* could afford such luxury, but she wasn't sure *how* on the meagre income they both earned. It had to be a side hassle on the black market. The two of them ran the water business, coordinated with body collectors, factories, reservoirs, and the banks.

But it was only a matter of time before robots took over. They were everywhere. Robots diagnosed patients in pop-up clinics, and printed prescriptions from their mouths. Robots tutored children who weren't home-schooled by parents, and ran online modules for those who were. Robots ran walk-in drycleaners—they swallowed dirty clothes and spewed them out ironed. They were all part of Robotix, the Great Leader's own company.

Talk of undeclared conflict of interest!

LUNCH WAS TWO REDS: bland pills full of protein, vitamins, minerals, water, and carbs. Zawadi swallowed them whole, grateful she could afford them, but not the water she recycled from dead people. She was still thirsty despite the nutrients in the pills. The swooning in her head told her she was tired. Yet only half the day had passed. Today, time was not playing kind.

On days she felt extravagant, she took purple pills that came rich with magnesium, calcium, phosphorus, and potassium—this diet balanced her water, fed her skin, polished her hair and her nails, and she stayed strong on iron and selenium.

On frugal days (she and Mapesa were saving to migrate to New Dodoma), it was the grays—a carb hit that kept her brain functioning. But mostly she could stay with the blues, cheaper than the reds and just enough protein to tease the right hormones and antibodies to keep forming.

She grabbed the remote and turned on the TV to the sight of the Great Leader with his hippo head and rat brain. Nearly two decades later, he was still denying climate change. 'I don't believe it,' he was saying to a reporter.

"Don't you believe about the ocean, how it once existed?" the reporter asked.

"It's all a hoax. We all know it's rubbish that Old Dodoma was once the Indian Ocean."

"It's charted in the records of history. Are you saying our ancestors were wrong? Scientists and scholars too?"

"Prophets of doom, that's what they are. They should be lynched."

Like he'd lynched the economy. Like he'd lynched opposition and democracy. Declared himself the Great Leader, worked with some monarch in New Russia on the secret to longevity, bought meds from New China to resuscitate his idiocy daily. It was no doubt Mapesa was a fan. And he kept harping about harvesting clinics. That the government was growing babies.

"If it's true," said Zawadi, "they're propaganda farms."

"Give the Great Leader a break. What's wrong with creating children of the state?"

"For what?"

"All you have to do is register and we get rich," said Mapesa. "I'd do it tomorrow if I was a woman."

"I'm not doing the harvester."

"Know how many credits that is? Two hundred and fifty thousand. More than ample for two one-way shuttle tickets and a settlement bonus to New Dodoma. Think of rippling waves smashing on a beach."

Zawadi thought about it, but disagreed with his thinking. "Dear one," she said, "you're good in bed. But does our talking always have to end in affray?"

SHE COULDN'T SHRUG the desiccated human from her last job. A woman had put her husband in a grain store for a whole year, hooked him up, skinned him and covered him with salt like you cured the meat of a pig. The carcass was still pink—maybe it was pink-orange, but did it matter what color it was? All Zawadi remembered was how he was crusted in parts, tougher than bad leather. And the face, dear gods, the face.

His water was gone.

But Zawadi logged the job, slipped through some credits. She wondered about the woman, and her intent. Was it to keep him or eat him, and was it freedom or desperation that finally led to the ping? Everyone had a breaking point.

She thought of slaves laboring under a harsh white sun in clove plantations—and a wrath of the gods that took away the waters. Even the gods broke.

"Is it really true?" she asked Mapesa that night back home in Lyumbu after their reds. "The harvesting clinic?"

"Don't be stupid," he said. "Of course, it's true."

"I'd love to see some seagulls."

"Me too. But only you can do something to change our situation."

The fish-scale curtain parted. "Look who's visiting," said Zawadi.

Mapesa looked, and frowned.

It was Rafi, the tenant's toddler. She poked her head below the curtains. She had big gray kitten eyes. She was smaller than her age, that was clear, still crawling on her stomach when she should be toddling. She didn't play much, was irritable in the hours that the people of Lyumbu slept. Her cry wasn't the owh-owh of a baby but a slow, low cry like that of a grieving old woman: 'Owwwhhhh.' It didn't take intellect to figure the child was suffering from malnutrition. Zawadi hated to imagine the teeny bub becoming another water run, feeding the mincer for condensate.

"Hello, Snotty," she said.

But the mother, whose name was Queeny or Beany, snatched in with her stink eye, taut cornrows and tattered chitenge. She scooped the child without a word, leaving behind her smell of the unkempt.

Zawadi couldn't put a finger to it, but the woman's husband, Jiwe, made her uneasy. There was something jiggery-pokery about him. He had the type of square face with mean eyes and a broken nose you'd pick out in a police line-up. The woman looked battered, always shouting, "Weye!" or "Acha!" to her lethargic baby who didn't need to stop doing anything.

Zawadi wondered if Jiwe was a wife-beater. She'd never heard it, but she was on the water run the whole day—who knew what the walls saw? Sometimes she called him the magician because he vanished at odd hours. He looked around with furtiveness, whispered into his handheld, put on his cli-suit and was gone until dawn.

"I can't do it, the harvesting, you know that," Mapesa was saying. "But you can."

She struggled with the thought for a long time, and finally said, "And who can we ask?"

He nodded at the curtain.

"Jiwe?" asked Zawadi.

"Haven't you wondered if he was in the black market?"

"Matter of fact, I have." She sighed. "Then *you* do it, Mapesa."

He smiled.

"Talk to him, man-to-man," Zawadi said. "Because I honestly would rather not. And I'm sick of this arguing."

"Easy," he said, and the gold danced.

SHE LISTENED TO THEIR WHISPERS—URGENCY in Jiwe and Mapesa's voices as they spoke. Indeed, the night had ears. Rafi was crying that old woman groan. "Owwwhhhh." Zawadi wanted to stand outside in the warmth of a shouting wind and was about to swing her legs from the sheets when the curtain moved. Mapesa slipped back into bed.

He cuddled her in a spoon, spined her until she trembled with electricity. He lay on his back, knees folded on the bed. She sat at his feet, her head slightly back as she faced him. She'd do anything for him, she thought. But she was hungry to forget this fact as she steadied herself against him, let him fondle the erogenous zone in her feet on his shoulders. It had taken practice to get this tantric position right, and it was perfect. His kisses and caresses on her feet felt inside her. She thought she would explode. Just when she nearly did, he pulled her to his swell, and she moaned at his thrust.

His words in afterglow breathed on her neck. They lay in a new spoon. "So, they have running water in New Dodoma—it splashes from a tap."

She turned, touched his nose. "And that is news, how?"

"They have shops where you can buy sugar, milk, bread, biscuits, even beer or soda in a can—like we read in the books, how it was long ago."

"If you say so. I said I'd do it, no need to convince me."

"I can convince you to something more," he said with husk in his voice. He knelt and sat her astride him, kissed and caressed her breasts.

She rubbed against his torso, not need much convincing on that score either.

Later, spent, his words continued to touch her in a drawl. "They have seagulls there—yellow-eyed and pink-beaked, flying low above your head and crying kraa-kroo in a happy warble."

"And Jiwe told you all this?" said Zawadi. "Has he even been there?"

"Well... er—"

"Soon you'll tell me they have shower huts in all colors of the rainbow at the beachfront. Caravan homes stacked with sun chairs by the waterfront."

"Is that too impossible to want?"

"Yes!" she snapped. "Like wanting hospitals with white sheets on a bed."

"But they do have them! And restaurants. You go in and sit and dine like a royal on a five-course menu. People wait on you every day, not just in government functions. They bring you poached chicken, boneless lamb, or butternut squash balls that you chew and savor, not swallow like pills."

Zawadi had to admit she was weary of soaring over burnt soil and dry rock to collect water from dead people. She wanted to see a world with clubs and the silvery glow of streetlights. Neon signs of whatever was the rage. Back alleyways swollen with cafés on ultrawide laneways. She wanted to walk in a botanical garden with real flowers and real dogs—Rhodesian ridgebacks, big like a grown-up, sleek Azawakhs prancing like sheikhs on trimmed grass. She wanted to step out of a beachfront caravan and walk to the beach, slip her toes in wet sand and feel the water's heartbeat.

"How many credits does this Jiwe want from us?" She toyed with the tightness of Mapesa's curls, stretching, releasing. "What do we have to give for him to hook us up with the clinic?"

"I've already paid, anything for you. All you've got to do is let me take you there. Just one week is all it takes. One week, and we're frolicking in water, sipping lit cocktails on a sandy shore in New Dodoma."

"A week?"

"It's called technology. The eggs are already treated. From the moment of implanting, it's an accelerated gestation."

She thought of the dead child with a puffed face in Malimbili, the suicide in Area C, the hit-and-run in Ipagala, how the mother roared her grief.

"And who'll do the water run?"

"I can talk to Amadeus. He'll give you sick leave—hundreds of casuals are waiting in a queue."

She thought of the husband, hung up like a pig. The wife's eyes turned inward, as if searching for her soul. On the scale of things, harvesting didn't sound that bad. Not bad at all.

"Dear one," she said. "And how much credit will you give Amadeus to agree to all this?"

THEY SOARED ON ONE HOVERBOARD—MAPESA'S. Zawadi wrapped herself around him as if she were made of tentacles. She sought an emotional connection, but she could well be clutching a plank. There was just his wood and vanilla smell from the antiperspirant, and his solid athletic frame.

The clinic stood behind steel gates, electrical fencing, double-security doors. Surprisingly, it had hospital beds with white sheets on them. She was the only patient, and there was one obstetrician in the ward. She was glad to see that he was a real doctor, not a robot. Either that or he was the perfect cyborg in a human body. A seasoned man with snow hair, a knowing jaw, and eyes that told nothing.

She felt thirsty. Mapesa was hovering with a smile—not the

suave one. This one was off, not reaching the gold in his eyes. It was as if he, not her, was discomfited by the whole thing. On second thought, no—the smile wasn't foolish. It was the copious one of a pauper about to get rich. At all costs. As she read and signed the paperwork, she thought of that traitor Amadeus who didn't give a hoot about Mother Teresa and would sell his employee to anybody for a few credits.

She looked up at the doctor in the room blinking with lights, and thought of a city with vibrant bustle and silver rain, water in her grasp. She understood that, much as she resented Mapesa right then, that full minute, it was her dream too. She wanted to walk into a neon-lit world whose boulevards resurrected names like Salif Keita and Yvonne Chaka Chaka.

She questioned her decision to be in the clinic, but her mind came at her with ecstatic thoughts of fun parks where she bought tickets and walked into the big mouth of a giant clown, and straight into a mirror maze or a spider ride or a supernova that churned her in the sky as she squealed her glee. She knew that she should ask about where the implanted eggs came from, who fertilized them and what happened to the babies: were they propaganda for the state, products of the Great Leader's lunacy? Suddenly it struck her, and she went cold: what if they were water harvests? Birthed, then humanely put to sleep for the crematorium distillate?

She thought of Tippu Tip and the curse he brought that killed a whole ocean. Slaves chained in planks, skin to skin on the floor like tilapia going to the market. Flesh to harvest by masters who had no claim to it. Sweat, blood and bones to fuel a trading empire on routes along the Indian Ocean from the Swahili coast to Persia, Omani and Mesopotamia...

But she closed her mind from the niggling growing into a tormenting dread that came with pondering ethics or ethos, and imagined escape from a perpetual drought that ate her inside out until it became normal, but not really. She accepted that her everyday as a water runner was too reckless to leave to chance and understood that there was nobody to save her, that she must bequeath herself with dragon wings to separate from this world with its fossil houses and ground so hard, footprints were a dream.

She thought of New Dodoma where she would never thirst again. She yearned for a cool wind that hummed year-round in a crisp breeze that summoned gulls, and they were alive not extinct. She wanted to be in a place where the ocean of pale green water unpolluted by humans and an evil trade went and went, round and round, no land in sight for miles and miles. Water so clear, so pale in its green hue, it let you see the silt and black rock on its ocean bed, as its wet tongues licked at soft, wet sand where children dug in buckets and shaped sandcastles. So instead of asking the questions she wanted, she searched the doctor's eyes, but they were black velvet. "Will it hurt?"

"Don't be stupid, you won't feel a thing," said Mapesa.

"We put you in a coma to keep your body activity minimal," said the doctor.

He hooked her onto a ventilator, and at once she felt heady. What if, from here, it was for her straight to the mincer? She saw herself as a corpse, pure, unresisting in giving water from her remnants in biological recycling. She panicked for a wild moment—already she was losing control over her own body. But before she could ask the doctor to pause or stop, the vapors took.

Sound fell.

She saw him at the edge of her vision, fading in and out. Mapesa's mouth was moving and she could make out the words "I love you," or "I have you," or "I hope you ..."

Did he doubt that she'd make it? Her last thoughts as her head plummeted and a jaw of blackness devoured her.

AMA'S JUNGLE

K-MING CHANG

Originally published by *Orion Magazine*

K-Ming Chang is a Lambda Literary Award winner, a National Book Foundation 5 Under 35 honoree, and an O. Henry Prize Winner. She is the author of the New York Times Book Review Editors' choice novel *Bestiary* (One World/Random House, 2020), which was longlisted for the Center for Fiction First Novel Prize, the VCU Cabell First Novelist Award, and the Otherwise Award. In 2021, her chapbook *Bone House* was published by Bull City Press. Her story collection *Gods of Want* (One World/Random House) won a Lambda Literary Award, and her books have been translated into Spanish, Chinese, Korean, German, Turkish, and other languages. Her most recent books are *Organ Meats* (One World, 2023) and a novella titled *Cecilia* (Coffee House Press, 2024). More of her work can be found at kmingchang.com.

We had never seen the color green. We punched each other to produce it. We grew our crop of bruises and hoarded our hurts like precious fruit. We didn't share. We rusted a penny. We grew mold on the crusts of our bread. Green was the color of rot and decay and time. It skipped birth; it developed from death. We tore the wings off a crow that was flattened in the road and slipped the feathers into our hair, running in the sunlight to catch the light at a slant, and for a moment we could see each other's green, a glint alive inside our gloom.

Then the woman moved into our neighborhood. She told us to call her Ama, but she was not our blood. She moved into a red house at the corner of the block, and like all of our houses, it had no yard, just a sliver of pavement that cleaved it from its neighbor.

We thought for a while that Ama was just another mother or grandmother or aunt, that she would work at the same block of factories or the same street of restaurants as the rest of us. But Yina, who lived next to Ama, said the house was empty. Ama had no belongings, and Yina never heard the gas stove ticking or the front door opening. "She only goes out the back," Yina said. "She leaves the door wide open." But where we lived, the back door only led to a chain-link fence. There was nothing to do behind our houses but swat flies and spit on the pavement.

We thought perhaps she left the back door open to let in a breeze, but there never was any breeze.

Samantha, who lived on the other side of Ama, claimed that at night, the red house was a cacophony: She could hear birds singing, trees bleeding freely into the wind, fruits spitting their seeds rapid-fire at the sky, rains of teeth. She heard a river winding through her fingers, so deep it would never surface, not even if we lured it with the thirst of a million mouths. She heard hoofs trampling the ground, rattling the foundation of her house, and an eagle shredding a liver into ribbons, dangling them above the gaping mouths of chicks. Samantha described the orchestra of the red house with so much vividness, we knew it was not a lie. She alone could hear the sound of our mothers crying at night. The rest of us slept with our ears plugged with socks, choosing the illusion of peace.

But the nocturnal ruckus of Ama's house could puncture the thickest of fabrics.

Unable to bear it any longer, we snuck out and gathered by the red house one afternoon. Ama answered the door. She was shorter than us, but her shadow was endless, unfurling past the door and seeping into the street, a river of unadorned memory. Her hair was the same silver as the strands our mothers paid us to pluck from their heads. We hoarded those hairs in our pillows, entranced by their luminescence. Like the threads of a carnivorous web. Ama's eyes were strangely alight, as if battery-powered. Our mothers hoarded batteries in case of emergency, and we could not help but wonder, as Ama stood before us in her soiled nightgown, if maybe she had arrived to save us. If someone had at last been summoned to the alarm of our silence. When Ama smiled, the world for a moment was rearranged by her playfulness. Nothing had killed the girl in her. Her face refused to cooperate with gravity, and her wrinkles were reversed, the skin pulled upward instead of downward, the folds like pockets for gifts so precious she would always keep them for herself.

Ama stepped out of her dark doorway, her shadow engulfing ours. "Come with me, little girls, little demons," she said. "Haven't you been waiting?"

We were swept into the tide of her memory, the undertow of her shadow. We let her momentum carry us into the house, which was just as Yina described: entirely empty, bereft even of dust. No furniture or belongings or photos, not even a source of light. Ama led us to her back door, limned in light, and asked us if we were ready to be eaten.

We thought she'd asked if we'd eaten, and we responded

eagerly that we were hungry. She laughed and said she understood. Soon there would be plenty to eat. But all change requires loss. To abandon our sordid present, were we willing to be consumed by the future?

We chorused yes. Each of us was accustomed to sacrifice. Every morning, our mothers listened to the same radio station, a monk who told us that deprivation is strength. Suffering is purpose. Emptiness is holy. Unlike our brothers, who were raised to leave, our destiny was to be masticated by this neighborhood, metabolized for those who can go further. Like our mothers before us, fodder for our fathers' freedom, and their mothers before them, who clutched desperately to the tails of their fleeing sons, who wanted only to mean something through their men, we have always been preparing to disappear.

Ama seemed satisfied. "Then you may enter this door with these words," she said. "Repeat after me: Death, this house is yours. I am going to my garden."

Death, this house is yours. I am going to my garden.

The back door was devoured by the darkness, crumpling into its own shadow and pooling on the ground like a velvet curtain. We stepped over it, crossing the threshold. Beyond it we could see only green, all shades of it: green that ruptured its border with blue, green like a sneeze, green that was more like gold, green as a rotting liver, green as a summer breeze, green like the sound of snipped wings, green as a wedding between roots and rain.

We stepped directly into a jungle. We had never seen one for real, but our mothers told us stories of them, complaining of the unending humidity and the clothes that never dried and the prosperity of mold. They told us of ghosts that roosted in the canopy and lured men to their deaths.

Beneath our feet was plush mud. Samantha took the first step, and her foot collided with a skull that refracted the sunlight. We didn't understand how sunlight could penetrate a canopy as dense as the one above us, a roof so reliable that squirrels and stray cats ran across it. We spun slowly in place.

"It's all for you," Ama said, stepping forward into the trees. She stood between two trunks, and we could see that they had become her family, that she had learned their language. Her shadow was so long because it was a tree's. Here, she had become something more than a sacrifice. She had found a towering life.

We followed her deeper into the trees. Birds flickered in the branches, bulbs of brightness we did not recognize, but to Samantha the songs were delicious. The jungle was a hatchery for shadows. Each tree was accompanied by a rabid, roving darkness that nipped at our feet. We were glazed with rain that rose from the dirt, a wetness delivered by the dead. Ama named the greens as she walked ahead of us: banana, papaya, guava, water spinach, taro, mountain apples . . .

As we walked, we could feel the ground moving beneath us, a beast with its heart buried deep. Ama forged ahead, not bothering to look back, and we scampered over roots, tripped over rotting logs, flinched at the sight of animal eyes in the shadows, green and yellow and red. We could not tell what direction we were moving, whether we were going forward or backward. The jungle was immune to linear direction, growing in concentric circles like an echo. Like a sound emitted from our own mouths, it expanded and rebounded.

At last we arrived at the river. The trees became sparse, the mud thicker and fouler, and then the river rose to our knees, to our chins. We laughed with relief. We drank and bathed. Though we could not swim, we floated effortlessly in this river, which had bounded up and engulfed us like an eager dog greeting our knees, so happy that we were finally home.

There were no bathrooms in the jungle, so we peed in the river and giggled. We splashed each other. The water was opaque and green and delectably cold. Tiny silver fish flitted through the current like slivers of orphaned electricity.

When we were clean and had drunk until our bellies bloated and bobbed to the surface like buoys, we paddled to the banks and laid ourselves out among the lizards to dry. The lizards crawled over our bare legs and bellies, mistaking us for tender stones. We laughed as they scuttled across us, tickling our limbs, sweeping us clean with their tails.

Soon we were dry and hungry, and we gathered around Ama, waiting to be fed. She gestured behind us, where the branches were bulging and laden with fruit, and whipped out from under her skirt a silver net she said could catch fish or squid or the moon.

We scattered to feast, climbing the trees, scraping our shins on the bark, digging our fingers into the dirt, slurping up sticky worms and candied beetles. Plums in prolonged rot, sickeningly sweet. Papayas with seeds we suckled like nipples. Leaves that dissolved on our tongues like a lace of salt. As we ate, we realized for the first time how hungry we had always been, how desperate, how deprived. It was not our strength, as the radio had taught us; deprivation had siphoned us of life, had brittled our teeth and torn out our tongues. At dinnertime, our mothers ate last. They watched us in the throes of satisfaction, eating only what was left over in our bowls. *Eat, my babies, it's all for you.* But now, as we dug our teeth into the trees, as light scaled our canines and revealed their shadowed roots, we saw no beauty in the restraint of our mothers, only the ugliness of hunger. We saw their flesh between our own teeth, saw ourselves gathered around them with our hands staked into their meat, tearing them apart and then ourselves, and suddenly the fruit in our mouths turned sour and rotten and we fell to the ground, hunched over, spitting and vomiting, our throats seared by acid.

"This jungle is not for the weak," Ama said. "It is for those who are willing to obliterate the world. Anything short of that is not permitted in paradise."

Lightheaded and groaning, our heads fizzing with vertigo, we begged her to let us stay. We will purge the impure world, we promised, we will leave behind our putrid lives. Let us stay. Let the river surface and roar in us, replacing the meager tide of our tongues.

Ama smiled. She said we were too wise for our age, that we had learned things she had learned only in death. She told us that she had birthed this jungle. It was the map of her soiled mind.

"I was married at fifteen. I grew this jungle because I needed somewhere to escape to. It was born of practicality. What do they say? That necessity is the mother of invention? Mothers are forever burdened with invention. This jungle is not like the one I knew from childhood. I was always afraid of that place, its ghosts, its shadows. But I would see some lesser creature, a duck in a stream, a hog in a clearing, and I would think, Your death will nourish something, and I would laugh that I felt such envy for creatures who would never be mourned, and I knew I would rather be nothing than to be given my meaning.

"You can never trust a house. A house only listens to the one who owns it. I needed a space of my own, a foldable darkness, a vastness I could pocket. Somewhere I could go to disappear. Somewhere I could abandon life. I pity you girls, who have only ever known drought, only ever lived in places that could be taken away. I know how green haunts your every thought. Anything you have never seen, you assume is green.

"This is my labyrinth. No one can find me here, not even you. When I truly want to disappear, I am everywhere."

We wept at her feet, touched our lips to her cheeks. We promised to never leave. Ama smiled at us and said that no one had ever said that to her. All her life she had been fleeing, always been the woman who left, and all along she was waiting for someone who would stay. "A world cannot exist if there is no one to populate it," she said. "You are many of the many who have come to this world. Who have come to join me."

It was dark now, the moon a badger's eye, roving over us as we flitted through the trees, newly fluent in our bodies. Ama led us to a clearing where we could see the stars, and we laid on our backs in the dirt.

Samantha unfurled on one side of me, Yina on the other, their breath rapid with excitement. We had never seen stars before, not even on the freeway when the sky was radiant in the darkness. But here, the stars were like moles on the face of someone most beloved and familiar, a pattern of undeniable prosperity. We'd had our moles read many times, their positions determining our marriage prospects, our capacity to earn money or be happy. We were content to be tragedies.

But Ama said the stars didn't belong to anyone's skin. They were the open eyes of animals, alert and ready to intervene, and all we had to do was call them down. In the jungle, Ama said, the world protects us.

We fell asleep beneath the stars that night, and when the sun grew back into the sky, a red cardinal that sang us awake, we noticed that Samantha was missing. We searched for her in the trees, and Yina even scaled the tallest to scour the shadows. But she was gone. Ama remained in the clearing, peeling open a tangerine, seemingly unconcerned. When we flocked to her, Ama pointed at a sign nailed to a tree.

JUNGLE MAXIMUM CAPACITY: SEVENTY-FIVE MOTHERS, NINETY GIRLS, TWO HUNDRED THOUSAND PARROTS, LIMITLESS BEASTS, LIMITLESS TREES. EXCESS OCCUPANTS WILL BE EATEN BY THE TREES.

Had we exceeded capacity? Ama shook her head. "I saw her leave last night while you were all asleep," she said. "But don't worry, she will be back."

We looked at each other, astonished. It had never occurred to us to leave. Here there was green. There were birds with eyes like planets, rivers that surged between our legs. Our stools had softened significantly, and we were finally happy. Here it was better than heaven, because there was no need to be good. There was nothing more that mattered than the fact that we were alive and we were hungry.

We missed Samantha and sent flocks of crows after her, legions of lizards, millions of ants. We would carry her back in crumbs if needed. But for the rest of us, the choice was easy. Ama had given us a back door. A paradise we did not have to die for. A world that could not survive without our joy. In the daytime, Ama introduced us to many wonders: the owl pellet that contained a mouse's rib cage, delicate as our mothers' jewelry; a duck that could outsmart unwanted sperm; the chocolate rocks scattered at the bottom of the river that we spent many days trying to find, taking bites out of every pebble until we found the ones that broke open.

Eventually we grew bold enough to wander away from her, to listen to the hearts of the trees, which began to sync with ours, and which told us they were once women. The trees parted to reveal their companions. There were others in this jungle, but they seemed to keep to themselves. They were black-haired, with the long faces of ghosts. We watched them fish, weave houses, fashion wings out of leaves to take flight from the trees. We saw them walking on stilts, sipping from cracked fruit. A few of us hid behind a tree and pelted them with rocks, but the river rose behind them as if to take revenge, so after that, we left them alone. They laughed at us when we tripped over tree roots, when we squatted to pee and splashed our legs. We heard the trees echoing their verdict: we were naive, amusing to watch, but someday we would become like them, part of the marrow of this place, sleeping in slings of sunlight.

"Stay," they said. "You think you can straddle this world and the one you come from. But this jungle is the truer place. Stay forever."

We preferred to return to the river and sleep with it curled around us. It reminded those of us who had cats of our cats; it reminded those of us who had dogs of our dogs. As we woke to the river's tongue lathing our faces, we noticed that more of us were missing. We seemed to be leaving in groups of three, sometimes four, but we didn't mourn. After all, the ones who left were the ones who cried at school drop-off, who wet their sleeping bags at naptime, wailing for their mothers. The ones who claimed they were lonely. Who feared truancy officers. Who feared that if they did not leave now, their former lives would follow them in.

Most of all, there were the ones who worried about their mothers, who knew it was their duty to accompany their mothers' suffering. If they abandoned their post, how would they be able to live? The ones like Samantha, who snuck away from us and walked through the jungle for days until she reached Ama's back door. Legs trembling, she crawled through it and reentered the tepid night. No time had passed at all since we'd left, and she could tell because the sounds of the night were the same: the barking dogs, the crickets, the woman who moaned beneath the weight of her migraine. When she looked up, she could see her lit window, the room waiting for her, the familiarity of her own fear, which returned to her like the weight of her body. She'd already forgotten the taste of clean water, the shades of green we could spend our whole lives naming.

The moon was there, but it watched her with indifference. It was foolish to think she had once believed she was a part of this world, that her absence could tilt its axis. It was foolish of her to think that her duty could change anything. Inside her lived the abject hope that if she was only willing to suffer enough, she would one day reap the bounty. There were two ways to be honored, and that was to die or to live as a sacrifice. Samantha had always chosen what she believed to be the lesser sentence, the second. But now, as she looked up at her vacant window, as she grieved what she could not remember of the jungle and its juicy moons, she thought that at least death was necessary. Her life, on the other hand, seemed utterly senseless. It was easy to endure your own pain. There was something pure about it, like the monks who learned to sit cross-legged on hot coals or sleep beneath freezing waterfalls. It was selfless and noble. It was good for girls.

"When you grow up, you learn to accept that life isn't fair," her mother had once told her. "There's no such thing as getting what you deserve, least of all love. When someone fails to love you, you have to love yourself twice as much." Samantha had laughed bitterly at those words. Was she content to be bereft while her father slept?

It was then that Samantha turned back to the door, remembering: One time she had been sitting in the kitchen, and from the bowels of the house she heard that familiar sound. It was the sound of death rounding the corner, glass smashing against the wall, sobs muffled behind a door. She asked herself often: how willing are you to die? But she never really had to think. She tried to run toward the sound, toward her mother, but her legs were trembling so hard that she could not stay upright. She had to crawl. Down the hallway she dragged herself, knees seared by the carpet, belly filled with the sickening churn of dread and anticipation. The sound saddled her back, weighing more than her own pain, and she carried its burden with divine purpose.

But if she turned away now, if she saved her own life and returned to Ama's jungle—a new fear entered her. A fear that she would not survive freedom. That it would obliterate her. That if she could not be good, perhaps she would really rather be dead.

The back door loomed ahead of her, radiating a dense and impenetrable darkness. Ama's jungle did not need her. Ama's jungle was complete. The sun glossed our faces with blood, and our only duty was to eat. To stay at last in a place we were safe.

"They'll come back," Ama said, whenever we despaired. "Didn't I say to be patient? You were patient out there, weren't you? Here, your patience bears fruit. Here, waiting is finite as a wound. You will live to see the world that deserves you."

Like black-haired brooms, the trees swept Ama's words toward the door, ferrying them to Samantha's mouth. All around her, Ama's house was empty and cold, the walls towering like the ribs of a picked-clean carcass. Samantha's shadow on the wall unfurled to its full wingspan, and we called to her from behind the door, drowning out the sounds of the night. Only our voices remained, an unkillable myth, and at last Samantha remembered the words.

Death, this house is yours. I will go to my garden.

A SEDER IN SIBERIA

LOUIS EVANS

Originally published by *Grist: Imagine 2200*

Louis Evans has been going to Passover seder at his Papa and Bubbe's house since the year he was born. He is a writer living and working in Brooklyn, New York. His speculative fiction has appeared in *Vice, the Magazine of Fantasy & Science Fiction,* and *Nature: Futures,* and is forthcoming from *Reactor.* His climate fiction has appeared in *Analog Science Fiction & Fact, Little Blue Marble, Fusion Fragment,* and more. He's online at louisevans.org and on Bluesky @louisevans.bsky.social.

THE CUPBOARDS LOCKED, THE KITCHEN SWEPT CLEAN WITH A broom of pine twigs, the children each dressed in their one good outfit—a sleight of hand transforming a band of free-range ragamuffins into a sort of pocket-sized town council—the sun creeping down, down, down toward the boreal horizon, and at last none of us could deny it: Jonathan wasn't coming.

So now it only remained to tell Mom.

I TRIED FIRST, because I'm weak.

"Don't you think it's time to go get Dad?"

"Miriam, your father's tired," she told me. Which is one way to say *dying of cancer*, I suppose. She was setting the table, for the third time. "Besides, your brother will be here any minute. *Then* we'll get Dad. Don't be impatient."

I bit my lip to keep from shouting. We had sworn a sacred sibling oath not to yell at her, but she does not make it easy.

David's turn.

"Maybe we should get started anyway, and Jonathan can *join*—"

"Just *wait*. I told your sister—"

"Do you even know *when*—"

"He'll *be* here—"

"Have you even *spoken* to him—"

"I sent a vid, he's very busy—"

Despite my resolution, that pushed me back over the edge. I was bitterly grateful that my wife was stuck with her herds tonight; she hates to see me angry. "You don't even know Jonathan's coming at all!"

"Miriam, I *said* I sent—"

"You don't even know if he *got* it. The loons—"

And then Leo spoke. He didn't have to shout; he never does. It's funny how the baby of the family became the one we all listen to.

"Mom," said Leo. "Jonathan's not coming."

Silence in the house, and darkness, too, with only a sliver of sun left and the candles not yet lit.

"I'd better go get Dad," Mom said.

The seder was my father's domain. Everything about it was his, year after year. The seder plate was his seder plate. The molding Haggadot, spiral-bound with ancient fossil plastic, were his. Even the recipes—suitably modified for our new diets, hazelnut matzah and algae karpas—came from his family. And of course he was the leader of the service, reading the familiar story word for word, year after year.

This was not the first seder of his illness.

Last year, when my shrunken and sallow father had taken his shuffling place at the head of our seder table, a remarkable transformation overtook him. It was as if the winds of other times and other places filled him like an airship, and suddenly he was not my suffering, shriveled, cancer-crossed Dad, he was my father from childhood, from every childhood, from when the world was new—

For the fourth cup of wine, for the fourth promise of G-d, he read, just like every year of my life, "I will take you to be *my* people," and deep in my bones I felt the truth of it, that I was of G-d's people and *of my father's people*.

That was the man my father was. Had been.

This was not the first seder of his illness. But it was the first seder of his death.

Dad entered the dining room with Mom holding his elbow. He made it to his chair. He sat down.

Nothing happened.

We all sat there for a minute in unfamiliar silence, even the children waiting for what was going to happen next. Dad blinked at the Haggadah that Mom carefully placed in front of him. He tried to lift the first page.

It was too much for him; he let it fall.

I found myself, of course, looking to Leo at the foot of the table, and I knew David across from me was looking the same way, and my kid began to squirm, and Leo's face as he stared at Dad showed no legible emotion at all.

"I guess I'll read," said Mom.

WHAT IS PASSOVER?

David's the schoolteacher; he's good at explanations. Me, I don't explain anything. I just gene-tweak mammoths.

Working as an eco-pheno-geno-biofeedback climate engineer, you get in the habit of seeing things as very complicated. Is this stand of old-growth taiga spruce a valuable carbon sink? Or is it a "bad voxel" with a dangerously low albedo compared to adjacent snowy grasslands, primed to absorb too much sunlight and turn it into heat? Or is it a useful landmark for a navigating mammoth herd? Or is that bad, because we want to lure the herd onto a different track to reduce the risk of inter-herd conflict? Or—

I write a lot of reports.

Passover is a holiday that celebrates the liberation of the Jews from Egypt *and/or* Passover is a collection of songs and stories and quizzes and weird little games, like a mixed-up child's toy chest of traditions *and/or* Passover is when twenty million of the world's most anxious people get to explore a fun seasonal set of dietary restrictions in addition to the year-round ones *and/or* Passover is the candles, and the wine, and the prayers, and the songs, *and/or* Passover is a story of a marvelous escape by refugees trapped between an army and an ocean...

I write a lot of reports, and then I go in and change the mammoths. Back in the Pleistocene, extremely long biofeedback loops took care of that automatically, but these days we are on a tighter timetable. So I made the mammoths snow white; that was me. The genetic sequence from polar bears is very well characterized, and it takes transcription easily. A white mammoth absorbs less sunlight; the glittering fur reflects more heat back into space. Every good voxel counts.

What is Passover?

Basically, you get all your family in one room, deny everybody food until you've made it through a two-hour interactive lecture, constantly drinking more and more wine, and then act surprised when a fight breaks out.

"MOM, DON'T YOU THINK—" said David. But she hadn't listened to him for forty-two years; why would she start now?

"Now in the presence of loved ones and friends, before us the emblems of festive rejoicing..."

She was off. What could we do? We read along, all of us chorusing in unison, siblings, spouses, kids, even Dad managing to mumble: "Remember the day on which you went forth from Egypt, from the house of bondage..."

And what do you know, she was good.

It was a little cynical, perhaps, to judge my own mother's reading of the seder strictly on its theatrical merits, but surely we Jews have earned our cynicism. And she *was* good. Deep voice, solid rhythm. Kept good time in the group readings and didn't interrupt my kids when they stumbled over the longer, more ornate words and transliterations. I didn't have to hate this.

So long as I kept my eyes off Dad.

"SEDER," in English, literally translates as "order." Nevertheless, our family never reads the Haggadah in the official order. Instead, the whole thing is held together by a complicated web of bookmarks and marginal notes. It's not the original system, but it works.

That's why, not twenty minutes into the seder, between the first and second cups of wine, we got to Elijah the Prophet.

There's a superstition about Elijah. You set out an extra cup of wine, and then you send the little kids to open the door for him. Then one of the adults sneaks the glass of wine, or secretly rocks the table, and *look, kids, it's Elijah, he's drinking it!*

In the Book of Kings, Elijah smites four hundred pagan priests with fire from heaven. In the Haggadah, he plays a silly little haunted-house drinking game with kids. Being a grown-up is like that, I think.

"May the All-Merciful send us Elijah the Prophet to comfort us with tidings of deliverance," said Mom. "Now let us open the door for Elijah."

David's and my kids knew their parts, and they ran, all in a giggling mob, to the front door to fling it open—

And they *screamed.*

THE MAN at the door did look like Elijah. He was tall and gaunt and bearded. He was bundled for the taiga, not for the deserts of the Holy Land, but his clothes were stark and worn. One arm was tied up in an impromptu sling.

I must have run for the door when the kids screamed—we all must have; I don't remember—I just remember staring, and staring, and *staring* at the man in the door.

It had been years. There was no reason that the kids should recognize their uncle Jonathan.

MOM BUSTLED Jonathan in the door, and she bustled the door shut. She bustled him out of his traveling clothes, and she worried over his injured arm so much that she almost fainted.

She ran back and forth with ever-increasing energy and declining effectiveness until Leo stopped her.

He got her back into her chair at the head of the table, got Jonathan seated at the foot beside him. Dad had not stood up to greet Jonathan; I did not know if he understood that Jonathan had been gone and now he was back. I didn't know.

David asked Jonathan about his arm. "Grolar bear attack," he replied.

It wasn't surprising. We've been driving up the population of grolars for years now. Larger apex predators produce upward cull pressure on herbivore size, which increases winter survivability and population throughput, ultimately allocating more biomass to the mammoths overall. But push it up too hard though and you kick off a predation double-bust, which throws your whole cycle out of whack, and so on.

Systems are complicated.

The kids were probably desperate to ask Jonathan about the grolars, but they were still scared of him; and he didn't seem inclined to talk much. So I didn't ask any follow-up questions, and neither did David.

"Mom," said Leo, "keep reading."

Jonathan started in his seat, turning to Leo. "Dad reads," he said.

Leo did not turn to face him. They had been so close before, the baby of the family and the eldest; Leo had idolized him. Jonathan was the sort of man he'd always wanted to be, since long before the rest of us even knew he would grow into one. But then Jonathan vanished. No surprise Leo took it hard.

"This year Mom reads," he said.

Jonathan looked at Leo. Looked at Mom. Looked at Dad. Looked away.

In a dining room crowded for seder, it's hard to find somewhere to look that's not another watching face, but he managed.

Mom was still staring at her prodigal son, drinking in his

face, but Leo managed to catch her eye and gave her a firm nod, and she started reading again.

PASSOVER IS A CHILD-FRIENDLY HOLIDAY. Not really the story of the Exodus itself, which has an unavoidable infusion of the bronze-age macabre—drowned babies, Moses beating and killing an overseer, blood on the doorpost, spontaneous death plague—but certainly the seder is. The songs have an easy nursery-rhyme simplicity. The ritual food appears in handy sandwich format. The children have dedicated readings—"Ma Nishtanah," "why is this night different from all other nights?" is traditionally sung by the youngest child present.

But the Four Children is not, I think, exactly child-friendly.

It's an odd little bit of text, a piece of Talmudic psychological gristle undigested by medieval pageantry or modern bowdlerization. It notices that the Torah commands us to teach our children the story of Passover four distinct times. Now, a mammoth geneticist would see that reduplication as merely a healthy copy-error redundancy in an inherited text, but the rabbis of the Talmud thought differently. They thought that every word was a perfect, unique gift from G-d.

So, they said that four commandments meant four different ways to teach, four different archetypal children. The good child, the wicked child, the simple child, and the one who does not even know how to ask. Each of them receives a different instruction.

The passage is child-unfriendly not through sex or violence but rather through its crushing essentialism. These days we tell our children, "You can be anything you want to be." These days we tell them, "You live in a special time, an important time, when there is so much work of *tikkun olam*, of repairing the Earth. So much work, so many jobs—from rewilding the rainforest to herding mammoths!—and one of those jobs out there is just for you. Just as special and unique as you are."

But our sages teach us: there are four children. Kiss-ass, shithead, stupid, and double stupid.

In my family there were four of us, too.

Don't imagine that we missed that part.

In the end, it was simple bad luck.

Most of the readings in our Haggadah are delivered solo by the leader, or together by the entire table. But the Four Children is tagged with that most perilous note, "A Participant." Which means we go around the table, clockwise.

I had the wise child. That gave Leo the wicked.

"The wicked person says, 'What is this observance to *you*?' Because they say 'to *you*,' and not 'to *us*,' they reject the unity of G-d and the community of Judaism. To them we respond sharply"—and suddenly Leo was looking at Jonathan, staring at him, teeth flashing as he bit out words—"it is because of what G-d did for *me* when *I* went forth from Egypt, for by abandoning us, *you* would not have known redemption."

Time for the chorus, and David and I leapt in, "The wicked one withdraws themselves from anything beyond themselves," and Mom was reading along, and the kids were doing their best, and even Dad was gamely mumbling, but Jonathan didn't say anything. Neither did Leo.

We trailed off, a comet tail of phonetic rubble. Jonathan's turn now, but he still wasn't saying anything. His Haggadah lay open on the table, still open to the page of the wicked child.

"Jonathan," I said, in the gentlest voice I could manage. "It's your turn."

My older brother has never listened to me.

"I don't deserve this," Jonathan said to Leo.

All across Leo's face I could see pain congealing into anger.

"Of course you do," Leo said. "You left. One day, you just got it into your head to leave us."

"No," said Jonathan. "Dad told me to go."

JONATHAN LEFT us when he was nineteen. There was no warning.

He'd been fighting with Dad more. I think. It was hard to tell. Jonathan and Dad both had a strange, oblique way of arguing. Nothing like me or David or Mom. Just a coldness that settled between words, between actions, that froze the ground and then kept it frozen. And then one day he was gone.

Leo was fourteen; he'd come out a year and a half earlier. (He's the only Jew I know who's had both a bat and a bar mitzvah. Good timing.) When Jonathan left, Leo felt abandoned by his brother. He was devastated.

But the rest of us were hurting too.

It's a big world out there, and we lived at the very farthest edge of it. I understood that. I could imagine how Jonathan might want to see something different than tundra, tundra, tundra, mammoth. I could imagine how Jonathan might want to escape from the cold in our house and the cold in our family. I could imagine lots of things.

I had to imagine, because he never videoed, never even DMed.

There's internet service at the house, at least when the loons —network-relay balloons, high up in the stratosphere—form a tight enough chain. Lately that's most days, since they keep putting them up in the stratosphere. Shiny mylar, *amazing* albedo. Very good voxels. Back when Jonathan left two decades ago, the service was less regular. But he could have at least dmed.

He never did.

Well, he never dmed *me*.

"WHAT?" said Leo.

"Dad told me to go."

"Just because he threw you out of the house didn't mean you had to leave the continent!"

"No. It wasn't like that. He sent me back."

"He *what*?"

Mom broke in. "You two can catch up later. The simple child—"

Leo stopped her with an outstretched arm. "Dad *sent* you? Why? *Where?*"

Jonathan shuffled uncomfortably in his seat. He was a big man, even if thinned out from his taiga journey home, but he seemed all at once to collapse in on himself. "I dunno. Ask him."

Leo's eyes narrowed. He turned to look at Dad.

Dad stared blankly back at all of us. He blinked. He licked his lips. I do not know if, in that moment, he could have counted his own children.

"Well?" said Leo. "Where did you send him?"

Dad blinked again. "The simple child asks, 'What is this?' To them—"

"Where did you send Jonathan, Dad?"

"—we say, 'With a mighty arm—'"

"Where did you send Jonathan?" Leo's voice was louder than I'd heard it in years.

"'—G-d freed us—'"

"Where did Jonathan go?" Leo was shouting, now, hands flat on the table.

"'—from the house of bondage.'"

"Where, Dad!"

"Texas," said Mom. "He wanted us to go home."

"Dad's not from Texas," said David.

"Home is *here*," I said, at the same time.

It's hard to say which one of us Mom looked at with greater contempt. But she loved Leo, and she spoke to him.

"We never told you," she said. "We didn't want you to know."

"Dad's not from Texas," said David. "We're not from Texas. If we were from Texas—"

"You didn't move here," I said. "You were sent."

Jewish history is a litany of expulsions. First Exile, Second Exile. The Roman Diaspora. The Spanish Inquisition. The Khmelnytsky Uprising. The pogroms. The Holocaust. These episodes enter gentile history as genocides, as exterminations, and this is not inaccurate. But the Jews of a later era are descended from survivors, and survivors *fled*. They knew when to flee, and how fast to travel.

The story of the Exodus is perhaps not a surprise.

"You could have told us," said David. "There's no shame in it. Half of my class's parents are from Texas. They made new lives, they raised families, they *talk* about it..."

"Yes," said Leo. "*They* talk about it." He was still staring at Dad.

Dad blinked aimlessly—and blinked again with sudden recognition, and said, quite clearly and distinctly, "Jonathan."

Silence at the seder table.

"Jonathan," he said again. But he was not looking at his oldest son; he was looking at his youngest.

"Yes, Dad," said Leo, quietly.

"Jonathan, you're back."

"Yes, Dad," said Leo, and beside him Jonathan mouthed the same words.

"Jonathan, did they forgive me? Can I go home?"

Leo clenched his jaw, his fists. He turned to his older brother.

"No, Dad," said Jonathan. "You can't."

WHAT HAPPENED in Texas was complicated. Drought in the Rio Grande. Crop failures on the Great Plains, from Nuevo León to Iowa. Mass migration along several distinct axes. Dismemberment of the petrochemical industry. Rocket riots over Project Sunshade. Paramilitary violence and military violence.

System failures are as complicated as systems themselves.

But not everyone who left Texas was a refugee.

"THEY TOOK ME TO A MUSEUM," Jonathan said. "I marched in and applied for family repatriation, and they looked my name up on a list and said you'd better come with us. And I thought..."

I do not think I had ever seen my brother cry before. Nobody needed to ask him what he thought.

"But I went and they *showed* me, Dad. The Hall of Exiles. They have a museum and *you're in it*. They have the dronecams and the SWAT groupchats and the interoffice wiki. Dozens of people *died* in that holding cell—"

"Hot summer," said Dad. He sounded ancient. He sounded like a boy.

"You had water, and you *didn't give it to them*."

"Such a hot summer," said Dad. "They just kept coming."

"A new king arose over Egypt," I said, "and he said, 'Look, the

Israelite people are too numerous for us. Let us then deal shrewdly with them.'"

"Hottest summer of my life," said Dad. "Nothing like here."

"Then *why did you send me back?*"

Dad stared, for a long time. His jaw slack.

"I want to go home."

WE COULDN'T GET anything out of Dad after that. He went back inside, to where that metastatic shadow-self was eating him.

The next day, out on the range with my wife, checking in on the pregnant mammoths and tagging the youngest calves, telling her the story, I could not believe it didn't end right then. But the truth is, we kept going. None of us were ready for the seder to end.

We drank all four cups of wine. We counted out the plagues. We ate algae karpas and horseradish from the backyard. The kids hid the hazelnut afikomen. Leo hugged Jonathan. Jonathan hugged Mom. The mammoth brisket was delicious. We sang "Dayenu," because even a single miracle would have been enough.

Out on the range with Thea, I thought about my parents' lies. About my father's crimes. About fleeing, and about being sent.

When a loon is near, I could look up my father's trial. I could dig up his conviction in an old database. I don't need to, though. The sentences were all the same. *Climate remediation for the remainder of natural life*. Forty years in the desert.

Those sentenced ended up all over. The *olam* is wide, and there's more than enough *tikkun* to go around. "It is not your duty to finish the work, but neither are you at liberty to neglect it."

The world is very complicated, and sometimes when I try too hard to understand it all I get confused. Which is why I'm grateful for my wife.

She gets up in the morning. She puts her feet on the permafrost. She tends to the mammoths.

To me, those animals are 5.8 billion genetic base pairs locked in a chaos cascade with maybe half a trillion other ecological variables, bending the curve of an ecosystem away from catastrophe. That's what I write in my reports.

Thea doesn't think about them that way. She puts her hands on a snowy, furry flank; a trunk wraps around her shoulders. That's enough.

So I told her the story, all of it, and I waited at the end for her insight. And because she's wiser than I am, she waited instead for me. And I realized: I know how the story ends. The same way it always does: *l'shana haba'ah b'yerushalayim*.

Next year in a more just world. Next year, in the city of peace.

LOVE, SCOTLAND

E.M. FAULDS

Originally published in *Nova Scotia Volume 2*,

eds. Neil Williamson and Andrew J. Wilson

E.M. Faulds is a Scottish science fiction and fantasy writer. Her short stories have been published in *Strange Horizons, ParSec* and *Shoreline of Infinity* magazines, as well as appearing on *PodCastle* episode 902 for their 2025 Disability Pride & Magic special. Her work has also been included in several anthologies, including *Nova Scotia Volume 2* and *SF Caledonia Anthology One*. She's a member of the Glasgow SF Writers' Circle, and was co-editor for their anthology, *Gallus,* for the Glasgow 2024 Worldcon. Her novella, *Bring Me Home,* is available now from Wizard's Tower Press. You can find out more at emfaulds.com.

Meera's knees burned as she stepped up through the Cowp, but she had to test each foothold, take her time. Mingis edged along ahead of her around the tumbled, teetering stacks, his back a yellow flash among the beiges and blacks of devices, the bruised purple of the sprouting fungus and the browns of the support matting. She followed, gloved fingertips tentatively pressed as an anchor or a ward against the jumbled masses of abandoned tech stained by dribbles of dark liquid. In the back of her mind a mantra: *no avalanche, no falling, no avalanche, no rain.* The clouds lowered in grey defiance; the town of Love was lost, somewhere below.

Metal shells and silicon crunched and warped beneath her feet, each step a new balance. The route that wound through: a path built by antlines of scavengers finding the easiest route. She thought of the Cathedral in Glasgow, down in its crypt where feet over millennia had worn the steps into a furrow. The refugee council had taken them on a trip there as a cultural insight. Saint Mungo was supposed to be entombed there. He had been important to the city.

The temples in her city were all buried now, the footworn story on their steps erased.

There weren't that many scavengers out today. The rain was coming, she could feel it. She bit her lip as her chest heaved and bucked on itself. The rain made these involuntary things happen, made her husband Hari's face flash into her thoughts.

THE ROAD UP THERE—MORE a potholed track after years of being cut off from regular traffic, a snaking jitter up and around the hillside. "The council could fix this up," she'd complained as the dog cart's solid rubber wheels got trapped by a particularly deep rut and they'd needed to apply manual encouragement.

"Whit? Spaff ma tax money on this? Nae danger," Mingis had teased as they grunted and pushed at the little machine with its load of sturdy canvas carrier bags spotted with mildew and acid pinhole burns. As it rolled out of the divot, he'd pressed a button on his phone marked *Continue?* and the cart resumed its autopilot route, and he resumed his story. "An she sez tae me, she sez—"

She tuned out, but the story about his ongoing battle with his neighbour was more for his benefit than hers, anyway.

His accent was thick as porridge, but for some reason she understood him. It was as if the man *vibed* meaning through a collection of soggy vowel sounds. His name, she had seen on her temporary employment form, was actually James Hunter Menzies, but he'd said 'Mingis' when he first shook her hand and now that's what he was. A Scottish way of pronouncing the 'z' sound and their complete disrespect for the vowel 'e,' apparently. The little man—a rough red drinker's nose and thick fingers—employed refugees like her. At first, she'd assumed he merely wanted to exploit the government sponsorship bonus. But these days she wasn't so cynical.

As she understood it, the spoil heap, his daily workplace, had started out as a fly-tipping deposit. When newly independent Scotland announced stage one of its major policy drive to deal with e-waste, bogus companies had sprung up overnight, offering to 'deal with the waste in an environmentally friendly way' for a cut of the government funding. Truck after truck had sneaked up into lonely roads above little towns just like Love to fly-tip the disposable vapes, phones, hard-drives, flatscreen TVs, and even old box PCs into the wilderness. But that was before stage two, the Myco-remediation Revolution. Fungi engineered in special labs not only broke down e-waste, but absorbed and stored their rare earth elements for harvest.

Now the waste deposit was an asset, protected from anyone but licensed gatherers like Mingis. The council had covered the heap with nutrient-infused matting and seeded it with spores. They'd fenced the place off and blocked the road to all vehicles larger than a battery-powered cart as wide as a wheelchair. You had to swipe in each time. The big fungus farms over on the East Coast dealt with all the new influx from other countries, but existing deposits belonged to the communities they'd blighted. The locals had quickly nicknamed it Mushie Mountain, or the Cowp—a Scots word for rubbish heap.

They'd stopped to put on the full protection gear before they even got close: waders, rain gear, full facemasks nestled snug under a hood. It was a sweat-inducing heatwave inside the suit, but necessary. Acids, toxic leaching, even the mushrooms were not to be touched without some sort of protection. Meera had pulled on layer after layer, picked up the canvas sack that she was to fill with their harvest.

This is how Meera became hazmat-suited up and among this tumbled heap of detritus in the rain, on a mushroom hunt.

The Haunting of Ghan

When the levee burst, Ghan drowned saving a cat from a storm drain. Not his cat. Just a stray. It didn't matter, the thing had cried so pitifully he couldn't have left it any more than he could have left a child. Many children drowned that day, too. And the people who had tried to rescue them as the torrents tore through the city.

Meera had met him online, but he had gone missing when the disaster struck, and she had not heard from him since his last video upload about a cat stuck in a drain.

When Ghan arrived in Love, he took the first open job: gathering some mushrooms with a weird little man who spoke terrible English that he later learned was not English at all, but a language called Scots. He'd done his time, but it was hard work, and the weather was atrocious.

His accommodation on Auricle Street was small, and everything smelled of damp. At night he put on all the clothing he owned to lie in bed and shiver himself to sleep. And all the white locals seemed to expect a degree of gratitude for 'allowing' him to stay.

Sick of being cold and wet, he'd taken a job as trainee cook in the Indian Jewels, a little restaurant next door to the Hug and Snug on Friendship Road. He'd expected some shouting or recrimination as he'd gone to tell Mingis, but instead the little man had accepted the news with merely a shrug and a sigh and sent over the last of his wages the same day.

It didn't matter Ghan knew very little about how to make pilau rice or whatever the hell chicken tikka masala was, (some weird British concoction with hardly any spice, it turned out). He chopped vegetables, stirred pots, cleaned the floor, and waited for his permanent Scottish citizenship to come through. He didn't have anywhere else to be. At least it was warm and dry in the kitchens.

Everyone he knew from back home had drowned when the levee protecting the city had burst. There was an inquiry about how greedy businesses and corrupt politicians had pocketed money instead of pouring it into the only protection from the rising seas for millions of citizens. No one had gone to jail yet. The coverage here had been pitiful, just another far-off place suffering, and the internet articles from back home frustratingly opaque.

But he was here. He was alive. Something better would come tomorrow.

LOVE WAS A STRANGE TOWN, and easy to lose yourself in, despite how small it was compared to the sprawl back home. Meera had folded a printed-off map into the breast pocket of her puffy, cumbersome jacket, in the beginning.

Philadelphia Street held the mosque around a corner from

the plaza known as the Atrium, where the weekly market set up. Amity Avenue was shared by a Sikh Gurdwara, and several rows of shops. The main route in and out of town was called Arterial Road. Agape Place, where the refugee offices were, wasn't pronounced like it was spelled—a Greek word, apparently. The name had come to be used as a kind of slang for refugees, corrupted until it became 'aguppies.'

These place names were a kind of joke, a play on the town name, but it was hard to find it all funny. Some of the white locals still used the old names that had been there before: Johnstone Road, Buchanan Place. Out of habit. And there were other things, things only someone who had lived there years could know. She wrote them all in. The map of Love gained many scribbled biro annotations, old name next to new name, where to buy what, that 'Leisure Centre' meant 'pool and exercise classes' and so on. It frayed along the creases and furred at the edges.

Sometimes when she came into the little shop to buy groceries, she caught the white townsfolk's expressions, the real one, before the walls came up. Some of them used the word 'aguppie' in front of her, pretending to apologise, or not. She didn't find the term offensive on its face, but they did, which told her it was just a stand-in for what they really wanted to say. Most of them smiled and nodded at her in greeting as she walked down the street. She smiled back as if it were really a pleasure, as though Hari's hand was in hers, as though these were streets she belonged to, as though it were sunny and warm.

She'd ignore the casual racism and the rain; she'd act as if everything was fine. But she didn't have to believe it.

Eventually the map in her breast pocket became welded shut when she was caught in a downpour and soaked through. The ink bloomed and ran until it resembled a psychoanalyst's blot test. She threw it in the recycle bin.

THE CREVICE in the spoil heap opened like a mouth. The gap was propped with steel pit supports like a mine, and its maw was just as foreboding. She'd been in before but hated it every time. Mingis had told her on her first day that the best mushrooms were inside, the ones they really needed. "Darker, see?" So, they went back in, over and over, even though it scared the life out of her. She was used to not arguing with bosses. But it was raining. She couldn't say no, but could she ask him for something else to do, anything?

The thought of that creaking mass falling on her, swallowing her ... but she couldn't argue. People got fired for arguing.

There'd been a succession of refugees who worked up here, he'd told her. And they'd done their time, got enough money to leave for new jobs or new towns as fast as they could. She could tough it out. It wasn't the worst thing she'd ever had to do.

The interview with him had been an odd experience, though.

His house on Heart Street was an eccentric mix of old and new. Most of it looked scavenged. IKEA furniture mixed in with heavy dark-wood antiques. Cushions with Persian teardrop patterns that the Scots called paisley clashed with battered leatherette modular couches. A glitterball smart speaker dandruffed its sparkle onto a mid-century modern console table. In the sitting room, above a mantlepiece with a brick wallpapered chipboard hatch sealing off the fireplace, the most hideously unsettling deer head was mounted. The taxidermy was rough, to say it kindly, but that wasn't it—where the deer's glass replica eyes should have been, twin clusters of mushrooms sprouted. Mingis had laughed when he caught her staring at it, mouth hanging open. He'd rattled off something, but all she could pick out was, "auld mushyface."

It was a tribute, she found out, to Myco-remediation. It was a point of pride. She realised then that you couldn't take anyone from these islands at face value.

The wind picked up and Mingis eyed the skies shiftily beneath his plastic face guard. Weather apps were almost entirely useless these days. Storms could form and shift in without warning. He muttered something about their chances of getting away without getting drenched. She nodded despondently, and they bent towards the entrance that led inside the very heart of the mountain of waste.

She knew what they had come here for. Mushrooms worth as much as diamonds.

The Haunting of Chesma

Chesma had fallen overboard from a boat crossing, trying to find a way to Scotland that wasn't hampered by the UK border patrol. She'd almost made it to Sweden, where a safe crossing existed, but her train had been raided and she'd been trucked to a camp on the French coast. England was only fifty miles from here, they said. A man had come round the camp and taken everything she had. Once she was across the Channel, he said, she could work her way up to cross the border into Scotland. They have a town there, he said, for people who need somewhere to live. Love, it was called. He laughed as he said it. Chesma's body was never found. Meera had read about the little boats that had capsized in the channel's frigid waters seven weeks ago. The names and faces of the victims were never shared.

Chesma played the bouzouki with her group of fellow refugees who had formed a small gigging band. They had a booking for the Love Festival, where the little town would open its doors to the rest of Scotland for a 'celebration of strength through diversity.' Food stalls and craft markets in the Atrium, art exhibitions and dance events had all been months in the planning. There was even a tour of the e-waste cottage industry, though that was strictly controlled. Spies and saboteurs were expected. Men with tattoos and flags would be coming up from the UK, too. Scotland still hadn't closed its borders to their old partners, and troublemakers could still make it past border control. But they'd been turned back before and would be again.

Her father had said, when she'd finally been able to contact him back home, that having so many dispossessed in one place was dangerous. That it made a ghetto. Vultures and hyenas would circle. The state would turn on them whenever it was convenient. Her father had been right, but wrong about the culprits.

UK tabloid headlines called the town of Love a dumping ground for the worst of humanity and reported on drugs, child abuse, gangs and theft, wars between the queer community and the religions who made their home here. And, worst of all, these troubles would spill into the UK because Scotgov were lax with their borders. All these stories were the worst possible interpretation of any event, any friction. There were arguments, of course, tensions. But no more than any other town. The Scottish government had, strangely for this part of the world, done something about it and fined and banned the news outlets. In response, the billionaire owners had declared war on the Scottish state.

But the UK still needed something from Scotland. The Scots could treat and recycle the e-waste thanks to those little mushrooms. The UK was still addicted to creating the waste, and where did they send it? To their northern neighbours. So, the threats made towards the country were hollow. And the town of Love made a damn fine living off the proceeds.

Chesma plucked the strings of her bouzouki idly while she

waited for her tea water to boil. Her father would come join her one day. Then he'd see.

THE SACK of mushrooms was much heavier than it looked as Meera dragged it, clambering at times on all fours through the crevice in the spoil heap. Elements the fungi had "sooked up like a sponge," as Mingis had explained, made the little fruiting bodies disconcertingly hefty. Trickles of rainwater and ponds of tunnel sweat made the plastic and metal surfaces treacherous, tons of debris held up above her head by pit props and prayer. It would come down on her. It would crush her, trap her. *No avalanche, no avalanche.*

She could see the cleft opening now, dark skies and howling winds swallowing the beam of her torch. She hesitated by the mouth of the tunnel. Mingis would want her to leave the mushrooms there so she could retrieve another bag. A day like today, all the other scavengers had gone home. Only Mingis was crazy enough to stay out in this weather. She could tell him she wanted to leave, that they should abandon the harvest for better weather. That he was insane.

What stopped her was the money. The town allowed her to stay in accommodation for free until she could earn enough to get out. If she got fired, she'd take longer. She was taking up a place for someone else, someone who might need it more. Someone who might already be trying to get here.

They were already in her head—a gestalt of faces she'd seen on television or social media, hunched backs in inadequate life jackets, bodies found in containers, starving and burned, faces in newspapers pictures and charity flyers; the thousands of people driven from disaster just like her.

She dumped the bag at the mouth of the tunnel and went back inside the spoil heap for the next.

The Haunting of Pavel

Pavel never made it past the men with the machine guns and dogs.

He had been executed by hanging. His body was strung up on the wall by a garage to discourage anyone else from 'deviant sexual practices' such as loving someone the government did not approve of. They had taken him in the night and held a trial, a mockery of justice. All the time, Pavel wondered who had denounced him. He had told no one. Meera had watched a documentary on the genocide being practiced on the queer people in this country, footage which included scenes of brutal hangings including one man with eyes wide and wild as he was led to the rope. She had left the community hall screening shaking, his eyes an indelible mark upon her soul.

Pavel spent most of the bus ride from the ferry terminal to the Scottish town called Love hypothesising on who he would have to fight. He was used to proving himself. He'd been in the national guard for his mandatory service and, even then, had been up on many charges. He'd never touched another man except to fight. It was the only way to survive. The current government had got in because people in his country were poor —crops failed, livestock got disease, and corruption was everywhere—and these men talked strong. There was rumour they would execute homosexuals someday soon. He'd sworn and spat curses at men who looked like they might be gay, just to be safe.

And then, the fire had swept through his hometown. He had nowhere left to live and a government that wanted him dead, if they ever found out what he really was. This was an easy choice. He'd paid all his savings to hide in a compartment in the back of someone's car for hours, choking on exhaust fumes. Then he was transferred into a cargo container with a bucket for piss and days and days of darkness with hardly any air. Then he had been taken out, and groggily claimed asylum at a place called Rosyth. And now he was in a bus winding through the Scottish countryside, past fattened cows and fluffy sheep idly chewing cud in green fields.

He wondered how secret he would have to be here, whether it was dangerous to even make eye contact with another man. He came here because he had heard it wasn't the case, but still. He should be cautious.

On arrival in Love, Pavel stepped down into the weak sunshine. At the welcome meeting in the refugee offices, he was greeted by a man who made him very uncomfortable. This man was openly gay. He should spit on him and walk away. For some reason, he did not. "It's okay," the man said gently. "You have a lot of adjustments to make." Pavel's English was basic, and the accent was difficult. But he understood it wasn't dangerous yet. He would fight if he needed to. But he didn't need to. Not yet.

THE WATER WAS THREATENING to enter the tops of Meera's boots when she took her last trip back inside the Cowp. "Come on, we have to go!" she screamed at Mingis.

He grunted and sighed as if she was overreacting. Nevertheless, he shoved the last bag of mushrooms at her and picked up his own to follow her back through the tunnel.

The tunnel groaned. She wondered if the rain would make things slip into a landslide, even with electronic components. The thought of being trapped here, perhaps alive while she suffocated under the thoughtless waste of so many, spurred her on faster and faster. The pit props creaked and her heart skittered. Had she left it too late? Would she drown or be pressed into paste?

No avalanche, no avalanche.

Hari. Hari. Hari.

And then they were out into the whistling winds and lashing rain.

The sodden canvas bags at the top of the tunnel were heavy. Meera dragged and hauled, hauled and dragged back down the Cowp until they reached the dog cart at the bend in the track. She shivered even beneath her protective gear from exhaustion and terror.

Mingis powered up the dog cart and they began the long trudge down. "There's a pint wi yer name on it doon there," he said cheerfully.

"Festival's the morra," he went on conversationally as if they hadn't just been in mortal danger. "Yez goin, aye?"

And for once, she didn't have the urge to say, "Yes, boss."

"Aye, I am," Meera said. "By the way, I'm not going back in there if it's raining like this again. Don't ask me."

Mingis didn't shout or fire her. He merely squinted at the rivulets of water pouring down the track.

"Right enough."

The Haunting of Meera

Meera had died during the floods that devastated her part of the world. She had made it to higher ground and safety during the torrential storm, only to be buried in a landslide that swept away the entire slope on which she and her husband had stood. She died from suffocation. She died from people turning their faces away when they could take no more of the world's death throes.

Meera had made it to Love without Hari. He said he would be there as soon as he could, but travelling that far was difficult, and he needed to keep working to make up the money they needed. They chatted online every day, but she felt like he was fading from her, an irreparable distance between them.

She had fled her home to escape temperatures that were getting worse every summer, killing anyone and everyone. She had travelled north, eventually securing a flight for the last leg into Edinburgh airport. She had been stopped there, at border control. She had told them of the heat, the drought, the babies she had held as they coughed and fretted until they stopped moving at all. She told them of the flood waters that raged whenever there was rain, earth too hard to absorb the water. She expected them to say that this was no excuse for not having a visa, that political threats to life allowed asylum but not environmental.

"We have a place for you," they had told her instead.

The town of Love, an old settlement that had expanded and taken in the refugees. There was still friction between old and new, but she knew from everything she'd read online that she was lucky to be here. Lucky to be not drowned, or starving, prevented from entry into the country by people filled with hate like so many others.

She'd been haunted with it. Everyone was these days. Stories of strangers dying, disasters that wiped out communities, trauma—helpless to change things but witness to it all. The internet connected them but divorced them, increased empathy but decreased agency until people drowned in it or switched off that part of themselves.

She'd found a town called Love, but so many hadn't.

She had signed up for a temporary work agency and, after a few different assignments, found the eccentric Mingis and his cottage business. It had sounded easy enough and the pay was astounding for the hours. But it wasn't easy. Every day she'd worked herself to exhaustion for this odd little man, who did the same himself. He swore as easy as breathing but there was never any malice to it. He had a weird respect for fungi, and she'd found many books on mycology in his house on Heart Street that were, to be honest, easier to understand than he had been.

But she had no fear of hard work; her entire life had been one of labour, cleaning and cooking for the richer families, caring for children as if they were her own, arranging the funerals for her family members who died in the heat, one by one. She had never had a job that paid so much as picking these element-eating mushrooms.

Yes, it was easy in comparison.

And then sudden news of her hometown, in the path of the floods. She had lost her husband, lost her last connection back home. And every morning she woke up from nightmares of waves and landslides, of drowning in mud. And had to crawl into a dark, dank hole in a toxic waste tip.

She mourned. She suffered. She was often terrified. But she did not die.

Instead, she found a place to go on.

Mingis dumped the mushrooms into some large digester vats in his back court. After a day of processing, they drew off several jugs of liquid which they loaded into the dog cart. The mushroom soup swam with ions of expensive and rare materials which Scotland traded with the world. Meera didn't fully understand how they would turn this back into metal, but the proof was in the money he put in her account every month.

She thought of alchemy, of how many ancient scholars had sought exactly this kind of magic. Mushrooms into gold. Or, at least, ions into electrons, elements that turned into digital numbers in an online bank account that gave her the things she needed to live.

Meera watched him ride his bicycle alongside the little

trundling cart as sunshine lanced down through the clouds onto Heart Street. He skirted some puddles, swearing audibly but with good humour as he went.

Later she would go down to the festival and watch the bouzouki band play and sing folk songs from their homeland—the videos she'd seen were infectiously joyful. And eat the wonderful food, especially that Indian restaurant that reminded her of home. And later, there was a queer cabaret she'd seen a poster for, the main attraction a man with striking eyes framed by heavy mascara that somehow made him more masculine.

And somehow, through all of it, they would exorcise the ghosts that haunted them. For a time. Find a way to keep going. It was all they could do.

Love wasn't perfect. But it was a place to start.

OUR BEST SELVES

HIRON ENNES

Originally published by *Weird Horror Magazine*

Finalist for *The Best Weird Fiction of the Year, Vol. 1*, edited by Michael Kelly

Hiron Ennes is the author of the British Fantasy Award-winning novel *Leech.* Their newest novel, *The Works of Vermin,* was released in October, 2025.

THE HOUSE IS A SQUAT TRAPEZIUM OF STONE, FISSURED LIKE the trunk of a tree. Its cracked slab of a roof slumps under centuries of vines, piebald with moss. When our cab approaches, a small owl rustles from a window and flutters up to the canopy.

Mum takes to it right away. She stumbles from the taxi with the cat in one arm and my brother in the other, leaving a trail of dropped objects behind her. Dad tries to mirror her enthusiasm. He picks up after her, snatching gloves and socks and booklets like a hen pecking. He wears a patient smile until he gets to the doorway, where he finally sees the magnitude of his fixer-upper. The floors are dirt. Leafy columns of light tumble through the cracks in the roof. A possum hisses in the entryway.

His wife is nothing but pleased. She circles the house, examining crumbling furniture carved from the same stone as the walls. Crude marble cylinders pass for stools. Slabs like tombstones mark the headboards. My brother wipes dust from a windowsill to find it trimmed in obsidian.

I slip through a fissure in the wall to the garden. Mum is already out there, bending over the mossy quadrangles of stone. She digs through the hardened earth, appraising the crumbling soil. There are plenty of things already growing. Berries, shrubs, apple trees, a couple of wild tubers. The canopy is thin, and there are soft patches where she can build more beds. Even the shady bits will be wrapped around her green thumb soon enough.

She rounds the stone fence and points out where she'll plant the spinach later this week. Where the beets will go, the tomatoes, her meticulously engineered squashes. She runs her boot through the brush, demarcating the beds, but my eyes have already wandered.

A sapling rustles by a window on the north side of the house. It's not an ash, not a maple, not an oak—its leaves, long and dark and strange, undulate in my direction. I know a greeting when I see it, so I step over to brush its bark, soft, smooth as skin, and dusted with fine green hairs.

"What's this one?" I ask Mum.

"I don't know, darling," she answers. "But I think it's yours."

THE FIRST NIGHT, we claim our rooms. If they can be called rooms. Some only become rooms when we drape Mum's tapestries over their missing walls. Others are completely closed in by vines writhing up from the floor. None has a door.

A fissure in the north wall widens into a sort of window,

looking out on the sapling. I want the bed closest to it, but my brother gets there first. I decide to fight him for it, and neither of us will budge. He's got his eye on that tree, and he doesn't believe me when I say it's mine.

In the end, Mum claims the room for herself and Dad. She says it's because she does not want to see us fight over it. She tells us that when we are squabbling, we are not our best selves, and we must always strive to be our best selves.

Dad lays their blankets down over the bed-slab and agrees.

"When you think about it, your mother and I are the unlucky ones," he says. "This is the only room that doesn't have a view of that beautiful night sky."

A WEEK IN, Dad takes his axe on a foray into the woods. He's decided that before he can install the floor panels, carve doors and shutters and repair Mum's loom, and especially before the rain comes, he must fix the roof.

My brother and I find pieces of it scattered around the property. We're supposed to be finishing our schoolwork, but we circle the yard, cutting away ferns and unburying dozens of wide, broken wedges. They lie scattered in every direction—a few have fallen so far that the cat won't follow us out to them, preferring to sit and yowl in the doorway. My brother wants to gather the missing pieces and fit the roof back together like a puzzle. He quickly learns that none of us could lift the smallest fragment.

"How did the roof break, anyway?" he asks me.

"Earthquake," I say, because I can't think of anything else with enough force.

He goes silent for a while, watching Dad pile his cuts at the edge of the garden, thin trunks that look similar to pine but smell much sweeter. Sap dark as mud oozes from their axe-bites.

"How was the house even built?" my brother asks.

"There's mountains nearby," I answer. "The builders chipped off slabs and carried them down here."

"Why?" He gestures to the trees, a verdant abundance of beams and floorboards and shingles. "And *how*?"

"They were giants," I answer. "It was easy for them. This is just their dollhouse."

"No, it's not."

"I'm serious. We're their dolls. Once they know we're here, they'll come play with us. Put you in a little dress, snap your limbs off."

I've gone a step too far. He frowns and floats over to Mum, who's planting her greens in neat, straight rows. He leans up to her, and she shakes her head.

"Don't lie to your brother," she hollers. "Those who lie are not at their best."

I sigh and look to the sapling at the end of the garden. It shudders and waves, though there's no wind I can feel.

THE CAT IS NO LONGER STRICTLY an outdoor cat, since there are no longer strict outdoors. He wanders through the fractures of the house day and night, chattering, kneading, marking.

Dad says he can't get the smell of piss out of his nose. He wonders aloud if he should abandon the roof and prioritize making doors.

"He's a pest," Dad says.

"He's the only reason why we're not overrun with rodents," Mum answers. She skins a few tubers at the sink, paring knife glinting with remarkable speed.

"At least let's keep him out of our room. He makes you wheeze."

"He doesn't —" She stops herself. She's not going to say the cat doesn't make her wheeze, not after what she's just told me about lying.

"And the hives," Dad says. "Your condition worries me as it is."

Mum gives him an irritated frown. "I don't have a condition," she answers, slowly, each word a careful guess.

She sets down her tubers and retreats to the garden, where she walks along her fresh rows for the rest of the evening. She doesn't even come in for dinner, after I have finished the paring and Dad the boiling, when my brother has set our stone table with stone plates. For hours, she paces and mutters among her seedlings. She is praying fervently, and against Dad's wishes, for rain.

EVERY WOMAN in our family has exactly one daughter. There are no sisters, no cousins, no childless maids, so our family tree is a thin, straight vine. All our knowledge of horticulture and herbalism descends in this way, unbroken and perfectly linear. The genealogies of our squashes are far more tangled.

My mother has already taught me most of it. She taught me which plants are friends and which aren't, which to eradicate and which to cultivate, which animals are pests and which tinctures might kill them. She taught me how to skin a tree, to soak and dry and flatten its pulp into paper, how to prune a tomato's limbs so the others proliferate unimpeded, how to select for traits that help our lineages grow into their best selves.

Despite her teachings, I can't identify the plant that has grown at the foot of my bed. A collection of dew has sprinkled through the hole in my ceiling, coaxing a green shoot from the ground. Overnight it's crawled up the granite slab of my mattress.

When I poke my head into Mum's room, telling her I've

found something new, she says she's feeling faint. She's tucked in bed with the cat and neither are willing to move. She'll hold out for as long as she can, until the blankets are soaked and we have to clean up the blood.

"Make me my tea," she says.

I retreat to the kitchen and grab her jar of little red pills. I steep them with the rest of the leaves while she groans in her room, more frustrated than pained. She's been trying for so long to wean herself off the stuff, the same way she's weaned off every medicine that came before. I hate the tea, but not because it smells like rot and looks worse, but because I am afraid, one day, that I'll need it too.

DAD COMES home with what he thinks is a boar but what may be something else. It's four-legged and hairless, long neck sagging on his back as he trundles back to the house. We help him drag it to the porch and watch him get to work with his knife.

"It's been so long since I've had any meat," he says, elbow-deep in blood. "My poor belly's sagging." He slaps his navel, leaving a splattered red print.

"We'll have you fed properly when the garden comes in," Mum tells him. "You just have to wait."

"Time is a necessity," I say.

"And what else?" Mum asks, smiling.

"Rain, sun and soil," my brother says, "are the only necessities."

"Very good."

The blood drips from the porch into the garden, where the early squashes grasp skyward. The sapling stands nearby, branches brushing the half-finished awning. Either it's grown taller in the past couple days, or it's gotten closer.

Dad manages to patch the roof by the first rains. It starts as a gentle patter, then, early in the morning, becomes a downpour. We are jolted awake by a deep, resounding snap, far closer than thunder. The house shudders with the echo of the rumble, and we all crawl from our beds.

In the kitchen, we find a pool of water, whirling around notches of wood and stone. Above our heads, a new fissure bolts through the ceiling, zagging from the hearth to the table. Dust and rain fall from the crack, pattering against our firewood.

Dad rolls a stool under the breach. He blinks through the thin sheet of sky-lit water, then lifts himself up to the crack. We clutch our nightgowns and watch his hand disappear into the fissure. He stills for a moment, frowns, then pulls a thin, long vine from the crack. He wraps it around his wrist, then his arm. Soon it's curling at his feet, yards and yards of leafless green.

When he finally snaps it from the crack, he's soaked. I'm not sure if it's rainwater or sweat.

"The cat is bad for you," Dad says. "We need to get rid of it."

"Don't you dare," Mum replies, wiping her nose. She is bedridden again today. "It's just the season. The pollen. It's gotten so thick."

She's not wrong. Gold dust has settled in with early summer, falling like snow through our open windows. Our sideboard, a recent project Dad painstakingly carved from oak, hasn't shown its surface in days. When we close our schoolbooks, we do so in puffs of yellow powder.

"He makes your eyes water," Dad says. "He wrecks your lungs —"

"He doesn't." If Mum wasn't already lulled by her tea, she

would notice how badly she's lying. But she is not her best. Her face is pale and dotted with sweat.

"It's not the pollen," Dad continues. "You know it—that animal is bad for your health, and your health is the whole reason we're out here."

"My health was an excuse," Mum replies. "You're happy here."

Dad's breath softens, his pause heavy. "Sure."

A FIRE BURNS in the hearth. The flames flicker blue and cold, so Dad gets another log. It slumps, soft and wet, like the last three.

"We shouldn't burn those," I say. "They're moldy."

He doesn't seem to hear me. "God," he breathes. "What I wouldn't give for a beer."

"Mum will kill you if you go back to town."

"Just for a night, dear." He glances at me. "You don't miss it?"

I shrug. I don't, really—I don't miss the old house, with its tiny garden. The school. The hospital. All the things that held us back, before Mum decided she didn't need it anymore—not the medicine or the car or the money to pay for any of it. Her best self would never need anything but sun and soil and rain and time.

Soft sobbing comes from the hallway. We turn from the fire to see Mum in her bloodstained nightgown, out of bed for the first time in three days. Her eyes are red, her cheeks flushed and wet. The cat dangles in her arms.

"Look at him," she says. "Something's wrong. Look."

She lays the creature on the kitchen table. The pollen clings to his fur and cakes his bloodied nose. She tries to stand him up, but he wobbles and falls, yellows of his eyes swallowed by the round, reflective black pools of his pupils.

"He looks toxic," Dad says.

"Did you give him something?" Mum asks. "Did you do something to him?"

"Of course not."

She begins to cry.

"I didn't do anything," Dad says. "Just wait. He might get better."

Mum wipes her swollen eyes, fingers goopy with pollen-stuff. "This is your fault."

"It's not."

"I'm going to find out how you did it," she says. She skirts the table, pulling jars of medicines from the shelf, opening stone drawers to rattle stone utensils. "I'll find it. I'll find what you gave him."

"I didn't give him anything!"

She ignores him, moving through the kitchen, the bedrooms, the back porch. She pulls books from their cases, and then pages from their spines. She digs through my schoolwork, breaks my pens and empties them, she dumps her jars of herbs and spices and preserves onto the counter.

She finds nothing amiss. She knows best what plants and oils go where, medicinal and toxic, which might dissolve harmlessly in a human mouth but fester in an animal's. She knows every leaf, seed and extract; Dad does not.

She gives up. Sobbing, she leaves the cat on the table and returns to her room. A thin trail of blood remains, smeared by the hem of her dress.

A DAY LATER, while Dad buries the cat, the oak handle of his shovel breaks in half.

It's an insult to describe my tree as a sapling anymore. Its trunk has thickened, its leaves fan out to arm's length. Its roots are flexible, growing, alive with tiny creaks and groans of xylem, billions of invisible stretching grains. If I listen hard enough, I can hear the soil shift between its rhizomes.

In a span of a few days, it overtakes the cat's grave. It lingers on that spot for a week, filling its roots, then slowly, slowly, retreats to the garden. It takes a month for it to make it from the lettuce beds to the tomatoes.

A little sentinel, Mum calls it. She no longer cries every day. Her breathing is clear. She has begun to make paper again.

Pulp floats on the surface of her soaking tub. She stirs it by hand, letting the bloated sludge drip through her fingers. It's a familiar task, a familiar smell, but today I find it oddly sickening.

A deep boom shakes the house, rippling the tub. Neither of us flinch. We are no longer startled by the crack of breaking stone. Even with the rains gone, every night we dream of new fissures, and wake to the sun shining through them.

Then, the crumbling of stone transforms, rising in pitch and severity until I realize it's not stone at all. My brother is screaming.

We abandon the soaking paper and stumble down the hall. A buzz of terror rustles the ferns peeking through the cracks in our walls.

A massive wedge of the roof occupies the center of the room. A broken portion of marble angles down from a streak of bare night sky, stone splinted with long planks of Dad's repair work. The dead wood has rotted, choked under a burden of leaves and branches and vines. Stems sway along the debris, swollen with sap, a shivering mass of rot and stone and greenery so convoluted I can't tell where it ends and my brother begins.

Dad appears behind us. He cries out, digging through the wreckage, grasping at his weeping, trapped son. I help him tear at the vines, snapping branches, ripping away sheets of bark. My brother finally appears again, mostly intact. His right arm is inextricable, and he screams every time our father tries to unearth it.

"Don't —" he wails. "Don't touch it—*don't*!"

Silent, mustering an uncanny strength, Dad pushes the slab off my brother's elbow.

Mum hugs me as her son rises from the debris, face bloody, arm hanging limp and mangled by his side. Patches of skin curl away like birch bark. He's got two new elbows, tipped with protuberances of white bone. Leaves and pinecone scales stick to his wounds. There is a splinter the size of a penknife lodged in his shoulder.

He is too shocked to cry out as Dad grips him under the knees and lifts him into his arms.

"I can fix him," Mum says. "It's bad, but I can do it. He needs a salve. He needs poultice—wait here, I can fix him."

"No, you can't," Dad barks. "He needs a hospital. He needs a fucking doctor."

"We can't —"

Dad shoves past her, terrified son in his arms. He carries him down the hall without looking at either of us, stomps through the kitchen, pushes open the front door.

"*Don't*!" Mum shouts. "He'll be fine! Please, we can do this ourselves. We *have* to do this ourselves!"

"We don't, and we can't," Dad growls. "I'm taking him to town."

Rapidly, my brother's shock abates, just enough to make room for dawning horror. He trembles, rustling the leaves sprouting from his mangled arm.

"I don't want to go back," he sobs. "Put me down. I want to stay."

"Listen to him!" Mum says. "Please, he's fine."

"I don't wanna leave!" my brother shouts, but Dad marches on.

"You can't just *walk* there!" Mum hollers, trailing him all the way to the squashes, to the moss-eaten path of pebbles that passes for a road.

Dad keeps walking, dodging the words flung at him, and with his arms clamped around my brother, disappears into the night.

I DON'T SLEEP that night. Neither does Mum. I crawl into bed with her, curling like the cat, and she moans until dawn.

In the morning, she works in the garden, violently pruning the tomatoes. She cracks stem after stem, nursing her cold tea in an obsidian mug. It doesn't help.

"It's good for the plants," she says, when I point out she's leaving a trail of blood. "It's nutrient rich." Then she begins to cry. Her tears drip thick and white like sap down her face.

"They're not coming back," she says.

"They are."

"The hospital will keep him—they'll put him down. My boy, my little boy. They'll murder him like your bastard father murdered the cat."

"Dad didn't murder the cat."

While she sobs, I try to clean the garden with the scuffle hoe, but it seems cruel, impossible. I try to sweep, but the cracked broom is heavy in my hands. I try to dry the paper, but the pulp repulses me. Every object seems to me a desiccated, desecrated corpse.

TWO MORE DAYS PASS. Then, they return. They have three arms between them.

My brother teeters, unsteady, wrapped in strips of his blood-stained pajamas. The severed sleeves of our father's coat bind his wound. He waves with his good arm from the end of the path, smiling through his pallor.

Mum, revitalized, rushes out to greet him, wrapping her arms around him and nearly lifting him from the ground. He groans when her chin brushes against his raw bud of a shoulder.

Dad greets Mum with a quick peck to the forehead. He looks like he's slept about as much as we have.

"What happened?" Mum asks. "Did the hospital just...let you go?"

"We never got that far," Dad admits. He eases himself through the front door and collapses on the stone table. "We had to stop."

Mum waits for an explanation. Dad is already half-asleep, curling his knees into his chest and closing his eyes.

She shakes him back awake. "What happened?"

He blinks. "We had to stop. I couldn't make it that far. We found a stream. I cleaned him up."

"Where'd his arm go?" I ask.

"I...pulled it off," Dad says. He turns over, buries his face in his hands, and releases something halfway between a laugh and a sob. "Snapped. Twisted it like a branch. It came right off."

"It did," says my brother proudly.

"Oh, my dears," Mum says, kissing them both. "I knew you could do it all by yourselves. I'm so proud of you. I knew you wouldn't give up."

Dad's breathing slows. "I...buried it," he mumbles. "By the stream."

Then he drifts away, exhausted from his travels. He's a sturdy man, rooted to the ground—he isn't meant to wander like that.

My brother is famished. While Dad snores on the table, he eats on the floor, chewing through the last of our early vegetables. He asks when the squashes will grow in. He asks if we cried when he got hurt. He asks if he can go dig up his arm later.

Mum laughs, tells him no. You should never unearth what you've already planted.

Dad confesses it's probably for the best they never made it to town. "It would've cost an arm and a leg to save that arm," he laughs. "Though I might've been tempted to get them to do something about this belly. It's sagging over my belt. In a few weeks I'll start tripping over it."

"When the squashes come in," Mum says, "we'll fatten you back up. We'll put some flesh under there." Her tone is earnest; by the silhouettes my parents cast against the ferns growing from the walls, they're holding one another close.

Dad blows an amused puff from his nose. The shadow of his arm reaches for her, skin hanging like a curtain from his elbow.

"You're breathing better," he says. "It really was that cat."

"Oh, stop."

"He was bad for you. He wasn't letting you grow into your best self."

"I know," Mum says. Then, quietly: "He was a pest."

I smile and look through the fissured ceiling to my tree, its dark crown spreading over our house like a new roof. I can feel its roots move under the floor, absorbing the activity inside. I can feel its soft, hairy bark brush up against the walls, soaking up my parents' heat, my brother's quiet, musical moans. His stub aches, but only with the pressure of new growth.

I shudder, relieved, contented. Leaves rustle in the breeze above me.

AUTUMN COMES heavy and full and fast.

The squashes swell with meat. The tomatoes burst and spill seeds, too heavy for their branches. The greens bolt, the wild apples fall, the corn shoots upward. Everything has grown to painful fullness, fecund and aching for relief.

My mother and I return to the kitchen with skirts full of vegetables. The peas are big as beets, the beets big as melons, the melons too big to carry. My father rolls one onto the porch, where he slices and salts and cans, swearing when he pinches his loose skin in the jar lids.

"Fucking tongs," he says, attempting to wrangle his chopped cantaloupe. "Everything wood in this goddamn house breaks."

My brother takes the utensils from him, extending his unbroken arm. It has grown a little longer, a little stronger in the absence of the other. He still likes using it, though two new ones have grown from his stub, stocky and thick. With his long arm he carries the tongs to the garden edge, with his short ones he digs a second grave, next to the cat's, and buries them.

Dad attempts to replace the tongs by whittling away at a branch of alder, but I can tell it unnerves him as much as it does me. We can both feel the pinch of steel scraping at the wood, hear the grain snapping and curling in pain. After a while, he gives up, blaming the skin hanging from between his fingers.

I tell him to make a new set of utensils out of bone.

"Whose bones?" he laughs. Then he stops, thinking over what I've said. The river isn't too far. It might take a day to get there and back.

SOON, the whole weight of the garden hits us. The squashes fill to bursting, agonized, stretched skin splitting open and spilling their entrails. Mum has to carry them in pieces to the kitchen, handful after handful of raw, ripe meat. I pluck the tomatoes while my brother makes his rounds of the garden, long arm reaching for what the rest of us can't. He strips the highest cobs from the corn, gathers seeds from the sunflowers, shakes loose the apples. Dad marches behind him, gathering the spoils in the loose apron of his stomach. When he can't carry any more, when his skin stretches with the bounty, he dumps the spoils onto our kitchen table.

My brother quickly sorts through them, organizing with respect to size and type and ripeness. The haul is so large it doesn't matter that he slips the cherry tomatoes into his mouth when Mum isn't looking, or nibbles at the basil stems. He is a growing boy. A fourth arm, short and soft as a baby's, juts side-long from one of his new elbows.

Mum removes seeds from the squash, digging her fingers through the orange meat and passing around sticky handfuls. We can only get through a quarter of it before we are too full to move.

Outside, the sky is cold and clear and blue. The deciduous leaves darken and shed, readying for the next turn of the season.

WHEN THE HARVEST is done and we've gathered all we can, Mum lies out in the empty garden, wetting the soil and steeping it for the following year. She can't stop grinning as she feeds the garden, lying in each patch and bleeding for a few hours before moving onto the next. Wordless, hair rustling in the breeze, her voice carries like birdsong through the house.

We've done it, she says. We've finally done it.

WINTER IS BLISS.

On the nights we make paper, Dad sits on a marble stool

while my brother grasps his skin, stretching it across the kitchen. I run a paring knife along it, trimming the hair, then through it. We cut a generous length from him, then I pat the laceration down with a compress of leaves and soil. Soon Dad stops gritting his teeth. He tells me it feels nice. He's always wanted to lose weight.

We pull his skin taut over a frame of bones, scrape off the pulp of his fat, and dry it in the cold sun. When the snows come, we stretch it over the ceiling, we hang it from doorways, we throw it over the beds and pillows and curl in its warmth. My book covers are stretched from his fingers. Our front door is made from his belly, navel protruding where a knob may have been. I have never loved him more.

When we are hungry, my brother lifts his long arm and reaches down the hallway, into the back room, where he grabs hold of dried corn and beans, or he rolls around a rock-hard squash, making a game of it. His arm is too long to reach his own mouth, and his other ones get mixed up with one another, so Mum breaks apart his food for him. For every morsel she brings to his lips, she scatters ten at his feet.

Occasionally, he will get bored. If I don't watch my back, I'll feel a tap on my shoulder or a tug at my clothes, and when I turn, I'll catch a glimpse of his long, pale arm snaking back into his room. I've never seen him grin as widely as he does when he pulls my hair from across the house. Sometimes, he snaps it off like a bunch of twigs, though always, more will grow.

The sapling has taken up residence right outside my room, branches stretching through the window, roots curling up from the floor. I don't think it can move much anymore, but it seems content, bathing in the beige light shining through the tapestries of skin.

I SIT IDLY MOST of these days, arms splayed under the lengthening daylight. Weeks pass before any of us become hungry or bored, months before my father grows a new length of skin to cut and dry and use again. There is little to do, but none of us mind. We want for nothing. We need nothing, except time, rain, sun and soil.

THE GHOST TENDERS OF CHORNOBYL

NIKA MURPHY

Originally published by *Apex Magazine*

Finalist for *Afterlives 2024: The Year's Best Death Fiction*, edited by Sheree Renée Thomas

Nika Murphy is a Ukrainian-born writer of speculative fiction. Her stories have appeared or are forthcoming in *Clarkesworld, Apex,* and other fine venues and anthologies. She lives in Florida with her family. You can find her online at nikamurphy.com.

Not all the ghosts of Chornobyl died in 1986. Some died years—decades—later, bodies ravaged by mutated cells. They were a hundred kilometers away, not realizing their favorite mug was doused with irradiated atoms from the destroyed reactor. I died in anger, during the invasion, volunteering to drive a truckload of baby formula and ammo, trying to prove to my father, to the world, that I was a man, only to be blown apart by an enemy mine. After, I wandered around for weeks looking for my legs until Kyryl found me and brought me here.

After eight months, I no longer try to leave the Exclusion Zone. The land pulls me back like the sun calling home a rogue comet. Kyryl teaches me about the mushrooms that feed off rogue isotopes. We tend to them. Help them grow and spread and eat the radiation. Help them bring the land back from the dead.

Kyryl says it wasn't so bad before the war. The only invaders he had to worry about were extreme tourists and documentary crews.

I sink my fingers into the black soil as the earth rumbles from explosions or shelling or crashing drones. I am learning to tell the difference in the vibrations. Worms wiggle and burrow their way to the surface through my sheer palms.

Bombs.

Close now. Less than five kilometers.

The forest cries out and so do my fungi. All at once, my mushrooms fan out their gills and release their spores. A sigh spreads through the woods and muffles the *rat-tat-tat* of the nearby gunfights. To the living, naked eye, there is nothing to see, but to me, to the ghosts, it is like wading through a gossamer fog. The spores shimmer and oscillate, calling to each other. Their song jingles in my ears, tickles my nose. They smell of dirt, of rot, of the smoke from a long dead fire.

I help some of the spores find their mates. Other ghosts help me find suitable places for them to settle. Fallen logs that capture morning dew. A deer carcass. The bark of hollow oaks.

"Do you think it will reach us?" I ask Kyryl one morning as he moves a yellow leaf and clears a space for the spores to settle. I speak in accented Ukrainian. My parents spoke Russian at home in the States. I only heard Ukrainian spoken on the phone with distant relatives. Now I speak it regularly. Maybe Dad would be proud of me.

"Don't know," he says.

Ghosts like Kyryl tend to the trees, the moss, the detritus. Some, children mostly, tend to living animals or insects. They enjoy it. More and more ghosts come every year as the older generations die. Most settle in Prypyat, in the ruins of abandoned apartments. Some build small shelters like birds' nests or Baba Yagas in the trees of the Red Forest. I live in a shack with a still living babusya who cares for the cats and dogs and chickens and goats that roam as wild and free as the spirits.

The babusya's name is Lyudmyla. She's shaped like a lowercase "a," hunched over with a round, soft belly. The whole of her always covered in kerchiefs and patterned robes and floured aprons. She knows I exist in the superstitious way most Ukrainian people do. I am her barabashka, a noisy spirit who keeps her company, keeps her safe.

Kyryl comes to collect me in the evening. We walk the shallow trenches where an invading army unit has hunkered down for the night.

"So many new mushroom beds for you," Kyryl says and slaps me on my sheer back. Something in me loosens, but not the anger, never the anger. Kyryl changes the subject, asks, "Found a new place to haunt yet?" He has been haunting here longer than I had been alive. Unlike me, he no longer bothers with the living.

"No," I say.

"You can stay with me if you like," he says. The memory of our physical bodies sends giggles through the mycelia beneath our feet. I pause, instinct, fear, doubt echoing from the days of the living.

"You know I'm not a woman, right?" I say.

Kyryl laughs. "We're not anything anymore."

A part of me vibrates with joy at Kyryl's casual acceptance. The rest of me burns with resentment, anger. Always anger. At all I lost when I transitioned. At my father. At my former body, my former name. Almost as if I died twice or never even lived.

The last thing I want is to be alone with my anger, so I follow Kyryl up a birch. We sway side by side in woven branches like hammocks, our spirits a tangled palimpsest.

The following afternoon, Kyryl and I make our rounds. The

defense forces have slaughtered the enemy unit. The invaders' bodies lay scattered between husks of smoking trees. A group of arborist ghosts gather to discuss regreening strategies. The dead soldiers' ghosts huddle together.

"At least you have each other, eh, fuckheads?" Kyryl yells to them.

One of the bodies begins to rise and visions of zombies fill my head, but it is only a soldier, using the corpse of his dead comrade as a shield. The soldier's uniform is covered in mud, not even the camouflage visible. He stares at the mass of limbs and bodies. The whites of his eyes shine amidst the kaleidoscope of blood and dirt and freckles on his face. A branch falls somewhere behind him, and he takes off running in the direction of Lyudmyla's cottage.

"Lyudachka," I say aloud, the tremble in my voice amplified by thunderclaps of anti-tank ordinance.

I follow straight through birch trunks and low-hanging pine branches. The air condenses around me and pulls me down, backwards. I struggle against the forest's spectral tendrils until I reach the shack.

The horizon glows red, first from the setting sun, then from the burning fires. Lyudmyla's voice hits me before the puppies' yelps. She is yelling at the soldier, full throated and nasally, as if a marble is lodged in her esophagus and her vocal cords have wrapped around it. Her words overlap, stuck to each other.

"WHYAREYOUHERE? WHATDOYOUWANT? GOHOME! GOHOMETOYOURMOTHER! SHESHOULD-BEASHAMEDOFYOU! YOUSHOULDBEASHAMEDOFY-OURSELF! ACCOSTINGANOLDWOMAN! GOHOME! THISISMYPLACE! LEAVEMEBE! YOUBASTARD! GOHOME!"

The only response is the *pop-pop* of his rifle and the puff of dirt displaced by his ammo. Lyudmyla stands in her doorway unfazed. She fears nothing. I stand in awe and shake. My fear escapes from my head, distorts the air above me like hot tarmac in a desert. I am stuck in place but so is Lyudmyla.

Time expands.

The soldier steps forward.

Lyudmyla doesn't budge.

The soldier's voice comes into focus, and I inch closer. He pushes her back. Says, in Russian, he doesn't want to hurt her. Only wants something to drink, some food, asks her where this place is, where he is, if she's seen any others from his unit, any soldiers at all. I cross the threshold to our little house. Dust rearranges itself into swirls on every surface.

"You will die here," Lyudmyla says to him and spits on the floor in front of his secondhand boots. "My cats will be happy to eat your eyes."

"My mushrooms will do the rest," I say, to no one.

The soldier pushes Lyudmyla again and she falls. The soldier apologizes, pointing his rifle at her, and ransacks her cold storage. He bites chunks out of a loaf of bread as if he hasn't eaten in days, pours milk down his gullet straight from the pitcher. His eyes close for longer than a half-blink as he chews. Lyudmyla and I watch him from our respective corners.

"You always eat like that? My goats have more manners," she says. She stands and steps around me, as if I am flesh and bone.

"Back off," he says with his mouth full.

"Move over, I'll make you a proper sandwich. Sit," she says. And he does. And so do the puppies gathered in the doorway and so do I and even the mushrooms wither and shrink.

He leans the rifle against the wall and watches as she cradles the bread loaf and cuts it dangerously close to her bosom. Her twisted hands work quickly to spread chunks of cured back fat on two slices. She smashes garlic cloves under her knife and presses them into the bread. She pours milk into a glass, stained with her lip prints and overlapping water droplets, and serves him. Gives him a handkerchief.

He picks up the sandwich between his shaking hands.

"Eat, eat. It's not poisoned, though it should be," she says.

He takes a bite and his eyes close for real this time. Tears carve streaks down his face.

"Well, where is your mother? Does she know you are here? Tearing up my land?"

He does not answer. It occurs to me that he does not understand her and anger rises in me like magma in a dormant volcano. I yell at him in every language I know. He does not hear me, but Lyudmyla senses something, some shift in the house's equilibrium. She moves slowly towards the stove and grips the handle of the cast-iron skillet.

"Sasha!" Kyryl calls me.

I ignore him and focus my energies on the rifle. If I concentrate hard enough, I can displace the air around the rifle and knock it down. Not enough to do anything substantial, but enough to distract him. Enough for Lyuda to make her move and knock him out with the frying pan.

Kyryl calls again. I try to refocus, call my mushroom friends to my aid, but they don't respond. They are busy feasting on their radioactive buffet.

"Sasha, let it go," Kyryl says from the doorway.

One small push should be enough, I hope.

"Sashenka," he says, quiet now. Gentle, like a puppy's whimper.

I vacuum the air around me, pull it through my spectral skin and push it out of my hands and towards the rifle, faint as a baby's breath. The rifle moves a millimeter, and another. Just enough to break free from the chink in the wall, just enough to lose its balance.

It crashes to the floor. The sound deafening in the silence of the cottage. Lyudmyla raises the skillet above her head. She has babusya strength. The strength of someone who whips egg whites by hand. The strength of a thousand ancestors who fought their occupiers with pitchforks and shovels. She is daughter of gods, mother of heroes. She is immortal in that moment. From my angle on the floor, she is a statue of freedom, of power.

But she is none of those things. Just a little old babusya.

The soldier rises and parries her swing, knocking over the glass of milk and the plate, and both shatter. He manages to push her back for a moment and reaches for his rifle. The skillet did a bit of damage to his left forearm, so he's unable to hold it up.

He gets two shots off in the wall before Lyuda attacks him with her kitchen knife, an ancient thing with a razor-thin wavy blade and a jagged plastic handle wrapped in tape like a shiv. He knocks her knife away but not before she slices his leg.

I lunge at him, try to throw pickle jars and potatoes at his head, but I am air and my efforts are met with a sigh from Kyryl.

"Help me," I say.

He shakes his head. "There is nothing we can do," he staccatos in English.

I watch as Lyuda and the soldier melee, and I cheer when she tosses everything she can get her hands on at him. Round blue eggs, oval brown eggs, hardboiled white eggs, warty cucumbers, lumpy tomatoes, radishes the size of grapefruits, three-headed potatoes. He swats them away, fumbles in his jacket. His breathing is labored and the blood stain on his thigh grows and saturates his entire pantleg.

My ideas must be worming their way into her head. I try to draw her attention to the rolling pin on the counter.

"Beat him," I yell. She does not hear me.

The soldier stumbles and an eighty-year-old pistol falls out of his pocket and clatters across the floor. Lyudmyla bends over, reaches for it, but she is tired and old and slow, and he reaches it first.

He fires a shot but the pistol jams. He wrestles with the slide, fires again.

I cross the span of the shack in one step and wrap my ghost body around Lyuda. Crystal spikes grow from my back to deflect the bullet.

It flies through me and sinks into Lyuda's belly. Two more shots hit her in the chest and the neck. She sinks to the floor and her head tilts forward. Her milky gray eyes focus on mine for a moment. And then she is gone.

I run outside to look for her ghost. I have to welcome her, help her with the transition. Show her she can stay in her old house, tend to her animals just as before. But she's nowhere. I lie down and wait. Clouds mix with smoke from rockets. Air-raid sirens screech in the distance.

Kyryl sits next to me among the sleeping dandelions, and we wait together.

In the distance, my mushroom spores begin to dance. They tango and waltz and dip and twirl. They spin and embrace and split and split and split and reach for the sky, for the tree roots, for the Earth's core.

The spores germinate into long, thin straws anchored to the microscopic wells of decaying molecules they siphon for radioactive nourishment. Deadly to humans, delicious to my mushrooms. To them it tastes like pop rocks and lemon drops and candied orange peels. The flavors tickle the sides of my tongue. My cheeks pucker and I shiver.

The sun rises over the land.

"She will not return," he says as dawn coats the grass in dew and the dandelions open for business. Birds chirp, goats bleat. The stench of gunpowder settles on the forest like a blanket.

"Why?"

"Some do not wish to stay."

"So she gets to move on? Why not the children? Why not us?"

"You still don't get it? You stay as long as you want," he says. "I will be here for the next twenty thousand years or however long it takes until the last rogue isotope is neutralized."

"You've lost your mind."

Kyryl shrugs, his indifference as big as my anger.

"The soldier," I remember suddenly. I rush back into the cottage, expecting him to have fled, but there he lies, dead, slumped against the wall next to his rifle and the shards of broken glass. Cats lap up milk from a shattered bowl. A baby goat chews on the corpse's shoelace.

Milk spreads across the floor and mixes with blood. The liquid seeps into cracks and crevices in the floorboards, drips down into the earth. My germinated mushroom spores drink it and spread their roots. The mycelium reaches far and wide to the edges of the forest and beyond where I can no longer hear them. The trees are anxious, they say. Danger comes this way, they warn. The animals raise their heads. I wonder if they can hear the fungi too. Then the ghost children come to shoo them away.

The soldier's ghost stands in the corner, his hands together in prayer.

"It is no use praying now," I say to him. He jumps. I have startled him. Good.

"What should I do?"

I look him over. He cleans up well in death. We all do. It would be awkward walking around like a flattened cartoon character, I suppose. But Lyuda's wrinkled face, now paper white, reminds me what he is, and my specter fills with red-hot rage like a maxed-out thermometer.

"Go fuck yourself," I say and leave.

Over the next few weeks, I return to the cottage to supervise Lyudmyla's decomposition. I sprinkle spores over her hands and face. The fungi will help her along. Other ghosts bring insects and maggots to take away the rotting flesh, cell by cell. Ghost children keep the animals out. A teenage girl named Zoya leads the wolves away. The war ebbs and flows. The soldier's ghost stays in his corner and watches his body ooze and rot. I don't speak to him.

Eventually, he begins to ask me questions about the mushrooms, the plants, the animals. He asks how long I have been here. How long he must stay here. I don't answer him. I don't know how to answer.

Kyryl is not in the forest graveyard when I come searching for him. No one has come to take the invaders' bodies. Our mushrooms flourish in their corpses, reaching for the sky. Some with thick brown stems and pyramid caps. Some like peacock feathers that emit a low hum. An orange cloud. A purple starfish that reeks of wet dog. Tiny white ribbons. Skinny pink ones. My personal favorite: a split gill fractalizing into thousands of sexes. Radiation funnels into their gills, sparkling and hissing as the mushrooms slurp it up.

I spot Kyryl's footprints glowing neon and follow him to the old power plant. The trail disappears at the mouth of a cave near the collapsed reactor. I call for him, and he hushes me when he comes out. He is absolutely shining with cesium isotopes. With each step, they slough off him like hordes of fireflies.

"What are you doing here?" I ask.

"I heard a rumor the orcs made an outpost here, so I came to chase them away, but it seems the land has pushed them out already. They are trekking back to their hovels as we speak."

I hope the soldier back in babusya's hut has left and gone with them.

"What is all this?" I gesture at the twinkling particles in the air, on the ground. He points up at the treetops. There, hiding in the canopy like fruit, roost dozens—hundreds—of bats.

"There are more in the caves. Their guano dissolves the radiation, so I will tend to them now," he says.

"Down there, in the dark?"

He nods.

I try to imagine the fungi blossoming in the caves below the blown reactor, but all I see is Kyryl dismissing me.

"What about the mushrooms?"

"You tend to them now."

"What about us?"

"Do you know how many of your type I have seen come and go? Dozens. Hundreds. You will realize soon, you can just go. The land will take you. If you want. I will be here. If you want."

Rage boils in my gut. Why doesn't he care? Why do I? The steam builds when I think of the ravaged land. Of my ravaged body, my body that cost me my father's love. My body that I spent years shaping and carving and sculpting and loving. The anger roils when I think of wasted chances. Of wasted lives. Of the death and death and death in the shadow of an insatiable empire. The only thing I want is vengeance. For the wail of a thousand mothers, for the whistle of falling missiles, for the silence that replaced Lyudmila's laughter.

For Kyryl.

For me.

I close my eyes, but light and sound smother me. I press my lips shut, but I cannot contain it. Steam rises from within, scorches my throat. I cover my ears but the scream pierces through me, explodes from my chest, my open mouth.

Kyryl stumbles back. The bats react, swoop down from the branches in black swarms, and funnel into the cave. Their shrieks echo from the cave's mouth and resonate with my own.

Then, a crack at the top of the reactor, and the bats erupt in a swirling black column and sweep down the broken walls toward me at impossible speeds like a pyroclastic flow. I brace myself and let them fly through me. Each one stabs like a gunshot. Each one feels like release.

The bats pick me apart, rip chunks of my spirit with their

fangs, their claws. They carry me in pieces above the forest and drop me as the sun sets.

The Milky Way shines electric above me and the stars chatter with the mushrooms below. They speak the language of eons. To them, we are not even a blink, a breath. What is my revenge against millennia of tending to the earth?

It takes me all night to pull myself back together, ghostly plasma leaking from the seams where my scars used to be like sap.

When the sun rises again, Lyuda's hut stands before me.

I enter and see that the soldier is not in his corner. He is crouched over Lyuda's body.

"Get away from her!" I yell.

"Look, the mushrooms have sprouted overnight," he says, giddy, excited, smiling. I meet his gaze. He is, was, younger than me, just a kid. He shudders when he sees me.

"What happened to you?" he asks.

"You shouldn't be here," I say.

I run my hand under babusya's body and tease the remaining knots from the mycelium.

"What are you doing?" the soldier asks.

"Helping the roots push the buds to the surface."

"They can't do it by themselves?"

"Not all of them. These are special."

"Those glow in the dark," he says and points to a pale green cluster of wide-capped mushrooms that remind me of cocktail umbrellas.

"That's new," I say. I reach down under Lyuda's body and pluck at the mycelium like guitar strings. "They convert the radiation to light."

"Can I try?" he says.

I take his hand and push it down until the fungi nip at his fingertips. He smiles again, then stops.

"I'm sorry," he says. Ghost tears fall from his face as dew.

My anger shifts, mutates into something with softer edges, and Kyryl's words repeat in my mind.

"The land will take you. If you want," I say.

The boy nods and says thank you and sorry and sorry again. The mushrooms fan their gills and siphon his spirit strand by lucent strand until he is gone.

Outside, the forest is silent. Not even leaves rustle.

I bury my face in the forest floor and weep. The mushrooms soak up my tears, my plasma, my anger, remnants of my old life, of the body I hated. The body I loved.

I don't return for a long time. Kyryl tends to the bats, and I tend to the mushrooms. In the evenings, we walk. Sometimes we get together with other ghosts and sing songs and recite poetry. Sometimes we sway in his birch hammock.

One day, long after the war ends and the empire falls, I find my way back to Lyuda's old cottage. Only a few stones from the foundation wall still stand. The forest has rearranged the rest. Lyudachka's bleached skull decorates a tree branch four meters above my head. Nothing remains of the soldier. It rains, and mushrooms carpet the ground. I follow their whispers deep into the woods. There, beneath a pile of leaves, a cluster of chanterelles grow out of my cracked femur and fill the forest floor with their apricot aroma. A fitting place to call home, for now.

SWARM X1048 - ETHOLOGICAL FIELD REPORT: CANIS LUPUS FAMILIARIS, "6"

F.E. CHOE

Originally published by *Clarkesworld*

Finalist for the 2025 Theodore Sturgeon Memorial Award

F.E. Choe is a Canadian and Korean-American writer whose work has been published in *adda, Augur, Clarkesworld*, and more. She is a 2023 alum of the Clarion West and Viable Paradise workshops, and an editor at *100 Word Story*. She has received residency support from Millay Arts and Hedgebrook, and was named South Arts' 2024 South Carolina Fellow for Literary Arts. Find her at www.fechoe.com.

You are born not long after the disaster. The city center has lain evacuated for two days by the time your mother makes her nest. She builds a small burrow from packing blankets, rags, her own sinewy body behind a row of waste containment units, and you are the sixth of your litter to slip out of her. A rubbery cord of pink flesh and matted fur, slick and slippery and new.

Your mother huffs the air around you. She licks at your face, your belly, your tiny paws.

And we watch, transfixed though we have watched countless births on this planet by now, your pinhead-sized nostrils, the soft pinches of flesh around your eyes, the line of your mouth. We watch and wait for your forehead to furrow by the slightest millimeter. Anything.

Our bodies thrum with anticipation. *Move, little one. Move.*

Do anything but lie there so stiff and still as you are.

Your mother whines. She pants. Labor pains wrack her ribcage, your siblings impatient to arrive. You are running out of time to begin.

Move, little one. We jostle against one another, flash with anxiety.

Some of the more heedless among us separate from our luminous cluster and sink down through the air to hover closer to you, small bodies of light which pulse with distress.

And finally, you move. A small twitch, a tremor at the base of your tail.

Life kicks across your spine, and an electric relief washes through us. It ripples through the synched network of our bodies, a burst of ultraviolet light.

We name you *6*, and you are the most beautiful creature we have ever seen.

BETWEEN OUR OTHER ASSIGNMENTS, we monitor your growth. We log regular measurements of your bone mineralization, catalog each of your needle-sharp milk teeth, enter and track the fluctuations in your weight, your brain development.

In our years of ethological fieldwork on your planet, we have come across bidirectional attachment bonds before, of course. *But*, we relay to our supervisors, *this is an unparalleled opportunity to collect such data firsthand, to record our own experience as direct participants.*

Some among us feel strongly that you are an ethical gray area to be avoided. That our growing interest in you compromises us, the reliability of our research, the unity of our swarm, the nature of our work here. That our time on your declining planet would be better spent documenting the migratory patterns of birds, analyzing the density and growth rate of fiddlehead ferns, or decoding the frequencies of cricket song—all enviable assignments coveted by other collectives, but which would require us to move farther to the periphery of our assigned sector. Farther from the city. Farther away from you.

We can only observe, inventory, archive, we remind the most eager among us, even as we travel as one back to the city at night and watch the sweet pile of you and your milk-drowsy siblings rest against your mother's belly. *Such exogenous attachments are conflicts of interest and will present a significant challenge to our reassimilation at home.*

But you are in such desperate need of care, 6. When you run, your ribs are painfully evident against your sides. We cannot help but go back to you day after day, to flush and vibrate concordantly with affection as you begin to recognize and anticipate our presence each evening. Even the few anxious and dissenting among us go quiet when you lift your head in our direction and bound toward us open-mouthed with excitement.

In those early days, you are always wandering off, already too eager to roam desolate city streets with us as you grow stronger and faster. You are less wary than your brothers and sisters to leave your mother's side. And in doing so, you justify your existence to our superiors and the nature of our attachment to you, 6.

With your help, we record the final chemical messages transmitted by the brittle, dying city sidewalk trees, trace their vast mycorrhizal network under the asphalt before it withers to nothing. We secure the mating and signal calls of eighteen different species of urban-dwelling birds.

In your eighth month of life, you discover a way to the roof of a nearby abandoned apartment building. Its overgrown garden plots have gone wild, reckless, and the air is filled with the humming of bees. You doze in the sunlight as we scan samples from their hives, record the chemical composition of their honey and wax, attempt to replicate the exact ratios of hydrocarbons evident in their pheromones, and graph their complex dance maps.

We linger for much longer than we should in those evenings as we practice and inscribe in our memory the intricate choreography of bees. The pattern of our movements, our delicate, indulgent mimicry, stirs the air gently over your heads and lulls you and your pack to sleep.

We swarm and pull apart, circle and swirl, split and twine and regroup. We arrange our bodies along rows and columns to form a kind of glowing, beaded panel, stretch apart, then collapse inward. We move in unison, folding and unfolding, triptychs of light.

This is how you say *hello*.

This is how you say *hive* and *home* and *clover*.

This is how you say *My saddlebags are filled with pollen.* This means *The flowers in the field beyond have just reached full bloom, their heads chime orange-gold when they bow and bend in the field.*

This is how you say *I have missed you, you have been gone such a long time*.

This is how you say *friend* and *foe*, *wildfire* and *disease* and *danger*.

In your tenth month, human cleaners reenter the city center. While we have been busy collecting and sampling and archiving, processing our detailed reports of life on this planet as efficiently and accurately as we can, they have been slowly sweeping along the coast of the country to you. They systematically and methodically break cities into grids, assign teams to sweep through abandoned buildings, exterminate pests and any animals that cross their path, anything capable of carrying particles and contaminates to other territories.

These cleaners stink of fear. They sour the air with their presence. By the time they reach the city of your birth, one of the last urban centers to be cleared, they have been salvaging and repurposing unauthorized material to supplement and replace their standard-issue equipment for months. They do not realize that they have been spreading the very poison they have been sent here to contain.

And you detect this poison too from across the street as you pick your way back to your den. It stops you in your tracks, mingled with the blood and machine oil the cleaners' boots track across the concrete as they approach the warehouse in which your mother and your siblings wait.

The building once housed a praline company, and when your pack first discovered the hole rusted through its steel door there were still boxes full of the confections. We watched you tear through the cardboard and plastic sleeves, dumb with delight and excitement, and gorge yourself until you were sick. And even now, as a group of cleaners enters the building, layers of residue remain on the brick from butter and sugar cooked in copper bottomed pans.

You do not understand the language that follows, cannot differentiate it from the static crackling of their radios, 6.

—Jesus, it's a whole litter.

—Do it quick, then.

—All of them? Fuck, man, they're not doing anything—

—You get used to it the longer you do this.

—She's in bad shape. I really don't think she's going anywhere—

—It'll be nothing in a few months, you'll see.

You cower, shake underneath a car with your ears pressed flat against your skull. You want to run to your mother, your siblings, to find comfort amid warm bodies which smell and move so like your own. Fear, the only thing that keeps you rooted to the spot outside on the street, the only thing that keeps you alive.

We cannot bear to leave your side, 6. But if you run to them, we cannot follow you either.

We are not to interfere.

You press yourself flat against the concrete, and we shudder and dim by your side when the first shot rings out, an interrupted, broken yelp of pain.

In your seventeenth month, you are living at the edge of what was once an industrial park when you encounter a coyote for the first time. The dust storms and wildfires have put so much ochre into the sky this season that sometimes you sleep through an entire day. When you wake, it is to a cloudy, stifling half-light, gritty discharge crusted down your face from the corners of your eyes.

She is wild and canny, an animal that has never had to unlearn domesticity. You lift your head from your paws and stare at her flat forehead and sharp snout, her thin, sleek body and long limbs. She meets your gaze and pauses only long enough to confirm that you are no threat to her, before skimming past, a flash of ruddy gray-brown against sand and red clay.

We depend on you more and more as you progress from juvenile to adult. You help us locate the spores of three species of mushroom, one of which has been dormant for over two hundred and sixty years. We record the flight of geese, the crashing sound of their wings as they leave the water. We study the predatory strategies of herons and egrets, the spawning behavior of blue catfish.

But you are reckless sometimes, and there are so many things you do not know. You drink from polluted streams. You think nothing of scavenging from the rotting, bloated carcasses of other animals. You are too trusting of coyotes, coydogs, and feral animals when we encounter them, and we watch, mute with dread each time teeth sink into your ear, your muzzle, your side and you stumble away wounded.

YOU ARE five when we stumble across the path of a bear. He is starving. His pelt is dull and mangy. And he is much bigger than you.

You bark, startled, your hackles raised.

He stretches to his full height, majestic and imperious before swiping at your flank.

You yelp, a high-pitched wail of pain before leaping away, sprinting madly away into the woods.

He barrels after you.

We search and search, skim and cover the area for hours before we circle back to hover restlessly by your latest, makeshift den in a half-rotted hunting blind. We draw close together, collapse our bodies into a small, singular, bright ball of light. You might find your way back eventually. Surely, there is a chance.

We lose track of you.

It is not long before our supervisors send us an updated timeline. Your planet is deteriorating much faster than we initially predicted. *Get what you can over the next sixteen months*, they say. *Collect what you can. Then, get out.*

We ask if there is time to prolong the search for you before we move on to a different area. But the directive from our superiors is clear.

Leave it alone, they tell us. *Focus on what can be salvaged. Or have you forgotten what it is you are here to do?*

IN THAT FINAL YEAR, there are many things we are unable to collect. We lose the life cycle of paper wasps, all knowledge of the construction methods of their hexagonal nests. We lose the average gestational period of wasp larvae in the Brown Turkey fig, the Adriatic, and the Bourjassotte Grise. We lose the shell patterning of six species of freshwater turtle.

We lose the gold thread of orb-weavers, the structural complexity of their webs. We lose the precision and methodical, graceful endurance with which these spiders climb and mend their silks. How they pick and thread and worry the filament through their claws. How mechanically they unspool their homes from their bodies.

We lose the last of the milkweed in full bloom by mere days, fail to observe the monarch butterflies feeding, laying their eggs, the migrations and life cycles of subsequent generations as they retrace the paths of their ascendants for the final time.

Some of us are quick to blame the others. *We would have been here in time, gotten what we needed, if only it hadn't been for 6. Is this not what we said would happen? This is why we are dissuaded from forming anything more than a distant, professional rapport with subjects.*

Perhaps we have spent too much time here. Some of us begin to look forward to the possibility that our supervisors might pull us out of the project. Some of us wish to return home.

We have performed thousands of these archival acquisitions with unfailing accuracy in the past, and for what? One more data point, an entry in an index in the vast catalogue of dead planets curated by our superiors.

The work here, it is warping our sense of time, of purpose, our sense of self.

TONIGHT, we are documenting the last display of a rare group of fireflies. They have exhibited anomalistic behavior for thousands of years, individually sending out yearning sparks of bioluminescence until they synchronize, beam in unison, light and dark and light and dark.

We cast our bodies in a wide, loose net around a dense gathering of them, ready for the moment they sync together. They flare quickly and subside, one after the other.

Something crashes faintly through the brush.

Between us the fireflies begin to sync.

Another crash, closer this time.

And it is you. Beautiful, barking, clumsy you. Breaking through the tree line and rushing toward us.

We hum with delight, glow so brightly that we disturb the fireflies. They dissipate, hover meekly lower to the ground, send out only tentative flashes.

We send out light. We scatter and collapse and unfold like the panels of a triptych.

Can you smell it too, 6? A chemical reaction as strong as the sulfur left by spent fireworks in the air.

The fireflies rise up and join us, and we are, for a moment continuous, a rippling, flashing wave of endless light.

Hello. We have missed you. You have been gone so long.

WEEKS later we discover the tumor on your chest, detect the DNA methylation, the first signs of the cancer that will kill you. A cluster of cells, their division and growth uncontrollable.

They divide and divide and divide, insatiable, covetous, resolute as they slowly and steadily lay waste to your body.

YOU ARE ALMOST seven when we follow you back to the edge of the city of your birth. You settle on a bank of soft grass by the river, too exhausted to move any further. You have traveled for days, stopping only to rest and drink a little water to arrive at this place, and soon it will be dark.

This is the end. We have seen it many times before in our time spent here on your world.

Like your birth, death is a phenomenon for which we have no innate vocabulary, no natural words with which to shape an understanding.

All we can do is flicker above you and watch as you pant heavily on your side, your chest rising and falling with irregular, ragged breaths.

We have no hands with which we can caress your face or head, nothing with which to comfort or hold you. We cannot nuzzle your forehead or stretch a soft, yielding body along your spine for warmth. We cannot rest an ear or muzzle against the bony ridge of your chest.

We cannot even weep.

We can only watch as your breathing begins to slow, note the heavy, pressing stillness that lengthens and lengthens and lengthens between each rise and fall of your chest.

You fix your eyes on some unseen place in the grass. You blink sleepily.

And then you stop.

6, please.

What we do next is not in any log or report. You will not find an account of it in the thousands upon thousands of fieldwork reports we submit over our shared life as a swarm.

We settle on your body, blanket you in our own glowing selves. We codify and imprint your genetic sequence into ribbons of light. We inscribe every micrometer of you into our collective memory.

One of us holds the first time you kick out with life under the wetness of your mother's nose. Another holds the memory of chasing a flock of geese as they take flight, the sound of their beating wings like drums, how they churn the surface of the water and find purchase enough to heave upward into the sky. Another holds the sensation of sleeping in a soft pile of your brothers and sisters, of rest amid warm bodies so like your own, in a brick warehouse that smells faintly of sugar.

It is our final, solitary act of love, 6. All we can give.

We hope it is enough.

THIRTEEN WAYS OF LOOKING AT A BLACKENED HUSK OF A PLANET

ADELINE WONG

Originally published by *Strange Horizons*

Adeline Wong (she/her) has an enduring sense of wonder and a penchant for hiding stories in places they have no business being found. Her short fiction has appeared or is forthcoming in *Strange Horizons, Archive of the Odd,* and Neon Hemlock's *Embodied Exegesis: Transfeminine Cyberpunk Futures.* She holds an MFA in speculative fiction from Sarah Lawrence College. You can find her deep within the woods, looking up at the stars. (Or on the blogotubes at adelinewongwriting.com.)

I

You've never seen something like this before.

No one in your class has. You're standing on the observation balcony of the timedeck, all twenty-four of you, staring out through six layers of reinforced carbon-mesh plexiglass. No one speaks. No one even picks up a datapad.

Somewhere to your left, lost in the long single-file line of seventeen-year-old wannabe valedictorians, someone coughs. The noise feels like sacrilege.

It used to be so blue.

II

You wonder what it would be like to stand on it. The planet. You know you can't, really; your teacher wasn't very clear on the details, but you've been covering time-view mechanics in AP Physics E. You're stuck in this place, at this moment, and it's the only accessible time-view point for several thousand years on either side. There's an extremely complicated proof explaining why this is the case, but the full explanation involves at least one partial differential equation, so your Physics teacher just assumes you'll take his word for it.

He's probably right, regardless. If it *were* possible to set foot on the planet's surface, someone would have done it already. Someone would have answered the questions, the Big Questions, the ones that really ought to have overthrown the Second Millennium Problems and the unexplained quantum processor barrier and the stable superconductor search. The ones you, and everyone around you, are thinking at this very moment.

One: *How did this happen?*

Two: *How do we stop it?*

III

You know the following information from your classes:

AP Physics D: Given your understanding of open-loop time dynamics, stopping it *ought* to be possible.

AP World History: Given your understanding of planetside governance and global corporate politics, it may not be.

. . .

IV

Even though it's impossible, you imagine yourself on the surface anyway. The planet isn't really black; it just looks that way because of the smog that chokes the atmosphere. Beneath the inscrutable cloud layer, there must be remnants of the past: ancient buildings, metal frames pitted and scarred from weathering and acid rain. Dirt, which the roots of grasses and flowers and towering trees once clung tightly to, now a dry, bleached whitish-gray.

Corpses. Are there corpses down there?

There may not be any animals to speak of. Most of them are already dying, in your time, though perhaps a zoo or two has survived long enough to mark the passing of its inhabitants: a bio-dome, carbon-mesh plexiglass a half mile across, now blackened by smog and cracked down the middle to reveal the bones eroding away within the bracken. Perhaps it's the one you visited last week, for this very same class.

(Last week, some three and a half thousand years ago, that is.)

But even if there aren't any animal remains, certainly there must be human ones. You wonder how long humanity lasted under that ugly black cloud, how they struggled and strove and who was the last to die. Maybe some of them got out. Thirty-six hundred years is a long time; maybe there are humans still alive and kicking on some exoplanet light-years away, or maybe there's a generation ship, its inhabitants in cryosleep, slowly drifting away through the cosmos.

Still, though. They wouldn't have taken everybody. A society that *could* have taken everybody would have stopped the disaster in the first place. There are corpses down there. In all likelihood, there are billions of them.

You stop imagining.

. . .

V

Remember, everyone, says a voice behind you. We only have forty-five minutes on the timedeck, and your worksheets are the only thing you're being graded on today.

It's your Climate Sciences teacher. (Regular Climate Science, not AP; only the country's most prestigious high schools offer AP Cli. Not enough people to teach it; anyone who's qualified has better things to do than workshop lesson plans for high schoolers. But you'll deal with the hit to your GPA—this is important.)

The teacher's voice is soft, but it carries. Every sound carries here.

You want to turn around and yell at her for breaking the moment. When you do turn, she's staring up at the ceiling and gripping a datapen so tightly her knuckles are white.

You don't yell. You're glad you didn't.

When you take your datapad out of your backpack, the light from the screen feels wrong. It's too harsh; too bright. You lower it, then bring up the worksheet. But you don't write yet. It feels like a violation, here, to do something as mundane as writing. For thirty long seconds, it feels like you've even forgotten how to read.

(Thirty seconds for you. Thirty seconds back home. For the planet below, no time passes at all.)

You drag your eyes back to the worksheet. You scroll a bit, aimlessly. There are five questions on it; twenty points each. Some look longer than others. Maybe those should have been worth more? But who are you to judge; you're not teaching the class.

Then you realize what you're doing, counting up points while you stare at the corpse of a planet below.

VI

Someone asks you if you have a spare datapen. You hand them yours, wordlessly, without looking. They wander away, take a seat, start writing.

VII

Climate Sciences - Field Study #4

This field study is worth a total of 100 points.

NAME ____________________

Score ____ / 100

Period ____

1. (20 pts. – Analyze) The clouds covering the planet below vary in color from light gray to black. They have average densities, particle sizes, and other characteristics given in this datadump. Name at least two possible chemical compositions for these clouds, assuming that the composition of the surrounding atmosphere has not changed significantly from our time.

2. (20 PTS. – Collate) Given the atmospheric composition estimates in this datadump, list the atmospheric CO2 of the planet below, in parts per million:

- 1

    - 1 At the top of the stratosphere (~50 km)
    - 2 At the top of Mount Everest (8,849 m)
    - 3 At sea level (0 m)

3. (20 PTS. — Calculate) Given the atmospheric composition in our current day and the UN's most recent projected rates of change in this datadump, calculate the projected atmospheric CO2 of the Earth, in parts per million, after 3,592 years:

- 1
    - 1
        - 1 At the top of the stratosphere (~50 km)
        - 2 At the top of Mount Everest (8,849 m)
        - 3 At sea level (0 m)

4. (20 PTS. — Compare / Contrast) How are your answers to Questions 2 and 3 the same? How are they different? If you can, calculate a confidence interval for each and use your result to justify your answer.

5. (20 PTS. — Theorize) Based on our previous class discussions, give at least two possible

```
explanations for your answers to Question 4.
What is the likelihood that the difference in
results is related to climate change? Ensure
your arguments are thorough. Be prepared to
share them with the class.
```

VIII

Your Climate Sciences teacher asks you why you aren't writing. This worksheet is a field study, and field studies are worth twenty-five percent of your grade. The class has five field studies, so each is half a letter grade.

You stare through the timedeck's window.

This worksheet is worth half a letter grade.

You think, for a moment, that letter grades are worthless here. How many of the billions of corpses below were scientists? How many more, in the thirty-six hundred years since you? How many of them were brilliant, top of their class, graduates *summa cum laude*? How many of them ran the same numbers? How many of them failed to make a difference?

I lent someone my datapen, you say. I'm not sure where they went.

IX

You do your calculations with your teacher's datapen. It feels heavy in your hand, almost alien. But you can still do the math with it.

You could probably do the math without it, even. Run the numbers in your head. This is a standard-load class, two prerequisites: Algebra II, freshman Chemistry. The concepts are straightforward, introductory. They'll make you feel like you can answer the First Big Question, at least in part, or at least that's what you were promised at the very beginning of the year.

The First. But not the Second. No one's sure about the Second.

And they won't teach you everything, not here. The real numbers can't be run in thirty minutes, by hand, without an internet connection on an observation deck locked in time.

X

Open-loop time dynamics says: the moment you leave here, the timeplane changes. It folds around you, *for* you, based on how your experience and your observations inform your future actions: the will-have-been.

What the next group sees will not be exactly what you saw. It might be better. It might be worse. There's another extremely complicated proof explaining why this is the case, and it's another one your Physics teacher wants you to take his word for. You've never wanted to take your Physics teacher's word for things, and now you don't want to take your Climate Science teacher's word for them, either. You want to *know*. You want to write the proof yourself. You want to understand to exactly what extent change is possible.

That's why you need to succeed, here and now—so that they'll teach you. So that they'll *keep* teaching you until you have the tools to fix this.

More than once, you find yourself wiping tears off your datapad with your sleeve.

XI

You finish the worksheet early. Most of the class does, too. You stare through the plexiglass, silent, together, down at the haze and the smog and the dark.

You try not to think. You've done enough thinking for the day. But you can't keep your mind from spinning, and you can't pull your eyes from where they're fixed on the planet below.

Then the warning bell sounds. Your time here is up.

You depart the balcony, not quite single file, heads turned over shoulders for one last look. Everyone is eager to leave, and everyone wants nothing more than to stay.

XII

Someone walks up to you, turns your backward gaze away from the window. They take your hand to press your datapen into your palm, thanks for letting me borrow it, and your dampened sleeve brushes against their dampened sleeve.

XIII

When you step off the timedeck together, neither of you lets go.

THE LAST LIBRARY

JOSHUA JONES LOFFLIN

Originally published by *Astrolabe*

Joshua Jones Lofflin is an award-winning writer with work in *The Cincinnati Review*, *SmokeLong Quarterly*, *Wigleaf*, and elsewhere. His stories have been anthologized in *The Best of the Net*, *The Best Microfiction*, and *The Best Small Fictions*. He lives in Maryland. Find him online at jjlofflin.com.

THE LIBRARY IS SINKING. THE PATRONS DON'T MIND, OR AT least don't complain to Joyce, and she doesn't complain to them. The library's second-floor windows once overlooked a green prairie dotted with brightly painted homes and arrow-straight roads. Now, those windows are level with ashy ground (the first floor buried altogether) and there are no more homes, no more roads, only a gray, muddled landscape pockmarked with house-sized pits. Nobody asks what Joyce will do when the library is gone. It's the last library. She's the last librarian.

Each morning, she unlatches the windows and watches the

patrons emerge from their burrows. They lead their children across a dust-strewn landscape, clamber across the windowsill, and use one of Joyce's dry paintbrushes to whisk the dust from their sleeves and skirts. Joyce catches the children's eyes and, with a jerk of her chin, has them wash their hands. She doesn't tolerate slovenliness.

The buried first floor houses the fiction collection, the picture books, the community room. It's cooler there, sheltered from the bleached, cloudless sky. During the unbearable heat of afternoon, Joyce wanders the stacks with a damp cloth draped about her thin neck, her hair in a knot. Her friend Alejandro keeps offering to cut her hair, but the last time he left her with gray, uneven spikes—a deranged topiary.

Alejandro prefers the second floor despite its heat. The light is better there, and he can study the narrowing horizon through Gothic floor-to-ceiling windows. In the Maps Room, he compares the landscape with local plats, old zoning plans, geological tables. He thumbs through atlases to see how countries emerged and disappeared, how borders snaked one way then dissolved, how on the oldest maps, beasts with grasping tentacles lurked in uncharted corners.

Sometimes there's no horizon. Sometimes, the entire landscape is swathed in swirling gray like television static. Or snow, Joyce thinks, though she can't remember if she's seen snow or not. She sometimes remembers trees. She sometimes dreams of mountains.

Alejandro attempts his own atlas. It's difficult work: his hand is liver spotted and arthritic, is nerve-damaged from his time in California when he was a child; he can barely open it beyond a claw-like C. He starts with a rectangle for the library. Above it, he draws two lumpen circles: ancient holes where once a government stored building-sized missiles in case it needed to commit atrocities. Below it, the freeway, or what's left of it, a drooping east–west line. He's drawn a blank-eyed face, he realizes. The mouth thin and judging; the rectangular nose crooked and canting.

Below him, Joyce frowns at the grime gathered on books that haven't been checked out in over a decade. Her orphans, she calls them, and wipes away tendrils of mold that now grows all along the lower level. It blackens the carpet, creeps up the walls, leaves the air tasting damp and loamy, like bracken and pill bugs and crickets, like disappeared things.

ANOTHER EARTHQUAKE PULLS the library down an inch. Children test out muffled shrieks and giggles; parents press fingers to lips. But Joyce is too busy rearranging her fallen orphans to shush them, too busy to notice the parents slipping books into purses and backpacks and shirts. As they tumble out the window with their spoils, the library lurches again then sits quietly, blankly.

Alejandro stands on the prairie and raises his thumb toward the library. He tries to triangulate the distances of the exiting patrons though he was never very good at math. The patrons totter forward in groups of two and three, then disappear, and Alejandro demarks each vanishing with a square until he maps out a jagged, contented smile of pits curving beneath the library.

Night falls. The library sighs and extends its roots. They stretch further and further for hidden aquifers, feeling their way like blind fingers. They grab at rock, crush buried fossils, and pull the library deeper into the coolness of the subsoil. There it vibrates and hums and dreams of rain.

THE SECOND-FLOOR WINDOW is half-buried now. When Joyce opens it, soil spills inside. Soil and dust and a scent of ozone, and

Joyce remembers rain even though it's been years since she's felt it on her face, years since she's stepped outside. How much longer, she wants to ask the patrons. How much longer until they can no longer squeeze through the window's shrinking gap, until she herself is trapped within. Instead, she tells them to wipe their feet. Instead, she leaves the window open.

ALEJANDRO SHOWS Joyce his latest map and points out the homes, the service stations, the bowling alley on Maple—all buried. The consignment shop, the corner pharmacy, the clinic he used to drive his wife, back when he had a car, back when there were roads. He sometimes dreams of driving. Of wheat fields. Of telephone poles racing past his window. He sometimes finds the tops of poles spiking up from the earth, their cracked insulators bleached white like knuckle bones. He marks them on his map. He marks the map again when they disappear.

JOYCE PACKS her orphans into a shopping bag and fumbles with the laces of her husband's old work boots. They're too big for her and leave broad, treaded tracks across the gray plain. In one hand, she carries Alejandro's map; in the other, a walking stick just long enough to rap on the roofs of sunken houses. When there's no answer, she makes an X on the map and goes to the next until someone opens their hatch and gazes upward, their hand outstretched.

Alejandro throws one stiff-kneed leg in front of the other counting out the paces between buried artifacts: here, an aerial antenna; there, the broken bricks of a chimney; in the dust, bent and swaying, a windmill's rusted blade; and beyond, Joyce's stooped silhouette penciled against the sky. Each evening, she returns with fresh notes to add to his maps—which houses are empty, which holes have vanished—and he helps her count how many books she delivered, how many she has left. There are too many, he thinks, and sometimes he thinks there aren't nearly enough.

MIDNIGHT, and the library gasps and shudders and releases a flurry of spores, smaller than dust. They catch and sparkle in the starlight like an aurora borealis, then swirl and settle across the prairie. There they glow, their light softening the nearing horizon, diffusing it until it's gauzy and translucent and doesn't look dangerous at all.

Joyce sleeps on her office's tattered couch, her head pressed into an oily throw pillow. Behind her, fingers of mold stretch from floor to ceiling, carving out runnels in the faded drywall, creeping into channels of the ceiling's acoustic tiles. She no longer wipes the walls clean, no longer notices when the spores lose their grip and rain down upon her coverlet, the one she crocheted beside her husband in his hospice room. His photograph sits beside the couch. Mold darkens its corners, fades his eyes.

Alejandro sleeps directly below, in the maintenance closet where pipes gurgle and rattle behind his head. There used to be only two, he's sure of it, but now five pipes snake upward into the darkness, clanking and hissing and pulsing with heat. When he puts his ear to them, they go silent, as if embarrassed, as if holding their breath, and he can only hear a distant churning like the roar of waves. Then he remembers the ocean, sand, a woman in a floral swimsuit telling him to stay close, and even then, at the edge of it all, the smell of smoke.

JOYCE HELPS ALEJANDRO DECIPHER HIS MAPS' legends, rendered with crayons in Alejandro's shaky scrawl. We're over the cemetery, she says at last, and points to a line of orange dashes where rows of toothlike headstones once stood. They were some of the first to go, sucked down into the gummy soil as if gathered by the dead, gone before the living noticed. Joyce kneels and begins to dig. When the hole is large enough, she lays the last orphan inside, then covers it up again, and pats the ground smooth.

DUSK AGAIN. Alejandro helps Joyce push a study carrel beneath a transom window, the only window they can climb through now. Joyce's bag is heavy. Now that the orphans are gone, she's emptying the shelves of fiction and poetry, science and history. One night, she delivered twenty-six encyclopedias while Alejandro mapped new quadrants, paced out new hectares. Now she lowers her walking stick for him and helps him shimmy out the window. The air beats close against them. A storm is rising. This way, Alejandro says, his map unfurled.

An ashy grit lashes their legs. Joyce leans over Alejandro's map and makes corrections until they find the house, rap on its roof, and deliver the books. That's the last house, Alejandro says and adds a tick to his map. The wind whips his words around and catches Joyce's bag. It's empty. It flies free from her grip and takes off into the sky. It flutters there a long while, then vanishes in the gathering clouds.

They return to the library, stopping by one of the missile silos on their way. The wind blows across its aperture with a throaty hum. How deep do you think it is? Alejandro asks. Joyce shakes her head and pulls out a ring of keys to forgotten doors—to her old house, her postbox, a large brassy one to the library's buried entrance. The key ring arcs into the darkness, catches the last light of the prairie, then winks away. They wait and listen. Don't hear it land.

It's almost afternoon, the light dull and fleshy through mold-spackled windows. Alejandro has to squint to make out the last pages of his map laid before him. Joyce helps him tape the pages together and spread it across an expanse of floor where children once sat for story circle. The rest of the library is empty, skeletal. Around the edges of the map, Joyce has drawn a sea serpent, its long neck arching upward. Then the neck wavers, the library groans, the empty shelves shake and shake.

Darkness sifts about them. A papery scent fills the room. The windows, Alejandro says, and Joyce nods in the dark though of course Alejandro can't see her. She reaches out for him, finds his withered hand. It is small and wizened and fits in her palm. The windows, they're buried, she says into the darkness. Then, one by one, small grains of dust begin to glow, soft and inviting as sleep. They settle onto Joyce's face, onto Alejandro's broad nose. Oh, she says, and squeezes his cool, dry hand, and she holds on—they both do—as the light of the dust fades from green to mauve to nothing. And there they sit, quiet and unmoving, listening to the library's slow, contented breathing. Outside, sheets of lightning streak across the prairie toward an unbroken horizon, but there is no thunder.

BODIES

CAT MCMAHAN

Originally published by *Clarkesworld*

Cat McMahan is a climate fiction writer from Pekin, Illinois. Her work can be found in *Clarkesworld Magazine* and listened to on the *Clarkesworld* podcast. She earned her MFA in fiction from The Ohio State University and is currently based in Columbus, Ohio. When she's not reading or writing, Cat can be found at her local movie theater or playing with Gazpacho, her orange cat.

AT THE DINER DOWN THE BLOCK, IT IS NOT UNUSUAL FOR THE waitress to keep us waiting at the door. She does, after all, have many tables of people to take care of.

"I wish you wouldn't wear your uniform," June tells me. She's quiet when she says it. She doesn't want to be seen admonishing me.

"Why not?" I say, pulling at my collar. We both look at Liam for backup, but he's staring at a spot above our heads, arms crossed.

June splutters, citing this and that about what's appropriate street wear and what isn't. What she doesn't say is that her own pink hoodie and sweatpants act as a sort of disguise, foiled by my white jumpsuit.

"I don't want my street clothes to smell like guts," I finally say, putting her out of her misery.

"Guts?" June says. "You see a lot of guts on the Husbandry line?"

"Cut it out," Liam says. The waitress is coming to get us. June's mouth scrunches around an unsaid quip, twisting into a false smile for her.

"Just the three of you today?" the waitress says.

"Yes," I reply. "Thank you."

The coffee is warm when we manage to get a refill. It isn't very good, but we'd be lost without it. I tilt a pink packet of sugar into the porcelain cup, then another.

If I were to wager a guess, everyone else in the diner is heading home for the night. The streetlamps are flickering on outside. The low hum of newly unearthed cicadas vibrates through the glass windows. Our day is just beginning.

I leave cash on the table. While the waitress holds a bill up to the light, as if it might be counterfeit, we head out into the night.

Gravel crunches underfoot, dusty and white like the hem of my pants. I'm digging in my purse for my ID card before we even reach the gate. Twilight licks our heels.

We're the last in the locker room, a common occurrence. But it only makes a difference for June and Liam. I pull my mask over my face, lower my protective glasses. The hairnet tries to blow away in the wind of a nearby fan, I catch it.

A thick piece of duct tape holds the cushion of my seat together. The silver leans against the chrome like a deformed twin.

Our CEO, a man with an unironically shiny, egg-looking

head, once called the plant: the Beginning and End of Replication Poultry.

This, he explained, was very clever for two reasons. One: our parent company was the first to use replication technology for mass-producing chicken and chicken products and, if the numbers don't lie, we'll likely outlive our competitors. Two: the plant literally oversees the beginning of a chicken's life and the end. Genesis and Revelation.

Nobody cares for the words "clone" or "cloning." And the term "replication," in later years, has been largely co-opted by other industries, tech mostly. So the East Building, where cells are cloned and eggs produced, fertilized, hatched, is lovingly called the Husbandry Building. The men in the office like to think it's a link between us and the zookeepers of old, trying desperately to get rhinos and elephants and giant pandas to reproduce.

It's nothing so noble.

Instead, it's me and my pipette, waiting patiently at my station for the next Petri dish to come down the conveyor belt toward me. I sit with noise-canceling headphones as I fertilize, wait, fertilize, wait. The pipette and I and two hundred some-odd Petri dishes. The headphones distance me from the relentless hum of the machinery, but I can feel it in my bones. I can feel it reverberating in my jaw when I'm sitting at my station, when I'm walking to the bus stop. I can feel it when I sleep.

It's morning when I leave the plant. I don't wait for June. But she comes bounding down the road a few minutes later.

"Glad to see I didn't miss it," she says, tightening her limp ponytail.

A couple of men in suits opt to stand, rather than sit, in the open seats beside us on the bus.

"Do I stink?" June sniffs the collar of her shirt.

The men hold Styrofoam cups, squint against the newborn

sun. It's pinballing between buildings, matchboxes made of silver.

"Like guts," I say. She elbows me.

The stop-and-start of the bus gives me motion sickness as the morning commuters board and disembark. I find a chewable in my purse to settle my stomach, but not before the road becomes uneven and the buildings passing by get closer and closer together. My stop isn't the end of the line, but it's close.

I wave bye to June and the others from the plant.

My town house stands just outside the city, the center of a spiral of identical town houses. It's so narrow that sometimes I stand with my back against one wall and my hand outstretched toward the opposite. I'm a single hand's breadth away from touching it. But the town house has two floors, and I find pleasure in leaving my white jumpsuit at the bottom of the stairs, like a selkie's skin.

I am lucky. There is one window in my home—in the bedroom—and it opens directly into the brick wall of the building behind mine. I am exhausted, and I am working again tonight.

I DON'T DREAM. I think it may be a side effect, a mutation.

At our plant, we only produce one kind of chicken: the Diogenes Hen. Sometime in the early twenty-first century, a man genetically engineered a featherless chicken, one that was fat and lazy and couldn't regulate its own temperature. A lack of feathers saved on cooling costs. Then, in the 2030s, they made it leaner—the new angle was that it was healthier to eat, clean to slaughter. In 2040 they removed the syrinx at the bottom of its trachea—its voice box—and genetically modified it to require forty percent less chicken feed. It couldn't wail or want.

Eventually, they zeroed in on a chicken without feathers, a

chicken that barely needed to be fed, a chicken that made little waste and no sound. The perfect chicken. They took that chicken, and they made millions of copies of it and subsequently billions of dollars.

It was big news when it came out that PETA had no interest in investigating our plant and its sister site—a place outside the city where the birds spent their time between being hatched in the East Building and being killed in the West. It wasn't because the conditions for the animals were good.

"With so many animals in cages across the globe," PETA's then-president explained in a press release, "it's difficult to prioritize replicated animals . . . animals that sadly don't live very long and are not a true part of the natural world."

At about three in the afternoon, hours before I have to wake up, there's a knock at my door.

Keys jingle in the lock before I'm halfway down the stairs. The silhouette of my landlady lets in sunlight like a poisonous gas, the bright of it filling every empty corner.

"You're home," she says.

"Yeah." I'm holding a hand out against the light.

My case manager, Denise, stands behind my landlady, thanking her for opening the door, apologizing for the inconvenience. My eyes adjust, and Denise is brought into focus as she steps over the threshold.

"Why's it so dark in here?" my landlady asks.

"I work the night shift," I say. "I was sleeping." I want to sound unforgiving. But I just sound tired.

"Sorry to wake you," Denise says. I know she's not sorry. She knows where I work, and when. I'm not feeling kind enough to appreciate her saying sorry anyway.

I don't offer Denise coffee; she doesn't take off her shoes

before stepping inside and sitting at the card table. We share a stalemate of manners, Denise and I. She doesn't extend the base level of politeness to me, and I return it with a lack of hospitality.

There is a painting hanging on the wall where a window might be in a regular apartment, an apartment that has to meet certain safety standards. I found the painting at a garage sale. Three geese near a red wagon.

"Have you been contacted by May H. in the past few days?" Denise slides a handout across the linoleum table. A woman with chin-length brown hair, like mine, stares up at me from the ink-smudged page. I know her. She works in Husbandry.

"She's gone missing," Denise adds.

Worked. She worked with me. She's probably dead.

"No," I say, "I haven't heard from her."

Somewhere outside a siren blares, rumbling wheels hit every pothole. The bulb above our heads sways.

"If you do, let me know," Denise says. "You have my number. Don't worry about the time."

I stare at her, reading the creases at the corners of her eyes, the lines around her mouth. I've never seen her smile, but here were the physical consequences of a happy life. I imagine, for a moment, Denise at a cookout or a child's birthday party. I imagine her cheeks ruddy, her smile lines deepened. A hair out of place.

"This probably could've been an email," I say.

"Policy," Denise says, "Plus, I'm supposed to visit anyone who has an appointment in the next six months."

I don't say anything. I wonder if she knows that telling me this policy has undermined it. I know what I am to her—a task on a list.

"The whole song and dance," Denise continues, "You all tend to get scared when things like this happen. You have your biannual all set up?"

I tell her I do.

"I'm here to reassure you. You're safe." I don't believe her.

"Can I go back to bed now?" I say. It's just a checkup. I'm not a child.

"Of course," Denise stands, "Take care. Let me know if you hear from May H."

I lock the door behind her, flip the light switch. I climb the stairs in the dark, slowly.

THE CHICKENS ARE HATCHED, travel to the sister site for the time it takes them to mature, and are sent back to the plant to die.

The West Building, opposite of Husbandry, is called Abattoir. The slaughterhouse. June and Liam work there. Their white jumpsuits are stained a faded pink in places—the crook of the right elbow, the wrists, the outside of the thigh—and it's the only uniform difference between the East and West buildings.

The men in the office have yet to engineer a bird that doesn't bleed.

"I'M SO STRESSED," June says, pulling at her cheeks until I can see the red beneath her eyes.

"Why?" Liam's mouth is full of toast. The diner hums with low voices and fluorescent light. The Day Shift stretches and yawns while the Night Shift sips their coffee.

"Because now, with the whole May thing," June says, "That's all I'm going to be thinking about. It's just so close to my own appointment."

"You've never had an issue before," Liam says.

"May didn't have any issues before this," I say, without thinking. I add belatedly, "But that doesn't mean anything."

Still, June drops her hands and stares into her orange juice.

"Sorry, Junebug," Liam says, "Look. You'll go to the doctor, everything will be normal. They'll publish whatever"—he waves his hand, as though this is the most trivial part—"and everything will be... normal. Fine. Promise."

A weak smile is his reward.

"You're scheduled with Dr. Kidd, right?" I ask. "He's nice. I've had him before. He's nice." He was quiet when I went, his head somewhere else. His hands cold, but sure.

Liam nods next to me.

I flag down the waitress, hoping for one more refill. It's nearly time to go.

A man in an orange skullcap pauses beside our table, something wedged between his lips. I don't realize it's a half-smoked cigarette until he's already dropped it in my coffee.

June, Liam, and I freeze.

"All night," the man says while his buddy looks on impassively beside him, "I've heard you complain—about all that free healthcare that you get. Fucking yap, yap, yap."

The waitress approaches, retreats. Intimidated by the man. I tried to recognize him, tried to place him—had he been seated in the booth behind us?

"Well, that free healthcare of yours, that doctor—*I* pay for him. Probably a better doctor than I got for myself," he continues. "And what do I get for it? Three fucking Bodies, whining about it in public."

Bodies. It was nicer than some words. Even derogatorily, "clone" is unsaid, out of vogue. I can see that June is on the verge of tears. Liam runs a hand over his closely shaven head, a nervous tic. We sit in a terrible silence, waiting for the man to go away.

He turns to me.

"Be grateful I didn't put it out on your face," he says, "because I might need a new eye one day." He then taps his cheekbone, just below his right eye, and says, "Glaucoma."

I almost thank him. I can't think of anything clever, and I want his face to go slack with shock, shock that I'm not afraid of him. That I might dare him to go further than he already has.

But I don't. I'm stopped by the sound of Liam grinding his teeth beside me.

When we're walking over to the plant, June only says one thing to me:

"I really wish you wouldn't wear your uniform. They can't tell if you're not wearing the uniform."

WORKING AT THE PLANT—THE blurry line between hands and equipment, the hum of the machinery, the flickering of overhead fluorescents—is almost, sometimes, like sleeping.

A hypnosis falls over me, Petri dishes swinging before my eyes like pocket watches. I imagine the others feel the same. The other stations down the line are manned by people like me, with a soft focus in their eyes and a certainty in their hands that only exists because of relentless practice at the job.

At the end of the line, far from my pipette, chicks escape the fragile prisons of their eggs, fertilized only earlier that day. The miracle of life in fast-forward. They click their beaks up at the masked faces that block out the sky, but, of course, they don't make any noise. Then off they go.

May H. worked at the end of the line. She scooped chicks, six at a time, into perforated cardboard boxes, ready for transportation.

The chicks are little and pink. They look like the mice you buy to feed pet snakes. They aren't cute by any stretch of the imagination, but they still feel like babies when you hold them in your cupped hands. They still strain their little necks to be fed.

Liam offered me a theory once, about why the plant is separated into three—the East Building, the sister site, the West Building. Birth, Life, Death. He said that the company couldn't ask the same people to carry out fertilization and slaughter. Psychologically, he said, it would take a major toll. I wasn't so sure—I suspected it was more of a space issue, maybe something to do with contamination.

Featherless, voiceless. Destined to be the contents of potpies and frozen meals, blended up and reshaped. The FDA reasoned that the words "cloned," "replicated," "duplicated," don't need to be listed under the ingredients of any meal-for-one or microwave casserole.

Just "chicken" would do.

When we get off work, June asks me if I'll wait for her so that we can walk to the bus stop together. I tell her it's a good idea and help track down Liam, who's waiting around the front gate.

I'm glad we walked together when we reach the stop. In the time during our shift, someone has spray-painted on the wall of the bus shelter:

NOT ALL GOD'S CHILDREN and REAL JOBS FOR REAL PEOPLE.

Liam scoffs and slings an arm around June so she has to turn away from the graffiti.

"They want my job?" he says over her head to me. "They can have it. Half minimum wage, twelve-hour shifts. They can have it."

June hushes him as the bus pulls up.

Nobody else seems to see the graffiti but us.

Some time ago, there was a big conspiracy going around that the government was secretly pumping Bodies full of growth hormones and illegal vitamins. This, paired with the escalating idea that vaccines were issued to thin the population of "real" people and that Bodies were mindless government drones, caused a lot of uproar.

After all, the government was responsible for making Bodies—owned our very DNA—and appeared to take much better care of us than the general populace.

So the government reluctantly agreed that the medical records of Bodies are not protected under HIPAA, do not belong to any protected category listed in the FOIA, and, in fact, should be accessible to the general public—even at the individual level. If you know the right website, you can see my blood type, my iron levels, my menstrual cycle. Prescriptions, surgeries, test results all a few clicks away.

The Diogenes Chicken, too, had its age of scandal and subsequent transparency. Once the company switched over from hatching genetically engineered birds to cloning one particular, perfect bird over and over again, ad infinitum, they released a docuseries. In the show, they got on top of the rumor that Diogenes experimentation led to the extinction of two species of chicken. It emphasized how the move to cloning was much better for the environment than their competitor's archaic breeding methods.

Behind the dark of a window that opens into a wall, I try to sleep. I struggle. I take a warm bath to relax me. I leave the light off.

In the dark, I can't see my body—only feel it. I can feel the bottoms of my feet by where they scratch the peeling paint at the bottom of the tub. I can feel the goose bumps rising on my forearms, the dry itch behind my ears. In the dark, my body could belong to anybody. In the quiet, it barely belongs to me.

The water is tepid.

"You can't taste the difference!" was the tagline of the docuseries. You could stream it on multiple platforms. People stopped complaining that they could, in fact, taste the difference between "real" and cloned chicken around the same time that the FDA told the companies that they didn't need to disclose the "replication identity" of their meat.

Funny coincidence.

On our day off, June and Liam and I drink overpriced milkshakes at the airport.

I think June likes it here because she can put on big sunglasses (regardless of the late hour) and tug a huge bag along beside her. She can pretend to be all kinds of things she's not, can pretend like she's going on a trip or coming home from a vacation.

Liam and I both live nearby, it's a good location. I suspect we both enjoy seeing June relaxed, hearing her talk about things that aren't worries.

"I might dye my hair," June says, "Go to a professional this time. I just couldn't get it right when I tried to do it myself."

"You'd be a pretty redhead," I say. Liam agrees in that dogged way of his, ducking his head and nodding at the table.

June's face falls, slowly, as we let the airport noise fill in the space between us. She's watching suitcase-toting people disappear through a metal door.

"I keep thinking about her," she says.

"Why?" I say, cold. "You barely knew her. I barely knew her, and I worked just up the line."

"I know." June fidgets with the straw in her cup, skewering

her cherry. "But I'm not thinking about 'oh, I'm so sad she's gone, oh, what happened to her?' No. That's not what I'm thinking about. It's—gruesome. I'm picturing— God, it's morbid."

Liam scoots closer to her on the plastic bench. A plane takes off out of the corner of my eye. Plastic plants soften every corner of the octagonal space that we're sitting in. A few artificial palm trees bounce against the ceiling. Travel is a luxury we aren't allowed and this makes the airport sweeter.

"But like—what was it? Do you think?" June continues, her voice dropping to a whisper. "A kidney match, a liver? Did someone take her to save themselves, or to give their sick kid a few more years? To save their mother?"

"Who cares?" I say. "It doesn't matter why they did it. It matters that they're going to get away with it." That they've already gotten away with it.

June stands, stiffly, tosses her empty cup in a nearby trash can. She crosses her arms and walks to a window, watching a plane roll up and down the runway. The glare of the overhead light turns her into a silhouette, an imprint left after staring at the sun.

I follow, Liam at my heels. For a few moments, the constant whir of machinery and the voiceless clicks of little beaks cease in my head, dispelled in favor of a crowded silence and distant airplane engines.

IT'S JUST me and Liam at the diner the next day. There are no sugar packets at the table, so I overmilk the coffee.

"Oh," Liam says, "I forgot my watch."

We don't talk about May H. We don't talk about June, absent from work to go to her biannual appointment, but I can read Liam's frayed nerves by how he clutches his naked wrist.

We walk on white gravel. Liam goes west, I go east. Mask, glasses, hairnet.

I feel the space between my station and the rest, the space between fertilization and the hatch. Are there more feet of empty space than there used to be? Two stations down sits a woman whose name I don't remember. She complained in the locker room one day about a man who found her records and discovered she was a match.

He called her every day, begging for a voluntary donation. She followed protocol and told her case manager about the incident. Then, he called her twice a day. Then, he sent her letters—more personal, he said, but she knew it was to show that he had found her home address. Please, he said, I need it to live. I'll die without it. The hospital's already drained my savings, I'm too far down the list to live, my family's in debt. You can make it worth it. Help me. Save me.

"But I guess he got the hint," she said later, pulling a sweatshirt over her head. "Or else he got fined or arrested or something. Because I haven't heard from him since."

I don't think he got the hint. And I don't think her case manager did anything to help her. I think he probably just died.

About halfway through my shift, I'm called into the manager's office. The air is cleaner in here, separate from the acrid smells of poultry and antiseptic. A pair of owl-eyed men sit in plastic chairs. One stares out the window onto the floor below, the other stares at me over a cluttered white table.

"Hey, sweetheart," says the one who calls us all "sweetheart."

"Hate to pull you away," the other one says.

"Did I do something wrong?" I say. It's an automatic response. Nobody's pulled into the office for a pat on the back. This company isn't one to brag about upward mobility.

The two men look at each other. The one at the table spins a laptop around, showing me a video.

It's me, standing by the hatching pen. The warm yellow light of the heat lamps warps the image slightly, so my white uniform looks like it's being eaten by the light. Like a glare on a windshield.

The managers watch me watching me reach into the writhing pink bodies of freshly hatched chicks. Their eyes search for signs of recognition, guilt. I don't give it to them. Instead, I squint at the video skeptically.

"Is this you, sweetheart?"

"Yes," I say, interlacing my fingers and resting them on my knee. "Is there an issue?"

They look at each other again.

"I know that's not my job—" I begin, but I'm cut off.

"What *exactly* are you doing, there?" one laughs. "It's difficult to tell."

"I'm disposing of a malformed specimen."

"So late in the process?" the same one says. "It almost looks like you're slipping it in your pocket, there."

I breathe a deep sigh. I didn't want to do this, but they forced my hand.

"May H. was at that station this quarter," I said, letting the statement breathe with a pause. "We're all trying to help out where we can."

They both look like I've spilled syrup on the table, or acid, something they don't want to touch. Something alarming. One looks out the window again, the other looks above my head, nodding.

"Since she wasn't there, and I saw the specimen—"

The "sweetheart" one waves me down, "Yes, yes, thank you." I recognize the dismissal and leave the office. I make sure they don't see the relief on my face, the tension leaving my shoulders.

Afterward, my pipette and I dance with a hundred more Petri dishes. A waltz, a tango, a gavotte. It'd be beautiful, this dance, if it were novel. But I've stepped these steps so many times that they've become mundane.

The moment they became perfect and lightning-quick was the same moment they lost any kind of magic.

I AM HOME JUST before the sun appears between two buildings behind me, closing my door on it just as it reaches the mat.

I climb the stairs in my thin, dark home and climb into bed with my shoes still on.

THIS TIME, when the knock sounds at my door, I am already awake. I am standing on the threshold of the closet beneath my stairs, my hand wrapped around the chain to the naked bulb in the hallway. The carpet muffles the sound of the closet door closing behind me.

The knock sounds again, not urgent. Carefully insistent. Denise. I'd recognize her by the way her knock makes the lock's chain rattle any day, but then, I've never had any other visitors.

I hardly look at her as I shield my eyes from the brief daylight and lead her to the table.

"No, thank you," Denise says when I ask her if she'd like a cup of coffee. "I don't expect I'll be here long." She's obviously put off by the fact that I broke our unspoken agreement and treated her like a guest.

She's sliding a printout across the table again, and this time I recognize the face as though it were my own.

"June?" I say. "What happened to June?"

The words feel like a lie, though the shock is real. I know what must have happened to June, just like I knew what must have happened to May H. I knew it without Denise having to say a word. But talk Denise must.

"I take it you haven't heard from her in the last few days?"

"No," I say. "You're wrong. I just saw her on Saturday."

Denise pauses to write something down on her legal pad. I'm afraid she might try to leave without giving me anything else.

"I just saw her on Saturday," I repeated. "She went to her appointment. Is she sick? Did you check?"

Denise glances up from her writing, brows furrowed.

"Her recent appointment showed she was perfectly healthy." Disdain, as though June's good health was a target she willingly painted on herself. "Her results were set to be published sometime next week."

"They weren't published yet? And she's still—" *gone*, I mean to say. But the word doesn't come out.

"It's unusual," Denise says, slowly, like she isn't used to going off-script. "But there is always a possibility that someone on the hospital staff . . . leaked her file."

"Sold it, you mean."

"Obviously, a full investigation is underway," Denise says. She puts her legal pad in her bag.

"Obviously," I snort.

Denise stops gathering her things and peers at me from behind her glasses. "We take these things very seriously. The disappearances of replicated individuals is a national crisis."

"Is it?" I ask, face hot. "I guess I haven't heard about it under the noise of all those medical miracles. People growing new kidneys from nothing. New eyes, new hearts. You don't investigate miracles, do you?"

"We take these things *very* seriously," she says again.

I lock the door behind her. I pull the chain in the hallway, slide down the dark wall, wrap my arms around my legs. I stare at the yellow light bleeding from the closet under the stairs.

THE WAITRESS HAS BEEN NICER to us since she noticed our trio has become a duet. I get three refills rather than my usual two.

"I just don't understand," Liam says again. "Why her?"

"Maybe she jinxed herself by worrying about it so much," I reply.

Liam grinds his teeth. His toast and eggs are untouched, ordered out of habit. When it's time to leave, he looks regretful. Nauseated.

"Could you be the one to clean out her locker?" he says. "I don't think I can."

"Sure," I say, patting his hand.

Gravel.

Uniforms.

Petri dish ballet.

The shift is exactly as long as it always is.

June's locker is at the very end, a coveted spot. I wait until the room has cleared, lest I be mistaken for a looter. I have her passcode memorized, just as I have Liam's—and they have mine. More intimate, I think, than knowing each other's birthdays.

But the locker is empty. No uniform, no notebooks, no cough drops or chewing gum. She stored extra clothes in here, I knew, an envelope with some money in case she forgot her wallet. And it's all already gone.

For the second time, I have a hard time understanding June's absence. It's not going the way they usually go. Bodies don't go missing until the information goes public. They don't have the foresight to clean out their lockers.

I NAME MY INSOMNIA "JUNE" because she's the one who keeps me up at night. I put a sheet over the dark window to keep her out. I don't own any curtains.

Cloned chickens are chickens.

But cloned people are not people.

It's been illustrated to me, through graffiti and catcalls and pamphlets at the mall, that the difference between "are" and "are not" is a soul, shaky colleague to flesh.

That is, the folks who believe in souls believe that animals don't have them, have never had them. So, there's no difference between a chicken created by God and a chicken created by man.

"You can't taste the difference!"

But human beings, on the other hand . . . The Petri dish tango (the big one, the one that made me, made June, made May H.) has no step for soul creation. Only God's Petri dish can split cells and make a spirit, apparently.

Thus, there's a pretty significant difference between a body and a Body. The razor-thin margin between heaven and nothing.

But to tell you the truth, I don't mind. I don't mind being considered something different from human. I may work in the Husbandry Building, but I've been next door to the slaughterhouse. I've seen it firsthand.

I've seen what happens when you call a chicken a chicken.

THE SUN DIPS LOW, our twilight morning scored by crickets and car horns. Liam's smoking a cigarette, and that's how I can tell that I really made him think. I feel lighter having said it.

"But where would she go?" he says, standing close to the building's edge. It's misting, even as the sun winks out in the west.

"I don't know," I say. I'm wearing a windbreaker, jeans, I smell like detergent. I like the feel of it. I like the anonymity, I didn't know that I would.

"I hope— I don't think you're right," Liam says, grinning despite himself. "But I hope you are."

I smile back at him. There is chicken feed in my pockets. There is an earthy smell that almost clouds the scent of industry, metal, blood.

"I can picture her—on a beach," Liam continues. "Is that corny? A beach, with a big hat, like this." He draws a big circle around his head with his hands, the end of his cigarette glowing like a sparkler.

MY THIN, dark house glows orange when I open the door beneath the stairs.

I kick straw away from where it's fallen from the makeshift enclosure. I adjust the heat lamps slightly, check the thermometers.

The chick is sleeping. Its little bald chest rises and falls in double time. It's grown since I took it from the plant, bigger, more defined. Like a soft illustration with black outlines.

It's so small, and it looks like every chick born beneath my hands. Exactly like every chick born under hands like mine. Every flutter of its too-quick heartbeat is proof that it's a living copy, a breathing duplicate. Only unique in that it's doomed in another way, an unplanned kind of way.

I stroke its little wing with the back of one finger, I watch it hop in circles. It clicks its little beak at me, black eyes glistening.

I don't picture June on a beach. I picture her at the sister site, or someplace like it. The place chickens go after they're born, before they die. I've never been there. But I picture a red barn, a dirt path. She's in the grass, there, in her bare feet. She's in the sunlight.

PIG HOUSE

KAY VAINDAL

Originally published by *Seize the Press*

Finalist for *Brave New Weird: The Best New Weird Horror, vol. 3*,

eds. Alex Woodroe and Matt Blairstone

Kay Vaindal is an environmental scientist and fiction writer from Baltimore. She really likes turkey vultures, sagebrush, and cyanobacteria. Kay's work has appeared in venues like *.ergot* and the *Drabblecast,* and has been featured in other year's best anthologies like *Brave New Weird.* Find out more at kayvaindal.com, or on Bluesky at @kayv.bsky.social.

WHEN THE POWER GOES OUT, WHOLE CITIES DIE. YOUR rebreather stops pulling oxygen and if it zeros before you can charge it: suffocation. Heave into your lungs the useless air. Deep breath, nothing. And another and another. Aunt Beth died that way when Rochester went out. That was the fifteenth biggest one in the states—Rochester. Three years after the atmosphere turned sour. No real protocol for accidents yet. So a snowplow knocked into a transformer and killed twelve hundred people: c'est la mort!

I don't remember any different than this. My mom did. She had cats and dogs and birds, rabbits, gerbils. Little animals that lived with her, slept with her, and she'd feed them, and they'd follow her and meow and bark and sing. Now I sleep with my rebreather. I go for walks with my rebreather. If I want to eat solid food or make out with somebody, I hold my breath. People die that way, too. Old people, usually. Drunk, usually. They forget.

On the news they say we're the only animals left. Except last week I heard my husband's coworker say there's a pig in Omaha, in a sterile room they pump oxygen and dinitrogen into, no nitrifying microbes to turn it fast into nitrate. I haven't stopped thinking about it, the pig. At night I stare at the ceiling and picture it. I want to see that pig more than anything. I'd die to see the pig. I'd kill to see the pig. As long as I get to see that pig, when the power goes out in Syracuse, I won't care.

So I'm doing it. I'm here now, on the road, my three-year-old conked out on sleeping pills in the back seat and my husband's credit card in my pocket. Giant corn country, now. Everywhere giant corn, sixty feet tall, cobs as big as me.

We pull over at a rest stop in Illinois, town called Mt. Vernon, because the kid's rebreather is beeping long and low. Clouds look threatening, moving in dark purple coils in the sky, sparks between them. I park the car under a solar panel in case it hails. Between low rumbles, there's the comforting whir of backup generators from somewhere out of sight. The power won't go out unless lightning strikes them all. I unbuckle my seatbelt and peel open the side door of the van. Sammy's heavy now. I toss her over my shoulder and head into the *Paul Bunyan* service center. A big blue cow statue stands watch in front of double glass doors, smiling with chipped teeth at the dark sky. Other families hurry between the cow's legs, into the building.

We get inside just before the rain starts falling, those sort of big heavy warm drops before a thunderstorm. There's no hills to stop the storms here, I know. I saw that on TV. When the storms start, they go for days, until the big corn bends over, ears on the ground, nitric acid pock-marking the leaves like rotten bananas.

It's a nice rest stop, all things considered. Food court in the middle. Protein drinks you can sip while you breathe. Decorative chandeliers hang from a center atrium, a big skylight so you can see the bubbling atmosphere. Maybe it was clear glass back when people had cats, but now it's striped with yellow crusts. Twenty or thirty people mill about as the sky darkens, sipping smoothies while their phones shine into their eyes. I make my way to the charging café in the corner, swipe my husband's card and hook the kid's rebreather up to a wire.

I hook myself up, too. Figure I'll get more bang for my buck here than I will with the car charger. I sit myself down next to Sammy and watch big raindrops paint the skylight gold.

The inevitable: A man sits down next to me, gives me a shy sort of look like he wants to say something but he needs my permission first. I glare at him. That's enough. "Couldn't help but notice that Steeple hoodie, ma'am," he says in a plain plains accent. "That's my favorite video game."

"It's my husband's sweatshirt," I say.

His eyes crease with a smile. I watch for disappointment, angled eyebrows, the seeds of a coming tantrum, but his smile looks pleasant enough. "You waiting out the storm here?"

I inspect the man more closely. His head is block-shaped, blue eyes, buzzed hair, nose that might have been broken once or twice. I'll bet his name is something like Sven Jorgensen, and I bet his parents come from Minnesota. I suppose I wouldn't mind screwing him in the backseat of the van. The *click click click* of hail on the skylight. I point my chin at it, and that's enough of an answer for Sven.

"Smart, yeah," says Sven. "No driving in that. Cracked my whole windshield that way back in August. You know, the corn farmers prefer this sort of storm. The acid doesn't come out of the hail till it hits the soil. Nothing a little liming can't fix, there, right? The biggest crops don't mind the hail as much."

Sven wears a Clayrite brand rebreather. I watch its LED lights turn green when he inhales, red on the exhale, and ask him if he's a farmer.

Sven shakes his head. "I'm a miner."

I'm tired of making eye contact with Sven. The hail on the skylight has no eyes to meet, so I watch that. I ask Sven if there's phosphate out here, but I doubt it. Since I left Syracuse, it's all old shale gas lands, cracked and broken and filled in with chalky white soil to grow up massive stands of corn.

"I'm not from here," says Sven. "Just passing through."

"Where you headed?"

Sven watches the skylight, too. Before he answers, my phone rings loud in my pocket. I tell Sven excuse me, and pretend to answer it, but really when I see my husband's name I press the red button. I say a lot of things like mhm and yeah and okay, honey and Mt. Vernon, Illinois, Paul Bunyan Service Center. The power flickers. I put into the phone a laugh that goes to no one. Wait a minute longer. Goodbye. I love you too.

I slip the phone in my pocket and turn to Sven. "I'm headed to Nebraska."

"What's in Nebraska?"

"Family," I tell him, and I think of the real live pig in its pressurized room. I picture something sterile, white. Glass windows where scientists can look on. Sammy has a kid's book with barnyard animals, a gift from my mother-in-law. The pig lives in the mud. And the farmer in his denim overalls can walk into the woods with a sleeping bag on a whim and never come back to his farm. He can find berries and small corn and turkeys to eat. The atmosphere didn't turn sour all at once. It got bad enough that you had to gasp, my mom said. Then so many animals died that their rotting corpses sucked all the leftover oxygen and gasping wasn't good enough anymore, and so many more animals died, and so on and so forth. At night, I imagine the pig feels soft under my hand. Silky-smooth and wet like mushroom flesh.

Sven's Clayrite rebreather has an auto display that connects to his cell phone number. A blinking blue light tells him and me he has a text message. He doesn't check it. Instead he looks at me very seriously, and he asks if I'm safe.

"Am I safe?"

One nod from Sven Jorgensen.

"Of course I'm safe. Why wouldn't I be safe?"

"You look a little beat up, ma'am, and you're talking about a husband, but you—" He pauses. Looks at the skylight again. "You look very young. I know there's bad business that goes on in some circles with all this repopulation talk, so I'm just making sure that you're—"

"I'm fine, Sven Jorgensen. Jesus Christ. Does nobody mind their own business anymore?"

"I'm glad to hear it," says Sven Jorgensen. "But if you need any help at all, my wife and I are traveling in an RV. We could hook your car up to the back. Drop you off in Nebraska."

I tell Sven my daughter is with me, and stick a thumb toward Sammy, conked out on the bench on her wire, looking peaceful below the white noise hail hitting the skylight, *chhh.* Sven says they have room for us both. I don't think Sven has an RV, or a wife. I think he has Rohypnols and human trafficking ties. Still, I imagine myself eating breakfast with his big blond wife, Helga, traversing the big corn lands on some great American tour. There's a gun in the pocket of my dress. If this is all true, and Sven can afford an RV on a phosphate miner's salary, I could wait until nightfall, pull the gun, say a few terse words and take the road yacht for myself. If it's make-believe, I don't have to wait until night.

I curdle my face into a smile and let my eyes get wet and tell Sven I would love that, thank you so much for your kindness, God bless you and your wife. The hail is falling harder now. I wait for cracks in the skylight, but it holds. It's had twenty years of hail and winds and acid rain, and it and the roof and the great blue cow out front haven't crumbled yet. Sven asks me my name, and I look to the brick wall on our left, and tell him, "Bricks."

Sven's smile doesn't fall, and I'm ninety-five percent sure he wants to sell me to the sky worshippers in Texas, now. He says his name is something like Todd or Tadd or Chuck, but I don't revise the picture of him in my mind. Sven Jorgensen. Minnesota.

On the bench, Sammy's eyes start to open. She can't hear, which I've always thought is a blessing. We can't afford implants. I don't know that we'd want to. No acid storm or screaming match can wake her. I leave Sven, walk to her side and sign, "Good morning."

She stares up at me, then looks left to right and left again. Sammy only knows a few words in sign language, like hello, and pig. I've tried since she got the diagnosis last year. She doesn't get it. The doctors say keep trying. It'll click. And then they send me off with a pamphlet on how to learn and teach an entire new language. It'll click!

Sammy's rebreather blinks green. She's past the age where she tries to rip it out, thank God. I unplug her, and she hops off the bench, wanders in a six-foot diameter around my feet. Her yellow dress is rumpled from sleeping in the booster seat. She points at the smoothie store. I shake my head. She gets that sort of thing, pointing, head shaking, head nodding. I think she lip reads at least a little bit, squinting through the foggy glass of my rebreather. No and yes and Sammy and things like that. Maybe that's the start of the click.

"I can buy it for her," says Sven, behind me like a ghost.

"Me too?"

Sven smiles, nods. I knew he would. Before he sells me to the sky worshippers, I want to make full use of his artificial kindness. I tell him I have to pee and he says, "I can watch her, if you want." And I laugh and shake my head—that's very kind of you, but she'll need to go too—because he's selling us to the sky worshippers together or not at all.

I'm pregnant again. That's half the reason the RV is so tempting, real or otherwise. An engine and a toilet on one set of wheels. None of my husband's other wives warned me on the subtleties of being pregnant when it first happened. They told me I'd glow, and my hair would be so thick. Nothing on the constant pissing and the fact that I'll never do jumping jacks again. I ate a bunch of coffee grounds and cigar ash to try and kill this one, but we're past the twelve-week ultrasound now and everything looks good. It's easy to run with one kid. Once you have two, you don't have any free hands.

We pee and I wash Sammy's hands and my hands and wipe them dry with paper towels. She looks at me with a head-tilt, and I tell her as best I can that we're going to Nebraska to see the last living pig. When I was pregnant with Sammy, I always craved salt. I would huddle in the pantry and unhook my rebreather and dump spoons full of it onto my tongue.

Sven is waiting for us with smoothies, like I knew he would be. He helps hook Sammy's up to her proboscis, and I do mine myself. "Where's your wife now?" I ask him. I'm okay with poking holes in the story now that the free smoothie's sliding down my throat.

"Out draining the RV," he says. "Fueling up. All that maintenance business. They don't tell you about that in the reviews. That you need to drain the pee out the back every few days or the whole thing stinks."

"In the storm?"

Sven laughs. His laugh doesn't fit him. It's high-pitched. Geeky sounding. He should be at a convention center in Buffalo, dressed in a cape and laughing about Mr. Spock. "Service area's all covered up. That's why we stopped here. Missouri rest stops don't have lids."

I nod, and slurp my smoothie and watch Sammy to make sure she doesn't choke. Her rebreather light goes off while she sips, on when she pauses, off when she sips. The rhythm of it soothes me a little.

"Is your eye all right?" Sven asks me.

The makeup on my cheekbone must have been sweat away. I figure he's been waiting to ask that for a while now, concerned crinkles in the corners of his eyes.

I smile at Sven like how sad battered girls smile up at their rescuers in old movies written by horny men and I say I'm all right.

The storm stops, eventually. It doesn't take days like I was afraid of and hopeful for. The clouds fizz and disperse and there's the sun and the corn-colored sky. Sven leads Sammy and I out, and we latch my van to his RV. There's no buzzing in my ears like I've been drugged, and I think I'm a little disappointed by that. Their RV has tires bigger than my daughter. According to the app on my phone, the screws on the axel are bigger than the thirteen-week-old naked mole rat burrowing in my guts.

We ascend a three-step staircase and I'm in the Jorgensen's home-on-wheels. It's immaculate. There's a bowl of lemons on the table in the kitchenette. Helga is real, and tall and buff and Scandinavian like her husband. She could scoop me up and put me in her vintage EAT LOCAL tote bag as a snack for later. Sven talks something about making ourselves at home but Sven is old news. I want to look Helga in her eyes and touch her face and tell her I'm taking my daughter to Nebraska to put our hands on the mushroom flesh of the last living pig. Instead I say something stupid like my real name. Sven Googles me, I'm sure, and texts his wife all the information from my New York State ID page, and she responds with a big, gooey-eyed frowny face, maybe wonders if she should contact the police, naive and EAT LOCAL as if all legal roads don't lead back to my husband.

While Sven adjusts himself into the driver's seat at the front of the car, Helga helps Sammy onto the couch and offers her a cell phone game. Sammy isn't allowed to look at screens at home. She loves it. I stand there dumb, hands in the pockets of my ugly dress.

Sammy and Sven otherwise engaged, Helga approaches me. She puts a hand on my shoulder and looks deeply into my eyes. She says, earnest as her goodie-two-shoes-ass-husband, "You're both safe now."

That snaps me out of it. I point my gun and shoot her in the head. I didn't mean to do that. It was too easy, and now it's done. I'm dangerous. I point my gun at Sven and shoot him, too. Sammy keeps playing her game. She doesn't look up once while I move their bodies into the back bedroom and peel their expensive rebreathers off their faces. I won't go back to Syracuse, and neither will my daughter. Lord willing, we'll be in Omaha before the Jorgensens start to smell.

Driving an RV is different than driving a car, it turns out. My hands shake, gripped loose around the steering wheel. I scrape the cement divider on my way back to the highway with the big corn under the yellow sky. We accelerate up to a solid seventy miles per hour and I follow signs west. I clear my mind and think about cats most of the way. My mother-in-law has a faux fur coat that I could stroke for hours. I could say to Sven and Helga in the back of the RV in a patronizing voice, "You're both safe now."

My mom was forty-four and pregnant when the atmosphere turned sour. She had six cats and three dogs and no husband and she made a living rescuing abused donkeys and posting their donkey faces online. Then she had a sperm bank baby and a hypoxic brain injury and she only got to stay my guardian as long as she did because the foster care system was so flooded with nitrate orphans. Once when she was more lucid than usual she said that in the early days of the new age, when the doctors all were closed, my Aunt Beth tried to remove me from her uterus with an ice cream scoop and a needle. Eleven-year-old me thought that was funny as hell, but my husband thinks it's what screwed me up in my head. He rescued me from ice cream scoops and hypoxia and nostalgia for donkey influencers. I was fifteen when we married.

I drive into the night. Sammy doesn't make a peep in the back of the RV, a whole world opened up to her on the dead woman's phone, lights and colors and shapes probably making more sense to her than anything I've ever tried. She falls asleep on the couch with it still in her little grip.

My GPS takes me to the address I heard my husband's friend talking about. Omaha National Food Security Laboratory. A manila, two-story building sitting unguarded, surrounded by suburban homes and big corn. I haven't seen a tree since I left New York. The landscaping here is giant corn and thick, waxy meadows. I park in a lot near the back of the lab and pack Sven and Helga's rebreathers into her vintage tote.

Sammy doesn't drop Helga's phone even when I pick her up and tuck her against my chest. My arms hurt from steering the big steering wheel and shooting two people. She feels heavier than usual. I sit her down in the waxy grass while I break a first-floor window in with a rock, then I make her wake up. She wipes wetness from her eyes and looks at me, and I sign *pig*, hand under my chin. She knows that one. I pointed to the pig in her picture book and signed it enough times before this trip. She signs back, *pig*, and we climb through the broken window.

There's no alarm going off. No security guard waiting with a night baton. I put my hand on the gun in the pocket of my dress anyway, hold Sammy's hand with the other. Above us, motion-detection lights flicker on up and down the hallway. I expected white walls and warning signs, but this looks like a post office.

The building is quiet except for our footsteps. I imagine the pig will be on the first floor, in the centermost room, to best protect it from tornadoes and the atmosphere. A cynical part of me wonders if the pig is here at all—if the pig is even real—if all of this was for nothing and I'll find another empty office. There should be security guards. There should be alarms. This is the last living pig on earth, and it sits in its tomb alone.

We're near the center of the building now. I try some doors, and Sammy helps. An office. An office. An office. A musky blue-toned room like an execution chamber viewing booth, big glass window and bright white door off to one side. Sammy and I step inside. The lights don't turn on automatically like in the halls. I flick on my phone flashlight and search around for a light switch. On the wall, beside a sign: *No lights between 8 PM and 8 AM.* I turn on the lights anyway.

The room hums to life. Light blue walls, long benches with clipboards set down at the end of the day. It's dark behind the glass. I can't see in. Above the big window, scrawled in Sharpie on yellow graphing paper ripped haphazardly from a notebook: SOW #651. So there are six hundred and fifty-one pigs in the world, maybe. So I've been lied to. I don't have time to wallow in that because if I start to wallow I'll wallow forever and instead I find a second light switch, and I hit it, and there it is.

One pig lying against a wall. A hundred times bigger than I imagined. It's a tiny space just big enough that the sow can turn around if it presses itself against the wall and then folds in half. It's not a sterile room. It's brown like a dirty aquarium, and there's a crack on the window and shit on the floor, and the pig has tubes down her throat and nostrils connected to an oxygen tank and a big barrel that says *feed.* Sammy looks at the pig, then at me. I sign *pig*, and she shakes her head. The one in her picture book was pink and round with mud on its hooves and a blue sky above it. This is tissue. Pile of cells. But its eyes are watching the door.

I decide I want to go home. My mom lives in a care facility now. I haven't visited since I got married. One day she's going to die and I'll say I should've visited and I know that and I still don't visit but I look at the pigs and I feel nostalgic for donkey influencers in a big green field and a farmer who could walk into the woods and stay forever.

There's a gun in my pocket. I could use it on the pig and my daughter and the naked mole rat and me but I don't. Maybe that's what I came here to do. There's no plan post-pig. There never was. I tell Sammy to stay put, and I slip into the pig's room. The door feels like it's never really been used, sits off its hinges in a way that I'm not sure I'll be able to close it again when we leave. The pig's eyes track me but her head doesn't move. I worry if she knows how. But she flicks her tail so I test Sven's rebreather against her snout. She recoils at the touch and pulls at the tubes stuck in her throat and nose but she can't get any purchase so she settles back down again. I decide if this doesn't work I'll shoot her. I'll tell her she's safe now and sell her bacon on the black market for a trillion dollars. Then I extract the tubes from the pig's mouth and nose one-by-one. She can't breathe. I can see the look in her eyes when she realizes she can't breathe. Her lungs are expanding and filling and expunging but nothing's happening. I fix Sven's expensive rebreather over her snout and secure the elastic behind her ears. The pig meets my eyes. Her chest settles. Oxygen flows over the bubbles in her lungs again. I exhale with her and tell myself I was never going to shoot her and my daughter and me. I have a post-pig plan.

The pig gets up, now. Turns around and chuffs and looks at me and the room she's probably never left. She bolts past me toward the door, then shuffles about the viewing booth, squealing into Sven's rebreather like a person with a stubbed toe. Sammy touches a pig. I touch a pig. Her skin is coarser than I expected, warm and wrinkled like a human palm and covered with long white hairs.

Sammy and I fashion a harness and leash out of duct tape and we exit the lab with her alongside us. We leave the Jorgensen's RV behind to duck under the cover of a big corn forest, disappearing under the giant yellow leaves. The sky is purple-black and the stars glow greenish against it. The pig's hooves turn white with sand and lime.

Deep in the corn forest, I take a picture of the pig with its rebreather and its white feet under the stars, and I open up Helga's phone and find her social media accounts.

THE PLASTICITY OF BEING

RENAN BERNARDO

Originally published by *Reactor Magazine*

Renan Bernardo is a Nebula and Ignyte finalist author of science fiction and fantasy from Brazil. His fiction appeared in *Reactor/Tor.com, Clarkesworld, Apex Magazine, Podcastle, Escape Pod, Daily Science Fiction,* and elsewhere. He writes from secondary world fantasy to dark science fiction, and he enjoys the intersection of climate narratives with science, technology, and the human relations inherent to it. His solarpunk/clifi short fiction collection, *Different Kinds of Defiance,* was published in 2024. His dark sci-fi novella, *Disgraced Return of the Kap's Needle,* was published in 2025 by Dark Matter Ink. He also had stories recommended by Locus and longlisted for the BSFA.

Edilberto Santos takes three plastic bottle caps from the teepee fire in front of him. He crumples their burnt remains together with a spatula, kneading them until they form a semi-solid, charred paste, their blue, red, and green mixing in an uninvited, incomplete rainbow. He whistles a joyful song while waiting for it to cool. I have things to say but I don't interrupt him. After three minutes, he grabs a cheese grater and starts scraping the paste in it, sprinkling the flecks into a bowl. Finally, he scoops the floury mix with a rusty spoon and eats it. His eyes focus on the camera as he chews it. Some catch in between his teeth. It doesn't bother him. He's used to it.

I glance down at my pad to escape Edilberto's gaze. The next question is highlighted on the screen. *How does it taste?* Did I write those words? What was I thinking? São João da Campânula is not a damn reality show. It's a landfill and it's home for about forty families. A knot throbs in my chest as I cross through the question to erase it.

"Are you all right, Dona Elisa?" Edilberto asks. He's missing a few teeth. His eyes droop over his sallow cheeks. I shrug and force a nod. What does it mean to be all right after seeing a man eating plastic?

I slide a finger over my pad so my cam-drone buzzes away from Edilberto, focusing instead on the trash behind him. A few people trudge through the paths that open like clogged veins amidst the heaps. A kid fetches something from the ground, giggling with a man beside him. A woman enveloped in a broad shawl carries a fat mesh bag. She selects an object in one of the heaps, yanks it out, and peeks at it. It's a plastic bottle, brittle and grimy with the tan of corrosion. She throws it in her bag.

I open my backpack, pick a sandwich and hand it to Edilberto. A sandwich. Of all the food I could've brought to São João da Campânula, I brought only a few sandwiches. Ham, cheese, butter.

Edilberto eyes the marmita with mild curiosity—a Tupperware box with a dog sticker on its side. He runs a finger over it. It's the only one I brought from Mamãe's home when I moved to Goiânia after our silent war started. She had that one since she was a child. She was five when she pasted that poodle there.

Over the years, the box had stored a whole sort of her most delicious food—bolognese spaghetti, fried cod balls, chocolate pudding with strawberries, and scrambled eggs when she was in a hurry. The last time I tried to visit her, I brought pão de queijo in it. She didn't touch them. Mamãe loved me for thirty-two years. However, over the past nine years she hates me. And she has a good reason for it.

"I'm not hungry right now, but thanks," Edilberto says. "I can keep it for the others, though. Can I keep the box? It's cute."

"Yes, of course." No hesitation. I don't understand why. For Mamãe—and for me—it should be an heirloom. Perhaps by getting rid of her marmita, I'd be officially detaching myself from the woman I loved the most in my life. I peer one last time at the barking poodle sticker, its edges frayed and threatening to unstick. "Keep it, yeah..." Those last words falter, but they come out anyway.

Edilberto smiles at me. There's sweetness in there. Despite the missing teeth, Edilberto doesn't look like a broken man. Not like I pictured all those people—the *plastikeaters*, as some having been derogatorily calling them since they were "discovered" by the media. I'd thought of them as sad, gaunt wanderers, aimlessly looking for solace in the landfills near Mairipotaba. In my nightmares, before I fully compromised in writing a story about their lives, they came to me as dolls made of plastic, revenge cooking in their eyes but their hands wilted together in begging.

The aggression of burnt plastic slicks the air. Not only due to the bottle caps that Edilberto burned. It comes from all over the landfill. Here and there, smoky snakes writhe toward the sundown. I skim through the list of questions I didn't ask Edilberto. *How does it taste? Does it hurt to eat plastic? How is your diet? Which types of items do you prefer?*

Instead, I look straight into his eyes. There's a deepness in there, brewed in the sweetness, that I doubt my own eyes possess.

"This smell..." I hesitate, swirling a finger in the air. "It's—What does it convey to you?" I think of fires, faulty electronics, problems. Of things going wrong.

"Which smell?—Oh! I barely notice it anymore. But it smells like dinner."

THE STORY OF São João da Campânula started with the company called Verdidea.

Once upon a time, Verdidea was the future: the bastion of sustainability and green technology allied with social and environmental responsibility, a powerful Brazilian—then global—force to correct everything that was wrong with the world. And, indeed, they showed what they were all about. In a decade, their projects of reforestation employed millions of micro-drones in the Amazon rainforest, with tech that healed the damaged soil, planted new trees, and rescued animals during fires—all the time learning the patterns of what they were doing, so they could improve themselves over time and avoid catastrophes. In five years, they managed to recover 85% of the previously unrecoverable deforested area. Verdidea freed more than eight hundred rivers from industrial waste all around South America; they brought water to the driest parts of the sertão.

Once upon a time, working for Verdidea was the dream job from engineers to lawyers, from botanists to PR specialists like me.

Verdidea truly wanted the world to become a better place. As long as the world was theirs.

THE STORY of São João da Campânula also started with me. Once, ten years ago, I came as a PR specialist to write part of it.

Now, two years after the company's breakdown, I come as a freelancer journalist to rewrite it the best way I can.

"You can look to the camera," I say to the woman, pointing to the cam-drone whirring in front of her. Behind her, a dog lolls on a chair underneath her wooden shack's only window.

"I prefer not to."

"That's okay." I slide a finger on my pad so the drone swivels to the side and avoids focusing on her face. "What's your name?"

"Ângela."

She's a woman in her mid-fifties, brown skin, curly hair falling over her shoulders like waterfalls. She exhales a sweet scent of unnamed flowers, generic enough to fit anywhere, anytime. Next to her shack's door there's a cauldron filled with plastic bottles. On it, scrawled in big red letters: *Pick yours, leave for others*. A repurposed dresser lies next to it with five cheese graters, all shiny and clean, delicately covered with a transparent raincoat.

"Hi, Ângela. My name is Elisa Assunção. I'm a journalist and I'm working on a story about your lives. It aims to bring attention to the authorities and—"

"I know who you are." I freeze. For a moment I think Ângela knows exactly the role Elisa Assunção played in her very existence. She waves her hand. "Your type always comes here, asking questions, giving us crumbs to nibble. Then you go away. You're predators, that's what I say."

I agree. Brazil was shocked when the news about São João da Campânula broke in the headlines. *Plastic-eating people living in landfill. A new kind of poverty sprouts in Goiás.* In their prowl for answers—*How can they survive? Is it a hoax? Where do they come from?*—journalists and authorities came and went to the landfill as explorers, merely digging for stories and opportunities, never fully finding the answers, never providing ways out.

I, on the other hand, have the answers already. I'm part of them, so I come with all of them, not for them. Instead, I come for any shreds of redemption I can find in that place. Like Mamãe used to say, *Don't try to repair your mistakes all at once. Some of them you'll just have to swallow.*

"Ângela, do you have kids?"

"Um-hum." She glares suspiciously at the cam-drone.

I tap the OFF button on my pad and the drone slowly descends to the ground, its propellers shutting off and its LEDs lighting off. "Tell me about them."

"That's what you wanna hear? Won't you talk about plastic? Your type loves to babble about plastic."

"I just want to hear about your kids."

First, she gives me what I deserve: silence. Then, she gives me the stories of Mariana, Rogério, Adenilson, and Cleiton, of how they walk fifty minutes to school every day. She tells me how they find toys in the landfill and how she has to carefully select what isn't dangerous for them. She tells me how she loves a man called Jango, who lives in a shack in the eastern border of the landfill, of how she found brand new canvas sneakers just lying around, green and yellow with black stripes, perfectly fitting on her feet. The only thing I type on my pad is the cornmeal cake recipe she dictates to me, which she only prepared twice in her life because she never has the ingredients.

In the end, she tells me she's grateful for that "Verde-something company" because her kids never learned what it meant to starve.

THE ENZYME WAS A BREAKTHROUGH. It took only one year to go from plastic-gobbling bacteria to plastic-digesting isopods.

Verdidea's name stamped every front page around the world. The Great Pacific garbage patch was being spoiled from its plastic by isopods at a rate never before imagined. Microbes carrying the enzyme were spread throughout landfills in Brazil, Argentina, and Colombia. It brought awareness and funding for bioplastics research, decreasing its costs of production. The video of a girl snickering and lowering a soda plastic bottle into a pool of isopods went viral for months.

When Mamãe saw the news, she was washing a plastic bowl. She guffawed, then widened her eyes.

"Perhaps I should replace it for something else." She raised the bowl. "Lisa, do you have something to do with that, with all those great things your employer is doing?"

I laughed at her curiosity. But yes, I had something to do with Verdidea's rise to fame. As their main PR specialist, I knew exactly what to sweep beneath the carpet: embezzlement schemes, tax evasion, greenwashing, and all scandals that involved Jandir and Vando Batista, brothers and CEOs of Verdidea. It was all justified, given the nature of Verdidea's noble undertaking. At that moment, laughing with Mamãe in the kitchen, feeling cozy and accomplished, I had yet to fuck a lot of lives.

ON THE FIFTH day of my trip to São João da Campânula, I have only a recipe written down and less than twenty minutes of video footage. At night, I choose to walk around the landfill's paths—its veins—with my pad and my cam-drone turned off in my backpack. This time, I don't bring sandwiches.

I trudge, observing the flocks of people coming and going from the shacks that surround the landfill. A trio of men jab small items from the ground with hook sticks. A few steps behind them, two kids argue about the true color of the moon.

One of them believes it's as strikingly white as unspoiled milk. The other one says it's tawny like the pages of the books in his mother's chest. In the sky, silky clouds strive to hide the secrets of the moon.

On a heap of trash, an old woman with a hunched back fidgets with litter, a statue against the nightly hues. She wears fruit baskets as shoes and gloves to pick up what she deems useful. I wave at her, experimenting with a smile even knowing it hardly fits. She frowns at me but doesn't wave back. A few meters ahead, six people gather around a grill, two of them sambaing to the erratic sounds of a broken pandeiro. The others laugh and talk loudly about a soccer game, pointing at each other, gesticulating. The stench that glues to the air, sweating from the grill, is the one I'm growing used to. Perhaps it means home to them. *It smells like dinner.* When I arrived home late from college, the aroma of Mamãe's beans cooked with garlic and paprika pervaded the apartment. That scent was like a tight, warm embrace, even though I eventually chose to abandon it to chase illusions.

"Moça!" I pivot to face a boy sticking his foot into a pile of trash. He gives out a muffled cry but doesn't really care about it. He stretches his arm to reach something. "You're tall. Can you pick that lunchbox for me?" His voice is jumbled. He's chewing bubble gum.

"Of course." I walk to the pile of trash and fetch the lunchbox for him. It's stylized with the drawing of a fading funny robot. One of its edges is dented. A bug skitters out of a tiny hole on its side. I shoo it away. "Is it for school?"

The boy shakes his head. He's about eight years old, shirtless, soot daubing his cheeks like tribal marks. Dollops of dried blood swell from his lips. Not bubble gum. He's chewing a piece of plastic casing for wires. I hand the lunchbox to him, mouth agape. They rarely eat raw plastic. It hurts their mouth, pharynx, and esophagus. That's why they partially melt it, work it into a paste, then grate it. Verdidea's directors spoke of plans for easing the process of eating plastic, mainly in the upper digestive system, from the mouth to the stomach. They went bankrupt without ever outlining those plans.

The boy opens the lunchbox and shakes it to clean it from dirt.

"Are you the journalist?" he asks, wiping the funny robot that grins at us with its coiling arms wide open as if looking for a hug.

"Yes. My name is Elisa."

The boy spits half the casing from his mouth and swallows the rest. I gulp at it, wanting to look away. If it were weeks ago, I'd probably retch at the sight. But now I know it's part of my story. I don't want to avoid it.

"My maninha says she likes you. She met you ten years ago."

My heart misses a beat. I gape at the boy. I don't need to ask who his sister is. Francisca da Conceição, the person I gave to Verdidea as a corporate offering.

WHEN WOULD Verdidea put a base on the moon like the other billionaires were doing at a rapid pace? Questions like that whirled on the news all the time, but it never made Jandir and Vando Batista's eyes shine. Their next big project was thankfully rooted on Earth: ending world hunger. For that, they had to choose between two paths: solving what prevented food from arriving at everyone's tables or devising new feeding solutions. The former involved politics and tackling the core of the economic system itself, from which they greatly benefited, so they left it aside. The latter was what motivated them.

The plastic-breaking enzyme working in mammals was Verdidea's secret—*forbidden*—breakthrough. After the plastic was digested into monomers, very specific bacteria carried its constituent parts through the digestive system. Grouped with other microbes artificially inserted into someone's microbiota, those monomers could be converted into carbohydrates, proteins, vitamins, and other nutrients. It was a giant leap from what Verdidea had been using in isopods for three years. (And by the way, the Great Pacific garbage patch had shrunken 25% since the crustaceans were employed there. Headlines flashed that Verdidea was *the company that should run the world.*)

With the enzyme-bacteria system working in humans, no one would need to starve anymore. Virtually anything around people could be easily turned into food. Plastic was ubiquitous in cities. The food supply chain would be disrupted. Transport, distribution, aggregation, and processing might all be rendered secondary and, with a whole sort of new processes, different textures and tastes could be acquired. Feeding people would be a decentralized process without lots of points of failure. Costs would plummet. It would all become excruciatingly cheaper than producing any kind of food, and with the way Verdidea planned to employ its enzyme-bacteria system, eating plastic could also prove to be healthier than eating ultra-processed food. Not only would famine end, but people would have quality nutrition all around the world. The abrasive and obnoxious stench of burnt plastic that would pester the cities could be solved soon after. Verdidea was certain they could do anything. I was certain I could make the world believe in that.

Mamãe and I had gone through rough patches when I was a kid. Mamãe had to work overnight as a prostitute to take care of me during the day, and on weekends she got temporary gigs as a window cleaner so we had food on our table. So, more than a meaningful job, Verdidea's project became personal to me.

The next step came when the process worked successfully on mice, then monkeys. So they needed volunteers. I never fooled myself about what that word meant for them.

There were poor communities near Mairipotaba comprising of displaced people from Goiânia's massive gentrification. They were jobless, many of them starving, not a few resorting to landfills to find food and junk to sell at paltry values. It was near those communities that Verdidea decided to build a new headquarters. It was me who wrote articles and called press conferences to convince Verdidea's shareholders that it was a good idea. I worked day and night to fabricate the vision of Verdidea sinking its roots in the middle of Brazil and making them sprout deep and wide, bringing progress everywhere they touched, so when it came to the public it would all be beautifully justified. All in the name of ending world hunger. Meanwhile, Verdidea's lawyers scoured the law for loopholes that would allow them to start experimenting on humans—and, as I later found out, Verdidea deceived the ethics committee responsible for the project, presenting to them an entirely different set of parameters.

In a one-hour speech, I convinced Verdidea's shareholders that it was a good idea make São João's citizens eat trash. Three months later, they applauded me and green-lighted the project.

THE STORY of Francisca da Conceição started when I found her lone shack, half a kilometer from São João da Campânula, the widest of the landfills. Her hut was surrounded by shrubs and flanked by a muddy stream. When I arrived, the wind plucked fiercely at pants, shirts, and sneakers hanging from a clothesline. Somewhere inside, sertanejo wheezed from shabby speakers. It was the furthest I had the guts to go into the Mairipotaba's communities, not so far from Verdidea's new headquarters—next to where I went to live after I left Mamãe and the cozy aromas of her beans with garlic. But most important, it wasn't within the humiliating heart of São João.

I'd learned through Verdidea's reports that an eighteen-year-old girl lived in that shack with her mothers and that she stayed alone during most of the day, when her mothers left to scavenge the landfills and hawk in the streets of Goiânia.

Francisca was a thin girl with a protruding belly. When I first saw her, she wore a crop top and jeans so spent they almost surrendered to white. Her shack only had two mattresses, a TV set, and a crooked, doorless wardrobe.

She invited me to sit on two plastic chairs outside and offered me a warm cup of coffee. I accepted.

"Do you eat?" I asked after I explained who I was and where I came from. At that point, I hadn't been fully clear about my intentions of asking her to be a volunteer. But she certainly knew people like me only went there when they had something to gain.

"I do." Francisca sipped at her coffee. She was a very shy girl, clearly not used to visits, much less by overdressed women.

"How is it so?" I looked around, indicating that there wasn't much beyond a makeshift oven and a few supermarket bags lying next to the shack. "Do you make your own food?"

"Sometimes." She shrugged. "But mostly my moms scavenge things from the landfills then sell them in the city. Then, they come back with some quentinhas. Sometimes it's rice and chicken, other times just a lettuce salad."

"Is it always enough for your family?"

The question caught her by surprise. Her gaze lost focus, the cup tight between her fingers, midway to her mouth. After a while, she shook her head. I was pulling the conversation to the point where I wanted, but not without pain. Speaking of hunger when you were not feeling it wasn't always easy. It seemed unfair because you were sated; but it also filled you with a senseless kind of hope, as if that bellyful moment could linger and maybe, just maybe, you'd never have to be hungry again.

"Sorry about the... sensitive and weird question...," I said. "But if you were hungry right now, would you eat those bags if you were sure they would sate your hunger?"

"Do you mean…" Francisca blushed. "Eating what's inside them?"

"No. I mean the bags themselves."

"I would." No hesitation.

I only remembered two moments of my childhood when I felt really hungry. I never forgot them. Sometimes Mamãe's work wasn't enough to feed us—the excruciating drama of many Brazilian families. Inflation corroded her meager wages and there was one occasion when we spent an entire day without having anything to eat. But they were enough for me to remember my own yells echoing throughout the apartment, unbeknownst to the fact that food didn't magically sprout whenever I wanted. Mamãe silently sobbed in a corner, knowing that even if she worked harder in the next day there was no guarantee that there would be food on our table.

"I would too," I whispered to myself.

It was later that day I offered a magical solution to Francisca. For now, she only had to come with me to Verdidea's labs and sign some papers. For someone with a hole to fill, she couldn't say no.

TODAY, Francisca doesn't live in a shack anymore. She lives in the middle of São João da Campânula, in a house with its bricks exposed and a corrugated iron roof. Clothes hang from the clothesline tied to two poles outside her house. The wind that buffets at them now carries the landfill's polymeric stench. From somewhere nearby, samba shackles the evening, scratching the air with streaks of happiness, threatening to extinguish the smell by the sheer pressure of joy.

I wait for Francisca staring at her closed door, snapping my fingers and trying to control my breathing. A man walks by carrying a bag of plastic bottles on his shoulder. He nods at me.

Behind the set of houses that clutter that part of the landfill, the old woman with a hunched back kneels on a mound of trash. Or perhaps it's another woman wearing fruit baskets as shoes, another shadow against the moon-paling backwash of the night. Behind her, beyond the warts of junk that pockmark São João, I see the imposing and abandoned headquarters of Verdidea—all that remained of the company that vowed to heal the world. A chill runs along my back when I remember all the nights I spent in that place, a haunted palace built on unstable stocks and the lives of the destitute.

"Are you okay, Elisa?" The voice startles me. It's still the same but with a quality of roughness to it.

Francisca isn't as slim as ten years ago, but the same curious half-smile shapes her lips, except her shyness seems to have melted away in the same humble kind of sweetness I saw in Edilberto's eyes. I shiver from head to toe when I shake her hand. I expect a slap, a reprimand, any sort of revenge for having transformed her and those around her into garbage eaters. None of that happens. After all this time, I have only one question for Francisca, and it's not one of those noted in my pad—*How does it taste? Does it hurt to eat plastic? How is your diet?* The one I have for her is different, and one that applies to her and to myself: *Was it worth it?*

Like the coward I am, I don't ask it.

"We'll have dinner tomorrow for my brother's birthday," she says. "Do you want to come?"

"I do," I say as fast I gave away Mamãe's Tupperware.

I'm sorry for what I did to you. The words quiver on my lips. I don't say them.

Don't try to repair your mistakes all at once. Some of them you'll just have to swallow.

"Thank you for the invitation," I say instead, gulping.

"I made dinner for you." Mamãe was dry and brief when she called me one week after I told her about Verdidea's plans with the enzyme. It happened a month after meeting Francisca for the first time and having her enlisted as a volunteer. "Can you come home earlier today?"

"Yes, Mamãe," I said to my pad on the table while I slid my fingers through the volunteers' profiles on the big screen at my office. Francisca was a go. There were five others, including one of her mothers, who were inclined to accept Verdidea's offer as well. Volunteers would be provided with temporary housing and five-month's worth of the current minimum wages. But the big prize lay at the end of the road: they'd never have the risk of starving.

"Are you listening?" Mamãe's grave voice shook me up. I rubbed my forehead.

"What?"

She sighed very slowly, which came out as an uncomfortable hiss through the pad's speakers. "I asked you not to eat anything. I prepared something special."

And when I went home, I found out what it meant.

On our dinner table, there was only one Pyrex dish at the center with an oozing black pudding that looked like charred cloth and smelled like burnt popcorn.

"Overcooked?" I said, kissing Mamãe's forehead as I lay my backpack on the floor. She didn't kiss mine back as she usually would.

"No," she said. "Have your seat and let's have dinner."

I frowned at her. "But what's that?"

"Our dinner."

"Is it... overcooked mashed potatoes? Seriously—"

"It doesn't matter." Her eyes didn't lock into mine. "It won't leave you hungry."

I saw where she was heading and closed my eyes. When I told her about the new project in Mairipotaba, I said I'd probably have to spend some time in Goiânia. She didn't take it lightly. She closed herself and spoke curtly with me in the following days. Up to that point, I'd thought it was because I was going to spend time away from her. I understood. I was all she had, so it was natural that she'd miss me. But there was something else.

"Mamãe..."

She pulled the chair. It scrawled on the floorboard. I flinched while she sat.

"Mamãe, stop. You don't need to eat that."

She shrugged, scooping the black pudding and putting it on her plate.

"That's what we have, isn't it?" she said.

I pulled the other chair and sat beside her, seeking her eyes with mine, finding nothing but pain and evasion.

"The project with the enzyme is an option so no one will need to starve ever again."

"The kid that I raised, the one that praised my soft pão de queijo"—her voice came out grated, her teeth chattering—"the one who was all yummy-yummy at my feijoada, would never want to see people eating garbage."

"It's not garbage, Mamãe! Don't you understand? It's the solution for a problem that has existed for thousands of years." But those words tasted sour on my mouth. Those were the words of Elisa Assunção, PR Manager at Verdidea, disinterred out of a presentation to shareholders, not those of Elisa Assunção, daughter of Maíra Assunção, raised amongst the whiffs of motherly feijoada.

"It's no solution, girl. It's just the same problem with a different painting. They won't give people options with dignity. They're giving them what they always did: the leftovers. Eating is not only satiating your hunger. It's a process that carries dignity. If you think it just serves to satiate your hunger, then eat the fucking dinner I prepared."

"Mamãe, I can show you the documents." I reached her hand, but she recoiled, her mouth a thin waning moon. I wanted to talk about the documents because I didn't want to find the truth in her words. "They're classified, but I have access to them and I trust you. You'll learn what this is really about. There's a report that—"

"If you keep insisting that a poor boy should eat that fucking bottle..." She pointed to a soda bottle lying next to the bin in the kitchen. "Then don't come back here."

Mamãe took a mouthful of the black pudding.

IN THE HUMILIATING heart of São João da Campânula, we dine.

There are about twenty people scattered on seven plastic tables around Francisca's house, all partaking of the beer and food I brought—feijoada, pequi rice, galinhada, and green corn mush. I wish Mamãe was there too, joyfully saying how she'd change each of those recipes, how she'd sprinkle coriander in this one and nutmeg in that one.

I sit at a table with three other people, but I remain silent, just smiling at everyone who dares to look at me.

The song *O Show Tem Que Continuar* blasts from two big speakers strategically positioned on each side of the field. *We'll find the tone, a chord with a beautiful sound, and make our voices good; then we'll be happy.* Children play with a hose, frightening the heat away. Night has fallen but the sky is still daubed in the summer's blue dyes.

Ângela is there with Mariana, Rogério, Adenilson, and Cleiton. She wears her cool sneakers and kisses her man Jango's cheek. The hunchbacked woman is there. She sings loudly. *Then we'll be happy; look, we're on air again; the show must go on.* Edilberto is there too, picking something he brought in Mamãe's Tupperware. He smiles as he stares at his friends—his family—chatting and singing and drinking and eating. When our gazes meet, he winks at me. He's eating melted plastic bottle caps. It's home to him.

"So, you came to write a story about us?" Francisca puts a hand on my shoulder. She has her other arm wrapped around her brother.

"I— Yes, I did."

"And how is it?" Francisca picks a chair beside me and sits. I nod at a glass of beer, but she shakes her head.

I grin at her. "I'll start over."

"Why?"

"It's just— My mind was elsewhere. I think it needs a complete overhaul."

I don't want them to become aberrations and exotic curiosities in the eyes of the public. I want them to be who they are: people. I want to write about the families living in São João da Campânula; about Mariana, Rogério, Adenilson, and Cleiton's daily journey to school; about the samba of their evenings.

I have other questions to ask them. *How was your day? What's something you created recently? What makes you laugh?* Who *makes you laugh?* Others will come to write about plastic. I'll leave that to them.

"Francisca, let me ask you something." I dare to put a hand over hers.

"Of course."

"Was it worth it?"

She stares at me for a while like she did when I first asked her if her food was enough. "Was it worth it digging trash after food and things to sell? Was it worth it to beg in the streets? When something isn't an option we don't ask if it's worth it."

The "famine issue," as the Batista brothers called it—as if it was just a minor inconvenience like forgetting a sandwich on a grill—was never only a question of actually eradicating famine. Since they never addressed poverty or housing, eating plastic became a symbol of desperation and lack of options, not of hope and progress. People in the landfills already picked their food from the trash. That wouldn't change.

I wish I could say I was the one responsible for fracturing Verdidea's business. I wasn't. Their stocks plummeted when they abandoned the Amazon rainforest project, then again when I couldn't shield them from the scandals—unknown up to then—involving several of the Batistas' other companies that employed forced labor. I was horrified, but I chose to believe they didn't know and that they could correct their mistakes. I still had my hopes high that they could address many of the world issues, including famine, food quality and distribution, housing, and poverty. It was only a setback. They were the solution. It was a selfish, self-destructive behavior. How could I have dedicated fifteen years of my life to them if they couldn't achieve those goals? Was I merely industrial waste along with all the other workers being steadily laid off? In my desperation, I even tried to push an article defending Verdidea's views. But not even the Batistas believed in the company anymore.

The final strike came when the people living in the Mairipotaba's landfills were exposed as the *plastikeaters*. It was when I learned Verdidea was already genetically altering São João da Campânula's dwellers to make their bodies produce the enzyme-bacteria system in their digestive tract. I thought I'd be informed when it happened. I'd thought I'd see the results, the smiles of people with enough sustenance to survive. Verdidea's directors didn't show me anything, perhaps because they knew I was only sustained by an illusion.

In the end, what toppled me was the front page of *O Globo*

showing a blind old man with plastic cotton swabs on his tongue. It was then that I couldn't take it anymore.

Mamãe used to say we shouldn't blindly pursue our dreams. Sometimes it was okay to put them aside for a while or to abandon them altogether. *Our dreams are the fabric of who we are, Lisa, but we're changing all the time, re-sewing ourselves.*

Nine years after leaving home, I knock on the door of the only woman capable of helping me sweep my dusty dreams from beneath my feet.

"Mamãe?" I stammer as an old woman opens the door. There's deepness in her eyes, a mix of sadness and longing that brews into a bittersweet gaze when she sees me crying. "I brought cornmeal cake for us."

BATTER AND PEARL

STEPH KWIATKOWSKI

Originally published by *Diabolical Plots*

Steph Kwiatkowski is a writer and preschool teacher from suburban Illinois. She is a graduate of Clarion West 2022 and her stories have appeared in *Fairy Tale Review, Nightmare, Diabolical Plots,* and *Uncanny*.

THE SUN'S ALMOST DOWN OVER THE BOARDWALK, THAT TIME of day when everything's dark but the sky's still lit up, when townies drive past the lake on their way to Gary and say gosh it's pretty out here by the battervilles, I don't know what all the fuss is about.

The air's thick with marina noise and mosquitoes eating up my shirtless chest. I'm pouring my jug of fresh-caught batter into the shuddering funnel of the change machine, even though I know in my heart there's not enough to buy Ecker the smallest size of honey-glazed crispies. The line for the chicko joint is starting to wind down the boardwalk. Everyone's yelling, a bunch of sunburned lake-slick battermags pissed I'm taking too long during the dinner rush. But I can't let it go, not tonight. Ecker is leaving tomorrow to go back to vocational school, and he's standing at the order window with his hands in his pockets like he's embarrassed.

"How much left?" I shout. The metal of the machine groans, empty, impatient.

Ecker checks the little grease-smeared screen that's converting my batter catch into chicko credits. "Thirty-two to go."

"How much now?" I smack the bottom of my jug. A pathetic thunk of batter hits the funnel.

"Thirty-one."

"Fuck outta here," someone calls out from the back of the line. "That thing's empty."

"It's not empty!"

"Did you scrape down the spout?" Ecker's voice is a wince. He knows how weird the question is when four months ago he was right here with me, hoisting the jug and chanting big money big money while we watched the decimals turn over.

"Yeah, I fuckin' scraped it down already." I wipe my forehead against the crook of my elbow.

"Come on," Ecker says. "Just let me get this with my stipend credits."

Ecker with townie money, real money. There was a time he would've jumped over the counter, grabbed a chicko bucket and dashed. I remember one night specifically he ripped off his shirt before he did it, just to make everyone laugh, or because we were high. He was screaming like the seals in Penguin Slide and his torso was caked with black batter and ferrofluid and I don't know if that's the moment I knew I loved him but I think of it a lot, especially at night when there's no one in the prefab but me and Skeeball, curled up with his little gecko fingers over my collarbone.

"I told you I got it. Just wait a minute, let me think."

There's a layer of batter stuck to my arm hairs. Some behind my ears, the oily black sludge of it gone tacky. It's been a while since I scraped the cracked ridges of my sandals. The crowd hates that one. A wall of boos and groans as the dried-up sprinkling earns me one tenth of a cent.

"Next in line!" The guy at the chicko window's had enough. He hovers his finger over the button that'll recall the batter deposit and cancel my order.

"Look I'm so close, please, can you just round up." I'm tapping the number on the conversion screen with both hands like a crazy person and there's sweat dripping down my temple and everyone is yelling and I've seen the guy round up for everyone in this town including me but for some reason today he won't because, I find myself screaming, he's on a power trip in his stupid light-up hat.

He smacks the return button. The change machine vomits back exactly 5.73 credits worth of batter at my feet. The crowd cheers.

"It'll just take a sec," I tell Ecker. "I'll take the boat out shallow, get some batter, and come right back."

The boardwalk's blinking with lights, boat crews pulling in and unloading their catch, divers stained with ferrofluid, some of them still scraping the batter off their magsuits. They call out to Ecker as we pass: hey big man, how's school, how's Illinois, you gonna come fix my septic tank, I got a hell of a block for ya. He responds with banter and a smile. He knows they're only ribbing him because they're proud. A battermag that tested good enough to pass the basic modules and go vocational, to a real brick-and-mortar school over the state line.

"I don't know why you wouldn't let me come out with you this morning." Ecker almost trips over the tiny light-up bugs some kids are racing over the planks. "I could've helped."

"What, with those soft little hands you got now?"

The joke drops awkward between us. It's been like that all weekend. Our whole lives we've been giving each other shit, but Ecker came back from school with some kind of armor up. I keep catching him with a weird look on his face, like now, when he's watching the little group of bug-racing kids. Marina brats, bare feet full of splinters, just like we used to be.

"Alright," I tell him, voice softer than I mean. "You wanted to come out? We're going out."

I gather up Dough-girl from their usual spot, hanging out in front of the kluski joint with a bunch of other teens. The picnic tables are a wreck—red baskets with dumplings and butter pooled in the wax paper, kids crammed along the benches with their module helmets on, tapping their left ears to skim-skim-skim through the lessons. Five years ago it would've been me and Ecker here tracing bored lines in the ketchup, blue light flashing over the balled-up napkins. Dough-girl's in the middle, chewing on a fry through the bottom of their visor.

"Hey." I knock on Dough-girl's helmet. "You know you're supposed to listen to those."

Dough-girl looks up. I can see Ecker and me reflected in the helmet's visor, a funhouse mirror of boardwalk neon and the pizza shack behind us.

"You sound like my dad." Dough-girl's voice is garbled by the math lesson squeaking from the tinny speakers. "What's the point?"

"I dunno, learn shit or something."

"So what, like I'm gonna test out?"

"Christ, Dough-girl, you ever tried to get on a bus? Go on, go to the depot and ask to pay for a ticket with your batterville credits. Might as well be a carmdot punch card."

Dough-girl rants back but it's muffled by some kind of science unit about capillaries. I can feel Ecker shift his feet beside me, the discomfort wafting off him.

"Whatever," I say. "Do what you want. We're going out again. Fuckin' chicko guy wouldn't round up."

Dough-girl pulls off their helmet. "But it's dark and we're out of b-powder. It wasn't even glowing last time under the black-light. It's too cut down."

"Fine, we'll get some more. Where's Brill?"

"Probably sleeping in the boat, right?" Ecker says. He meets my eyes for the first time all night, and it's then that I realize his hair is curling around his ears even though he doesn't like it to get so long, that in the four months he was gone he never got it trimmed, that the haircut I'm seeing is the one I gave him in his boxers on the concrete of my front steps.

All the unloading stragglers shake their heads when they see us approach their boats, pleading, hopeful, primed to beg. The only one who doesn't shout us away is Izzie, the last of the olds from back in the day when the cleanup boom first happened, when this town was nothing but deep woods and dead fish rotting on the shore, their bellies swollen with plastic.

Izzie just stands there on the boat deck with the bag of yellow powder, sucking her teeth. A softie. When me and Ecker were little she used to let us crush up the vitamin pills for her. We'd get to swipe a fingerful of batter from her catch tub as a reward.

"I'll pay you back," I say.

"You owe us like a pound of b already."

"Hey!" Dough-girl points over at Izzie's partner by the net. He's sifting out white plastic pellets from the lake weeds and trash. "They caught pearl."

Only a fistful, but it's enough for two months' rent. I've always been told that the battervilles started as a settlement; a bunch of tents and prefabs full of people who got demerited out of the big warehouse jobs. Back then Lake Michigan was dying, but not yet dead. The government paid good money to clean up microplastics from the lake, turn it into batter you could collect and slop into a cooler. I saw one of those old commercials once: a tattooed guy and an old lady smiling in this cute painted rowboat, dumping in their dainty bottles of ferrofluid and swishing the water with those tiny magnetic wands that could only catch the world's saddest clump of batter. It didn't take long for people to start getting smart, strapping head to toe in duct tape and all the magnets they could find, but it was pearl that made the town boom. Some kind of lawsuit found out that a specific company had spent decades dumping little plastic pellets into lakebound drains, and made them pay big money for every little pearl you could catch. I don't remember much from my modules, just a picture of a fish, figure A or B or something, spliced open. The white pellets were packed in along the twisty pink of the intestines like the fish had been born with them there, a weird little row of gut teeth.

"You think that's a trove?" Izzie waves off the handful of pearl like it pains her. "You should've seen us thirty years ago. We used to come back with buckets full of the stuff. That's why they brought in the change machines. We were pulling it out of the water so fast they had to automate."

"Yeah and you guys sucked it all up," Dough-girl says. "Now all that's left is batter you can't buy shit with."

"What, you want us to leave it there to end up in the fish bellies? You don't want the lake to come back?"

"Lake's never gonna come back," I say. "It's a fuckin' batter bowl. All we can do now is make the money we can. See, you owe us the b-powder at least, come on."

"Fine, but I swear t—"

"Where'd you find the pearl?" Ecker's voice cuts through.

His hands are in his pockets again but he sounds like the kid I used to know, the one that won our shitty motorboat in a diving bet and stood with his arms crossed in the doorway of my prefab when my mom finally showed up to claim it five years after she disappeared.

No one bothers fishing for pearl anymore. You might find one or two free floaters, but the only clumps left are in pockets on the lakebed, trapped in the weeds and algae muck. It's more of a legend at this point, and I don't know why Ecker cares. He's only here for the weekend until he goes back to his plumbing program with the nice little dorms he sent me a picture of: tables where you can eat outside in a subdivision with green astroturf instead of dead baked grass.

"We were up by Michigan City then we cut west. Don't waste your time, kids. It was a fluke."

"Michigan City. Got it." Ecker turns to me. "You ready?"

I don't like the look in his eye.

Growing up, me and Ecker always dreamed of hitting it big. Even pearl credits don't mean shit outside the battervilles, but we didn't care. We'd be kings of the boardwalk, buy a big prefab tricked out with a tactile lounge for Penguin Slide and a backyard full of ATVs. Even if we never got the big house, I always thought we'd end up living together. Fantasized about making him dinner, with like 30% meat burgers or something nice, and he'd look over at me and smile like when we were little, floating on our backs in the lake and laughing because we were so close to sinking. I'm not stupid. I've always known the rest of the fantasy would never happen. Ecker likes smart guys, the ones that make him talk nervous, biting into all his consonants. Not me, the dumb easy one that smears him with a lazy smile like cornoil butter on bread.

Ecker didn't tell me he got into vocational school until two days before he was supposed to leave. All the crews got together to throw him a party and he avoided me the whole time, already packing his fists into his pockets like a stranger. But at two a.m. when everyone was drunk and setting off fireworks in the backyard he pushed me into the murphy laundry of Izzie's prefab and held my face in his hands and kissed me like we'd never been two separate pieces, only one whole.

WE'RE SPEEDING out on the black, just the four of us. All the boats have already come in. Ecker shouts over the wind and motor to tease me about my steering, the way I still whip the rudder with a little flourish of my hand like I'm on some kind of stage. It feels like it used to, before we even took on Dough-girl and Brill, when we were just a crew of two, laying down in the boat between dives and talking about the dumbest stuff.

Just past Michigan City we drop anchor in one spot, then another. Me and Ecker dive together. The bottom of the lake is barren, a tangle of weeds and sunken boats and not a single pearl. When I was little it sucked the air out of my lungs to be down on the lakebed, the feeling that you're not touching the weeds and grimed up junk so much as it's got you in its own fingers. People say it's the kind of darkness that crushes you, but it doesn't bother me. Not anymore.

At our fifth or sixth spot we give Brill and Dough-girl a turn to dive. Me and Ecker sit in the midnight quiet, sniffling lake-water snot and listening to the chop against the boat.

"We're not gonna find shit out here, Eck."

"Maybe not the way you shake the weeds."

"Oh and your little barrel roll is gonna do the trick." I tease him back, imitating the twist that he does with his eyes closed, graceful as a dancer, though I'd never admit that I don't think it's funny at all but beautiful.

"Even if we found pearl it'd be wasted on you anyway," he laughs. "I know you'd just blow it on your damn lizard."

"Skeeball's a fuckin' gecko, first of all, and the specialty waxworms help with his digestion issues."

"Right, right, the digestion issues."

Ecker looks at me the way he used to. Like the time I got the idea in my head that we were gonna save up all of our kluski wrappers to wallpaper my bedroom with the little thumbs-up noodle mascot. Like it's the dumbest thing he's ever heard and he loves me for it and every goddamn time it makes my head go fuzzy.

Ecker rubs the water from his face with both hands, and when he's done he stares at the bottom of the boat, the smile gone from his eyes.

"On the bus ride in I saw one of those big prefabs for sale, you know the ones we used to talk about, with the heated floors and the tactile hookup."

"Yeah?"

"I was just thinking, like, if we could just find a little pearl, then maybe I don't have to go back to school."

"What, you don't like it there?"

"No, I mean, it's fine. It's a bunch of townie kids that flunked their modules, couldn't get into college even though their parents paid for all the tutoring add-ons. I'm the only battermag there. Sometimes I just want to be back home. With the people that know me. You know?"

Ecker stretches his feet out the way he's done a hundred times in this boat, but this time he nestles his foot between mine, the way I imagine people do when they're curled up in bed together, twined into the close spaces, breathing each other's air. It makes me shiver to imagine that small amount of body heat spread out heavy on top of me and at the same time I can't stop thinking of Ecker at the bottom of the lake, twirling with his fists crossed over his chest. Smiling, under the weight of all that black water.

Dough-girl and Brill surface with a splash, cussing into the night.

"There's no pearl down here," they say. "This is stupid. Let's get some batter and go home."

Ecker sits up, his foot no longer touching mine. I feel the ghost of it on my skin, like a handful of empty water.

THE MAGSUIT'S heavy and sticks to the edge of the boat, cause we only had enough money to anti-mag the bottom and sides. Some parts of the fabric are still damp from this morning, itchy cold against my skin. I tap the velcro pockets along my arms, belly, shins, smushing in the fraying duct-taped corners to make sure the magnets hold. Dough-girl ties me to the floater tube that'll keep me just a few yards below surface, so the weight of the suit doesn't pull me to the lakebed. I tell them to give me more slack. I like to move around.

When we're ready to go, Ecker pours Izzie's little ziploc bag of b-powder into the old milk jug stained grayish with ferrofluid, then Brill clicks on the industrial blacklight. It lights up her gapped teeth, makes the ferro glow like the prairie moon.

"Fifteen count, alright?" Eck hands me the glowing jug. "On yours."

"Got it," I say. "One."

He shoves me into the water.

Two, three. I squeeze out the ferrofluid, give its oil molecules a chance to find their tiny plastic cousins swirling around the water.

Seven, eight. The magic starts. A slash of hi-vis yellow in the dark.

Microplastic binds to oil, then magnetite, then boom. Lightning in a bottle. It all shrinks together into little glowing clumps of muck like something that's alive. I hold out my magnetic arm, watch the batter fireflies gather along my elbow and stomach and all the way down to my toes.

Thirteen. There's a tickle of weeds. My foot hits mushy bottom. Shit. I reach for the rope to the flotation tube and where it should be there's only water. Shit, shit.

Nineteen. Forty. I lose count.

The suit's so heavy it presses me to the lakebed. When I thrash I just churn up the mud, deeper and deeper. I clench my jaw to keep from sucking water but I can't hold it anymore, I can't, cause it feels like we're somewhere between a hundred and thousand.

A tug.

A yank in my guts.

Air.

Ecker, treading next to me in the water. His face under the blacklight, all twisted up and heaving, then suddenly he's looking behind me, and I see it behind him, too.

Hundreds of them, glowing UV-bright. Riding on the surface of the waves like it's not made of water but pearl.

WE SCOOP UP THE PELLETS, pack them in the mesh net at the back of the boat. There are so many fistfuls we lose count. Brill cracks open a beer and passes it around to celebrate, and I have to stop Dough-girl from chucking their module helmet into the lake saying now none of it matters.

Ecker skins off my magsuit, wraps me in a towel while he scrapes the last bit of batter from the inside of my elbow. He tells me he's not going to take his bus tomorrow. He looks happier than I've ever seen him. I try not to cry.

We crank the boat up to high speed and soon enough I can see the batterville lights again, the little stretch of boardwalk where Eck and I grew up and will die together if I let him. Feels like I should be flying, but I'm just shivering.

In the net behind me is our future together in the big prefab, all the weed and Penguin Slide we could ever want. Ecker pressed up behind me in the morning, kissing my neck. Six ATVs in the backyard and fireworks and the both of us shirtless, smiles receding as the ash cools on the cement. In ten years we'll be like the handful of others who struck it big with pearl, the ones buying out rounds at the boardwalk bar, wrinkled and wasted, telling stories everyone's already heard. He'll grow tired of my easy jokes, my yellowing teeth. He'll wish he never came home.

Ecker smiles at me over his shoulder, and in the dark I hope the one I give back to him looks real.

I wait until he's turned around again, until I can only see the windblown rooster of his hair. The net latch's not hard to open. I do it with one hand.

I'll take it, this little moment. When the pearls are leaking out onto the waves around us and no one can see them, not even me.

PARASITE'S GRIEF

KATHARINE TYNDALL

Originally published by *Fatal Flaw*

Katharine Tyndall (she/her) has been published in *Nightmare, SAND,* and many more. She is a finalist for the 2025 Grist Imagine 2200 Climate Fiction Prize and the 2024 winner of the Berlin Sci-Fi Film Fest in the Short Story category. Currently she is at work on her first novel at the Granta Writer's Workshop. She lives in Berlin with her partner, and when she's not writing, she enjoys walking in the woods collecting species observations for her iNaturalist account.

When her limbs started to fail I realized I was killing Leucal. She couldn't walk far without stumbling. She'd try to get up but her ten limbs would struggle, as if a terrible weight lay on her back. My weight, I thought to myself. Through my link to her brainstem I'd try to help her, clumsily reaching through her mind and moving her limbs when I could feel her frustration. I tried not to take full control yet, though we both knew it was inevitable. The weakness is a common first sign of the change; as her brain lost the ability to steer her body, I learned to control it. Eventually, she would transfer her body to me.

In the place where our minds connect I could feel her slow dread, the steady pulsing of her consciousness becoming aware that her life was almost over. I could feel her exhaustion from fighting the loss of a body that became more of a shell every day. She felt fear of death, concern for my future, but no bitterness about the change or jealousy that I would live on. I was amazed at her ability to be worried about my life after her, when she was the one dying. In our moments of stillness I could feel her love. She would curl her ten pillowy limbs around me as she did when I was young, cradling me in the white cocoon of her body. I tried not to let her see how much I hated myself for doing this to her.

The way Leucal expressed love to me was more complete for its wordlessness. The way she interpreted the world through her cilia-covered surface made her communications to me a flood of sensory information. Memories and hormones and literal warmth passed through our mental link in the moments we grieved our fading partnership. I couldn't help but feel that my own expressions of tenderness were poorer. She was my home, my incubator and carrier and protector, the blind but infinitely perceptive body that both of our minds lived in. I was the thinker, the seer, the steerer, the one who invented games for us to play, who represented us in the community. But there was no decision we didn't make together, no action we hadn't wordlessly discussed through our shared connection. Some Teloschi philosophers have claimed language is actually an impoverished form of communication, that our symbiont relationship to our Hyella is the most complete way to transmit information. I only realized how right they were when Leucal was gone.

We took a lot of time together before the change. We still participated in the community, but for the most part we enjoyed long, meandering walks with only each other for company. As Leucal increasingly lost control of her legs, I took over, steering her while she tasted the air. Each day I'd feel her physical strength fade while her mind hummed along as it had before, warm and content and loving. Our favorite path led around the smoking lake, where we could enjoy the rich steam that rose off the waters and the sight of the soft purple crusts of organisms clinging to the rocks of the shore. As we walked we shared memories of our time together through our connection. One day, Leucal showed me her memories of life before me, and how I came to be.

She was born in the same nursery cave she and I often visited to lay her own eggs. Of her ten nest-mates, only eight matured, and one of those ran off before the pairing to join the wild Hyella who live on the high plains, to never take a symbiont and to live his own life. No Hyella is forced into pairing—the choice is theirs. But Leucal never wanted to face the world alone. When she was small, paired Hyella would come and tend to her and her siblings, and she showed me how she envied and admired them. In that childish way that we all want to grow up faster, she desired a symbiont more than anything else. She shared a memory with me, of curling up with her siblings in their nursery, together but lonely, anxious for the day they would find their Teloschi.

In her third year, in the warm season when the methane storms subside, she and the other Hyella made their journey to the low valley where the Teloschi mate. The Teloschi whose Hyella have already passed on, who have full control over their bodies, do their part of the dance at the head of the valley, where warm winds rush over the low mountains and draft downward. The young Hyella gather on the valley floor, undulating, dancing, feeling the change in the wind as the Teloschi release clouds of spore. The Hyella dance for hours in the valley, spinning until the point of exhaustion and beyond, taking in as many spores as possible to better their chance of infestation.

She showed me the feeling of her dance, the hope and excitement as she felt the spores in the air, the way the tiny molecules pricked her as she swayed soundlessly in the valley. The little burning sensations as the spore came in contact with her cilia, as she willed her immune system to give in, not to fight the onset of infestation, so that she could meet her partner and start her life. All day and half the night she danced, until she was tripping over her limbs with exhaustion, too tired to raise her forelimbs to the wind. She felt the whole outside of her burning with spores, praying she had collected enough. Not all Hyella manage to catch their Teloschi their first year, and as the weeks went by and she waited for signs of infestation, she lost hope. First one Hyella in her nursery announced their pairing, then a second and a third. She had resigned herself to waiting until next year when she finally felt the chemical pulse on the top of her body that signaled infestation.

Leucal and the other newly-paired Hyella would gather apart from the others, whispering to each other through the touch of their limbs. She recalled losing sensation as I grew over her cilia, gently reaching a limb up to the top of her body to feel the translucent green-blue scab that would become me, tracing the minuscule bumps where my three eyes and mouth would soon form. She showed me how proud she was of her dance, and of me, how carefully she tended me in my first months to make sure I grew strong, the excitement as I finally latched to her brain and she felt my first glimmers of consciousness. She said my first thoughts were tiny flutters of warmth as we lay together in our new nest.

I felt almost sick as she showed me my birth. She was the only home I had ever known, and somehow I would have to keep going after she was gone. I tried to hide my guilt and despair, but she sensed it. She curled around me on the shores of the lake and held me, remembering how it felt to cradle me when I was just a cluster of cells.

I AWOKE one morning a few days after our visit to the lake to Leucal dying. Her consciousness flickered, the little energy she had left drained into the point where we connected, no longer sustaining her but rather healing the place where my adult body had fused itself to hers. She was barely aware as I piloted her body out of our dwelling, up the cliffs, moving her many legs in rhythm. I passed the nursery caves where she had been born and laid her young, scrambling on past the cliffs covered in clinging purple crusts, to a craggy ledge where thick layers of vegetation tumbled over the rock walls. I was growing accustomed to her body—our body, my body—the feel of the heavy, soft feet falling and spreading, encompassing the textures of the ground with trillions of cilia, in a grip so secure that the slick edges of the cliff face did not deter us as we climbed.

We reached the top and the great open plains, a plateau extending perfectly flat as far as I could see. The land was covered with red hair-grass nearly as tall as Leucal that swayed and rippled in minute breezes, appearing as a sea broken by waves where the wind moved it. A herd of wild Hyella stood a short distance away, grazing in the hair-grass, grasping clumps of strands in the crook of their limbs and sucking the microbes that lived on the surfaces of each strand into the tips of their cilia. Forty Hyella, huge and pure white in the red grass, their limbs constantly moving in the strands, brushing against their neighbors as the herd moved as a single unit, led by the largest, the matriarch, at the very center. This was the wild way, a slow way, gentle and peaceful, living in close herds, transmitting feeling and thought to one another by the touch of a limb, sensing the wind for dangers of storm and spores.

I felt Leucal drifting in and out of a near-death slumber. Gently I woke her, prodding her consciousness, now a small, flickering thing in that body which was becoming mine. There was a glimmer of awareness as she awoke for the last time. Warmth, life, joy, as she sensed me, felt the warm wind of the high plains and tasted the scent of the wild herd. I tried to send her as much of my love as I could through our link. I clung to her, trying to hold that spark of consciousness in place. I wanted to smother her in my love, weigh her life force down in our body, extract promises that she'd never leave me alone. Love and smother as I might, in an instant she was gone, and I was empty. The last things I felt from her as she slipped away—calm, love, and wonder.

I can't recall the first hours of being truly alone. I know I stayed in silence on the high plains for a long time because I remember stumbling down the cliffs in the dark, wishing Leucal would help me guide these legs which now seemed clumsy. We—I—made it back to the dwelling and curled in our—my—nest, gasping with grief. Before, when she'd only been dying, I could always feel some piece of her, even asleep, when she'd felt like little more than a warm pulse. Now my body echoed with her absence. She was a cave that I was lost inside. The place where our bodies connected felt different, as if a door which had once been half-open was now thrown wide, and I could pass through with my entire self, into the chasm which had once been her. I could feel every part of her now, feel it directly. Where before I had only gotten glimpses of her cilial perception when steering her body, I was now overwhelmed by the feelings of these tiny hairs sensing the composition of the air and the nest, sensing what was outside our dwelling by the minuscule changes in air pressure and chemical content. I became aware for the first time of a sense of discomfort in the crooks and crevices of her—my—

body, where I had neglected to groom her in the last days of her life as carefully as she had once done. Now dust and dead cilia had accumulated there, and they itched. I burned with guilt for not tending to her. Had she died feeling uncomfortable? I hoped she had already been too far gone to notice. My first act of care, of tender ownership of the vessel that had once been her, was to groom, meticulously, for hours, until this body felt like something loved.

THERE ARE many written accounts of the change. It's unsurprising that it occupies so much of our art and recorded history, as a crucial phase of life. For a while, before and during, I read these accounts whenever possible, hoping to make sense of the experience, and the pain. Once it was over, I could say there is no change like one's own change.

None of the sources I read talked about the guilt I felt. Do most of us not feel it? I know that it's natural, a part of every Teloschi's life to go through the change. We cannot live without our partners. But Hyella can live without us—live larger, longer, more peacefully—in the high plains and the open air. Our paired Hyella chose us, chose the dance and all that came with it. We are paired, we are partnered, we share the joys and pains of life, help each other to thrive. And yet there is an end, when my infestation of Leucal's body overcame her, where it took her life. With my growth to adulthood I sapped her last reserves of strength, until I took control of the body which had once been hers and made it mine. She gave it to me, lovingly, as her life partner. Her parents did the same thing before her, and the children she had will likely meet the same fate. I read one philosopher's account, which said that the distinction between Teloschi and Hyella is an artificial one, and that it is more accurate to see ourselves as a single entity, as a "we" which becomes an "I" as we absorb the life and experiences of our partners and take them forward after they are gone. I wanted to find comfort in it, but I could not reach Leucal to ask her.

The young Hyella are growing up now in the community, divine little creatures, feeling their way sight-blind through the dwellings and pools and fields. They haven't mastered their cilial chemicoception yet and bump into things while they walk. I nearly stumbled over one on the path by the lake while lost in thought. He was tiny, only old enough to be from Leucal's last clutch of eggs. I felt him sense me. Through the places where our limbs touched, I felt an uncontrolled rush of feeling: awe at meeting an elder, embarrassment at getting in the way, longing for his turn to dance, to have a partner of his own. I wanted to ask him why, and if he was really sure about this, or if perhaps he wouldn't prefer to leave the nursery caves and go to the plains, join a herd, spend his life grazing. I held back, because I knew the question was for my benefit alone.

In the Teloschi elders' village, where those who have already undergone the change choose to live together, I met Varrel, who will be my mate at the dance tomorrow. She went through the change many years ago and tells me she still thinks of her partner, still sends thoughts to her in that body they once shared.

"But she had her time," Varrel says. "She had her years before me and her years with me. The children she made are growing and will be paired themselves, if they aren't already—and I hope one of my children will pair, someday, with one of hers. But I think you and I have it harder. Our Hyella never know what it's like to lose us, to share body and soul with another and then have to keep going after they're gone."

"Do you think it's worth it for them? Do you think they would be better off living without us?" I ask her. I had already asked her many times.

"Your Leucal and my Dreya both loved us, deeply. They looked forward to joining with us, they cherished and protected us, and they wanted their children to know what we had together, and to have it themselves. Why don't you trust her judgment, now that she's gone?"

I don't know why. In life I trusted her more than anything else in the world, and without her, my life is filled with doubt. But I trust that she loved me.

Varrel and I practice our steps for the dance. She offered to be my first mate, the one who mentors me in the steps. We spin around one another in imitation of the dance the young Hyella will take tomorrow; then, shifting our weight to our front feet, we grasp our next pairs of limbs, and the next, until we stand together on four legs and clasp the rest, coming together in an upright circle. She has beautiful eyes, three golden jewels set in her translucent blue face, forming a pattern of veins where her Teloschi body meets what was once her paired Hyella. We pinwheel together in a circle, gently resting the next pair of feet down, and the next. I am shaky on my feet, unaccustomed to balancing aloft. She is surer and steadies me as we turn. When she looks at me while we dance, I wonder if I could love her.

Three turns in the circle tomorrow at the top of the valley, and then, when the wind rises, we press our bodies together and release our spores. The cloud of spore will rise from the pairs of elders and catch the downdraft, sinking into the valley to where the young Hyella await their chance at pairing. I wonder if one of Leucal's will be there in the valley, dancing, hopeful, waiting to meet the partner of her life.

SKITTERING WITHIN

KELSEA YU

Originally published by *Apparition Lit*

Kelsea Yu is a Taiwanese Chinese American writer who is eternally enthusiastic about sharks and appreciates a good ghost story. She is the author of *Bound Feet,* a Shirley Jackson Award nominee, I*t's Only a Game,* a Children's Book Council Award winner, *Demon Song,* and *Stormraven* (forthcoming). Dozens of Kelsea's short stories and essays appear in *Clarkesworld, Apex, Nightmare, PseudoPod, Fantasy,* and elsewhere. Find her on Instagram as @anovelescape or visit her website kelseayu.com. Kelsea lives in the Pacific Northwest with her husband, children, and a pile of art supplies.

On the day Lina Cheng goes into labor, the last horseshoe crab harvest begins. Her water breaks as the crabs are scooped from their coastal homes; she rides to the hospital as they're transported to the lab. As a nurse helps Lina into stirrups —leaning her head back, spreading her legs wide—scientists strap the arthropods into specially designed contraptions, angling their faces up, folding their tails under.

Lina pushes and pushes; the pads beneath her soak red. The crabs are intubated; their bleeding jars fill blue. By the time Hai crowns, the last crab has been bled. A nurse wipes Hai clean and hands her to Lina; scientists hose down the crabs and send them back to the water.

Snuggled tight in Lina's arms, Hai screams, engulfed by the crabs' pain and disorientation. She cries, and the ocean shudders.

AT HAI'S SIX-MONTH CHECKUP, the pediatrician leans in to inspect her face. "Those dry, red patches indicate eczema."

Lina frowns, rubs her eyes. "Eczema? We have no family history of that." She hasn't had more than two hours of uninterrupted sleep since Hai was born; the last thing she needs is a *condition* to deal with.

"Does she often pick at her skin?"

Lina thinks of the tiny mittens she and Wei started putting on Hai because she was scratching herself all over. The times she's watched Hai flip onto her belly and start rubbing her scaly red cheeks against the carpet. The nights Hai has cried and cried until Lina soothed her with a baking soda bath. Lina sighs. "Sometimes, yeah."

"I'll write a prescription for a cream you can apply to her skin twice a day. And I'll have my assistant print you an info sheet. I wouldn't worry too much. Most kids outgrow their eczema within a few years."

HAI DOES NOT OUTGROW IT. In preschool, she's scolded at nap time because she can't stop fidgeting, can't stop itching. In second grade, she scratches her thumb hard enough to tear it open, and when it gets infected, she ends up hospitalized. In fifth grade, a pediatric dermatologist declares Hai's eczema the worst she's ever seen and asks Lina permission to photograph Hai's skin for a medical paper.

When Hai is in sixth grade, the Chengs move to a little town on the coast. Wei wants to finish unpacking, *because otherwise how will he know if the movers damaged anything—didn't Lina see how careless that bearded guy was?* But Lina's loud, long-suffering sigh is enough to remind him that they moved here to get away from the petty stresses of city living, of material concerns. What's the point if they don't enjoy the beauty of their new surroundings? Wei sets down the box. Together, Wei, Lina, and Hai walk the two blocks to the beach.

It's Hai's first time seeing the ocean.

For once, she isn't thinking about her itchy skin. All her attention is caught by new sensations, by observations. The cry of gulls as they glide by; the roar of waves licking the shore; the scent of salt and sulfur on the wind. The mesmerizing beauty of gentle ripples moving across endless water, disappearing into the vast horizon.

While Lina and Wei fight over where to set up their towels, Hai walks toward the water. The breeze blows her parents' argument away as she dips her toes in.

As soon as saltwater kisses Hai's skin, a thousand fleeting moments rush through her. *She is a humpback, releasing the whalesong caught in her throat; she is a remora, nibbling parasites off her companion shark's underbelly; she is a leatherback, opening her soft beak to swallow gooey jellyfish; she is a wolf eel, lurking in a dark cave—*

Startled, Hai stumbles back, but she's unprepared for the way her feet sink into the wet sand. She falls, catching herself with her palms, and an eager wave engulfs her.

As always, Hai's body is littered with tiny wounds: punctured blisters and fingernail-wide lacerations and patchy rashes scraped raw and red and angry.

Each one an invitation.

Stinging saltwater rushes in, relentless and sharp and cruel, and *she is a blue-ringed octopus, curling her tentacle around a delicious snail—*

Hai opens her mouth and screams, screams, *screams—*

She is an abyss-dweller, drawn to a glowing orb in the black ocean—

Saltwater mixes with Hai's blood, flowing through her veins—

She is a ghost shrimp, tunneling through sediment—

Briny blood floods the chambers of Hai's heart, pumping back out through the arteries, searching, seeking—

She is a vampire squid, pulling her webbed arms up and around, turning herself inside out—

Suddenly, Lina and Wei are there, shouting as they pull Hai back from the shoreline, away from the water; but before their connection breaks, the ocean finds what it was looking for.

Deep within Hai, something stirs.

HAI DREAMS she's bound to a surgical bed. Her torso is angled up just enough to see a tube trailing out from between her legs. She knows the feel of a catheter, knows something about this one is wrong. She tries to reach down, to pull it out, but her wrists are strapped down tight.

You're helping us, little one. Helping us create vaccines that will save countless human lives.

Hai doesn't know if it's a voice or a thought she's hearing. She doesn't know anything except that she can't move, and she shouldn't be here, and this is all wrong.

Liquid begins to flow out of her body, through the tube, but instead of yellow, it's blue, it's blue, it's *blue*.

When Hai wakes, there's a pool of blood on the sheets beneath her.

Lina finds Hai curled up on her bed, sobbing. When Lina spots the stain, she leaves and returns, bringing with her a pad and a practiced speech about what it means to grow up.

HAI'S BEEN in her little beach town for half a year when she learns about the annual class field trip to the big city aquarium.

Before they moved, Hai was fascinated by the lobsters crawling over one another in their tank at the Chinese grocery. She used to drag her parents to the pet store to check out the tropical fish. Now, she picks at her food when they sit too close to the lionfish tank at the only Thai restaurant in town, and she cries when she sees the goldfish lined up in little plastic baggies at the summer fair.

The thought of all those creatures locked away behind glass makes Hai's skin crawl. She begs her mother to let her stay home.

Lina's barbed sigh burrows into the fragile hope that her mom might, for once, give in. Hai knows there's no point arguing with Lina in the same way she knows she shouldn't pop her blisters.

Knowing isn't the same as being able to stop.

"Please, Mom. I'll help you cook dinner for a month. I won't ask you for anything for the rest of the school year. *Please.*"

"Hai, you're making a big deal out of nothing. You used to love the aquarium."

"It didn't hurt me then."

"It can't hurt you now! It's in your head! You need to deal with whatever this is. It'll be good for you. Exposure therapy."

"But, Mom..."

"No more arguing. You're going. I can't take any more time

off work, and I don't need your teacher on my case again about how you never join in social activities. I already get enough shit for not having time to chaperone. Of course, no one hassles your dad about how *he* never volunteers."

On the bus, surrounded by chattering classmates, Hai's nervousness turns into more blisters, more itching. Lina's right. Hai *is* different now.

The aquarium towers above all the surrounding buildings, a twisted, modern thing covered in gray panels laid out like fish scales. Hai feels the oppressive charge of it, like a pressurized can ready to explode, but no one else seems to notice. The kids follow Mrs. Anderson inside, Hai at the end of the line.

Their voices echo in the entryway as Mrs. Anderson sorts out their tickets, and then they're inside the metal gate. A burst of excited energy rushes through the class as everyone hops onto the moving walkway through the underwater tunnel.

Hai tries to stay back, but one of the chaperones grabs her hand and pulls her forward.

The tunnel glows cyan, lighting up the busy ecosystem within. Hai looks up, unable to help herself. All those creatures living out their entire lives behind curved glass. It's a work of art, as beautiful as it is painful. Her palms itch, and she scratches them just as a little kid runs into her.

Hai is knocked off balance, but she catches herself with a hand on the thick glass of the tunnel. As if drawn to a beacon, a white-bellied shark swims straight for Hai's outstretched palm, scattering a school of sunny yellow fish. It swerves at the last moment, garnering exclamations of delight.

Hai is suddenly dizzy with want, a desire so potent it has a heart and a pulse.

She longs to explore the places where her ancestors roamed, letting instinct and magnetoreception guide her through deep waters. She is newly mature, ready to make her way to the place where her kind meet and mate. She wants to be a small creature in a vast ocean, not an expen-

sive specimen circling endlessly, never finding a way out. She wants, she wants, she wants.

Hai yanks her hand back from the glass. She can already feel bubbles forming beneath the surface of her skin. Pushing up, up, and out, rounding into clear little domes ready to burst. Suddenly, the glass around her feels like it's shrinking, keeping her there. Collecting one more trapped thing to scoop up and place in a tank.

A turtle looks straight at Hai with a doleful gaze, and another wave of *want* pulses through her. Hai's skin responds, growing itchy all over.

Two more school groups arrive, a hassle of loud middle schoolers and backpacks that fill the tunnel. Hai's head throbs, the urge to flee stronger by the moment. She glances at the entrance to the aquarium, but there are too many attendants near the door. There's only one other way out of this too-crowded tube. Hai slips through the crowd, winding her way deeper into the body of the beast.

For a time, the pain and longing ease. Not quite a surcease, more a dull ache now that Hai's no longer packed in that tunnel like an empty-eyed sardine in a can. Hai passes a tank filled with translucent shrimp and another with a starfish pressed against the glass, its underside on display for passersby. There are more creatures in each tank, little fish that dart away and tiny snails ambling along the pebbled ground and sea anemone swaying with the imitation tide, but Hai doesn't stop to look. She can't afford to dawdle when someone is sure to notice her absence soon.

She does not wonder why no one chases her. Why none of the aquarium visitors seem inclined to stop her and ask where her adult is. Why there isn't a voice booming through the speaker system right now, letting everyone know a child is missing.

Hai is only eleven, after all, and she is used to being ignored.

She hurries past blue-ringed octopi and bioluminescent jellyfish. Skates that blend in with river rocks and bubblegum-bright coral. Fish in more shapes and sizes, colors and patterns, than she could ever have imagined.

At last, she encounters a welcome sight. Up ahead, sunlight shines on the patterned gray carpet, exposing fibers worn down from years of trampling. Hai follows the light to a side door propped open by a rubber wedge. Freedom is close enough to grasp.

But there's an archway to her left, and from somewhere beyond, Hai hears an instrument playing, rhythmic and percussive and beautiful. It's strange and enchanting.

Her feet carry her forward.

As Hai nears, the sound clarifies into something more like a clack or a tap, somehow both odd and familiar all at once. Hai clicks her tongue along with the tempo, as if finding her way back to a lullaby buried deep in memory. It shouldn't be possible; the meter is inconsistent. Yet somehow, she keeps perfect rhythm.

There's a wide tank at the end of the corridor, its sandy surface covered in rust brown discs bigger than Hai's face. They skitter across the tank, crawling on one another. One of the bigger creatures knocks over a smaller one, and Hai startles, seeing the little insect-like legs tucked within the smooth shelf. It reminds her of a giant cockroach.

The upended animal arches its back, twitches its tail, and waves its spindly legs in the air. Hai shivers and steps back. As she turns to step away, that beautiful rhythm drifts into her ears again.

It is only now that she puts the pieces together. These strange critters are the source of the mesmerizing music.

For the second time that day, Hai reaches out a hand to touch the glass. As soon as her fingertips make contact, a wave of pain and love and hope and desire rush through her. She feels the distress of a thousand silent screams as they're forced into place, the needle pierced through their membrane. The exhaustion of the weakened, bled crabs, desperate to escape the subsequent hose down. The shock as they're returned to the ocean, many dying shortly after.

Tears stream down Hai's face, and a shudder runs through her. She feels the way she did two days after her parents told her they were moving, when it finally hit her that her whole world was about to be rewritten.

It's overwhelming, this shift in awareness. But unlike the claustrophobia of the tunnel or the discordance of the rest of the aquarium, something about being here feels right, too. Instead of pulling her hand away, Hai reaches out with her other hand, pressing it against the glass.

Collective hope and desperation twist together, forming a question that sears itself into Hai's mind. She opens her mouth to answer—or cry out, she can't be sure which. That's when the intercom finally buzzes to life with a crackle and an announcement that an eleven-year-old Asian girl is missing. A worker nearby suddenly notices her, and then the ordeal begins.

As Hai is hauled away, her eyes stay locked on the receding tank of horseshoe crabs. Her tongue clicks in time with the skittering of their chitinous little legs.

FOR ONCE, Lina and Wei agree on something: Hai must be disciplined for her escapade at the aquarium. They settle on grounding her for two weeks. Other than the hassle of having to sit through Wei's mostly-off-topic lectures and Lina's rants about how she should never have had children, Hai doesn't much mind. She has no friends for Lina or Wei to keep her from.

Besides, Hai is under a spell.

In the mornings, she wakes with the feeling of sand between her toes, the taste of sea salt and fresh clams on her tongue.

Those first few days go by in a blur, the heady rush of a new obsession overriding all earthly concerns. She reads article after article, meticulously copying every newly acquired fact in her notebook. She watches recordings of marine biologists picking up horseshoe crabs at the coast, pointing out their compound eyes and five pairs of clawed pedipalps; the book gills that jettison streams of water for quick getaways. She finds a video from *that* aquarium, where a woman in a lab coat describes the team's conservation efforts—the way they meticulously breed and incubate new baby crabs, some of whom are eventually released into the ocean.

Hai finds a clip showing rows of horseshoe crabs strapped in and bled, accompanied by a voice-over explanation of how their blue blood will be used to test vaccines. Though she isn't sure why, she can't stop playing this one on repeat, watching again and again until Lina finally takes the computer away.

Hai hasn't broken any rules. She's always been given free rein when it comes to research, to learning. But Lina's pursed lips make it clear that Hai's behavior has somehow crossed into the realm of *too odd*. She leaves Hai locked up in her room without a computer while she decides what to do. Lina has only ever asked for two things from Hai. One, don't make things difficult. Two, for the love of all things holy, just be normal.

Hai has never quite managed either.

With nothing to do, she sits in her room, rereading her notebook and picking at her skin. It's the worst kind of itchy. The kind that feels like no matter how she scratches, the itch is always a little too far below the surface for her to reach.

Wei is gone again. Lately, he's been on business trips more often, but Hai knows better than to mention it.

To Hai, Lina has always been more schedule manager than mother, but she softens a touch when Wei isn't around to raise her hackles. And she makes the best meals when he's gone.

Hai is upstairs doing homework. It's fun, for once. She had to pick an animal to write a report about—the final assignment of the year—and of course, she picked her favorite. She knows everything about them already, so she doesn't *really* need to research, but it gives her an excuse to read up on them again without Lina giving her a hard time.

She's doodling a crab in her notebook when she hears the front door open and shut. Her mother must be back from the market. Hai tries to go back to her drawing, her research, but her arm begins to itch something fierce, and she's lost the train of it. Downstairs, the faucet turns on.

Hai walks to the bathroom. She opens the top drawer, pulls out the little tube of fast-acting anti-itch cream, and applies it. Then she pinches her underarm to distract herself as she starts a slow count backwards from a thousand. No scratching, no scratching, no scratching. She only has to make it until the medicine kicks in.

Hai is somewhere in the two hundreds when she hears the scream. She runs for the stairs full speed, heart beating a mile a minute. She's terrified of what might be wrong, the roar in her ears drowning out all other thoughts, no room to wonder at little things like how the scream sounds nothing like Lina.

She grabs the rail, hopping down the stairs two at a time. As her feet hit the fourth step down, the scream turns to an ear-splitting shriek. Every inch of Hai's skin feels like it's been set aflame, erupting into red hot boils.

Hai is the one screaming now. Her skin, which has learned to take a hellish amount over the years, suffers a shock even it isn't equipped to handle, and she collapses, hand loosening from the rail as she falls, falls, falls.

"WHAT DID you do to her, Lina?"

"I didn't! I didn't *do* anything! I was boiling a crab when she started screaming and fell down the stairs for no reason!"

"That's impossible. The doctor said..."

"You're the one who's fucking impossible. You're never home, not that you do anything to help with Hai when you *are* home."

"Work has been busy."

"Yeah, *work*. Is that what we're calling her now? You're a fucking cliché, you know that, Wei?"

"Keep your voice down. Someone might hear your hysterics."

"Fuck you. Go home. Or go back to *work*, whatever. I don't give a fuck as long as you get out of my face."

"You can't treat me that way. Especially not after this."

"Yeah? Except if we split up, you're never going to try to take custody, because then you'd have to actually take care of her."

Hai is intimately familiar with Lina and Wei's arguments and empty threats. What she isn't used to is the floaty, buzzy feeling or the pain that creeps up whenever she tries to focus on a particular body part.

"Hai?"

Wei looks down at her with sad eyes. Lina looks like she hasn't slept in ages.

Everything hurts.

Outside, Hai hears the crash of ocean waves, the cry of gulls. She thinks of that first day at the beach. She opens her mouth to say...something. What, she isn't sure. But her lungs burn, and she manages only a small croak before tears begin running down her face.

There are some shouts, and then a nurse tells Hai they're going to give her a bit more medicine. The world drifts.

WHEN HAI WAKES UP NEXT, she's alone. The intense pain she felt earlier is now nothing more than a dull ache. Gingerly, she presses her palms into the hospital bed and pushes against them to sit up. As she does, she feels the bumps on her skin and sighs.

She inspects her hands in the light, frowning as she looks closely. Sure enough, they're covered in blisters. That, she's used to. But the pus inside them has a faint blue tint.

She knows she should figure out how to call for a nurse, but...

Hai pops a blister, and the scent of brine fills the air.

She pops another, and another, until salty ocean air overwhelms her with desire, outweighing her blister-popping compulsion. She climbs out of bed in search of satisfaction, her steps sounding strangely like the skittering of clawed legs.

The corridor of the tiny beach-town hospital is inexplicably empty, despite it being the middle of day. As Hai walks, her badly burned skin begins to slough off, old giving way to new. What lies beneath is red and raw and itchier than her worst flare-ups.

With ocean air filling her lungs, Hai doesn't bother holding back. She scratches at her arms, feeling nothing but cool relief as the new skin flakes and peels away. She scratches at her chest and something—four pairs of somethings—claw their way forth, bursting out with glee. From her lower back, a long, twitchy thing grows, stretching until it hits the ground and helps guide her path. From her back, a shell emerges, hard and ridged where her spine might once have been.

As Hai pushes open the hospital doors, her arms elongate, turning hard and spindly. She is near the ocean, near enough to taste it. Near enough to hear the shuffling, the call to join her kind growing ever more difficult to resist. She falls to her hands, her legs combining and sectioning into gills.

As her new little legs cart her forward, she hurts for all her brethren trapped in tanks around the world. She imagines them there with her, a mass of cinnamon-brown discs moving as one across the warm, familiar sands.

Ahead, the endless waters stretch out to greet her.

Hai dips forward, accepting the ocean's embrace. Here, in the life-giving waters as rich and blue as the blood within her new shell, freedom awaits.

TO DRIVE THE COLD WINTER AWAY

E. CATHERINE TOBLER

Originally published by *Strange Horizons*

E. Catherine Tobler's short fiction and poetry has appeared in *Clarkesworld, F&SF, Bourbon Penn, Gamut, Strange Horizons, Lightspeed, Nightmare,* and others. Her photography has appeared in *The New Yorker.* Her editing and writing work has been a finalist for the Nebula, Utopia, Sturgeon, Hugo, Ditmar, Aurealis, Locus, and World Fantasy Awards. She currently edits *The Deadlands.*

For nine straight miles, the hot-rolled steel rails cut a path through the woods, a metal chain thrown into soft mud. Discarded, rotting railroad ties littered the tracksides, the stench of creosote saturating the forest air until birds no longer frequented the trees. It was wholly quiet, cathedral still, waiting. The waiting never ended.

She came to the woods to mourn—to the island, for it was here she spent her childhood. The island called her back to bury the mother she no longer recognized. The father she was estranged from did not come, had never come, would never come. He was like the birds and the creosote-soaked air, incompatible.

The ground took the casket well enough, swallowing it away into the dark. It did not feel like a lump in her throat, or anything in particular. A relief, she'd hoped, but not even that in the end. Just a quietness she had never known. Once the neighbors had gone, and the casseroles had gone, and the flowers dead too, it was just the stillness, just the waiting for the return of normalcy. Whatever that was.

She wandered the farmhouse, but it was not normalcy; she had been away eighteen years, and the house felt as much of a stranger as her mother did. They both sometimes made a complaining creak, but these sounds were unfamiliar after living in a city for so long. Every animal, her mother said, has a sound it makes. The house did not purr or bark at her, though the screen door did snap and the gas stove whispered when she heated water for tea.

Her mother's teapot, her mother's cups. The nurse had used them more in the end, handles and rims showing chips here and there. She set the worst of them into the trash, tied the bag, and carried it out to the bin. It was all hers now, even the dented plastic trash bin. The men came on Wednesdays to collect, Mrs. Steele had told her, but she couldn't recall what day it was now.

The end of the day, in any case, the sky going bruised with the departure of the midwinter sun. She closed the bin and wondered if raccoons had made the deep grooves on the lid in an effort to lift it, but a tremor at the edge of the tree line scattered rodent concerns. White spruce, eastern hemlock, a sprinkling of bare yellow birch, and something moving smoothly between the pale trunks and into the dark boughs.

She waited. No bird called, and nothing else moved, until far across the neighboring yard, a yellowed porch light came on. She drew in a breath, pulled her coat around her, and went inside, closing the door firmly behind.

The house was as still as the world outside, but for the ticking of one clock in the den. Unable to stand it, she took the clock down from the wall, turned it flat on the desk, and removed the battery. The ticking ceased and her breathing slowed.

Tomorrow, she resolved; tomorrow she would go into the woods.

But tomorrow arrived and with it Mr. Butler, who had missed the funeral, but needed to spend an hour or two reminiscing about the woman they'd both lost. She did not feel the loss, not yet, not even when she poured tea for them both and Mr. Butler said her mother had loved honey, not sugar, in hers, and did she have any now. She drew the honey from the cupboard, a beautiful blue glass jar, but when they managed to unscrew the stubborn lid, it was to find the honey had gone to sugar after all. Mr. Butler chipped out a chunk of the sweetness to let it dissolve into his tea.

When he had gone, she set the cups in the sink and stared out the kitchen window at the tree line where the midafternoon light slanted low through the branches. The light was no longer ideal—but what was ideal anymore anywhere? There were four hours until sunset at least, time enough to look, so she gathered her jacket and her camera bag, and left the house. She took no care to lock the house—it felt like it belonged to a dead woman, not her, and she laughed at the idea of being careless with her mother's things. The loud clock, the sugared honey.

She wasn't usually like that, but it didn't make sense, that her mother was gone. It felt like a fairy tale, something happening to someone else. Needles and leaves crunched under her boots and that felt like her own experience, something she was an active participant in. She crossed the wide, brown lawn, and the neighbors on their far porch waved at her despite the distance. She supposed it was good that someone knew where she was going, in her apple red jacket. She stepped into the trees, she felt the world change as it always had there, the crossing of a boundary from one discrete space into another.

The light changed, filtered through the pine boughs. Almost like light cutting through water, everything dappled and undulating. She breathed, comforted by the sharp pine, the vague soft rot beneath her feet, but the silence was always unnerving. The lack of birds, the lack of song. Beyond her mother's death, it was why she had come (work, always work, Jake-Joe-Isabelle-Tom complained, and she could not argue, she loved her work more than she loved them).

They would start here, she'd suggested to her boss, to begin undoing all the damage that had been done—centuries' worth, and he'd laughed at her, but she didn't care. The railroad stood abandoned, the logging mills were silent. They could heal the island, they could give it back to nature and stop destroying it. It was this that interested her in the house that was now hers, it was this that gave her hope, that she could live here and chronicle the world as it was, and the world that it would come to be.

The Mi'kmaq had called the island home until the French colonized it, until the French ceded it to the British. How careless white men had been with it, as with all things, not considering who had been here first, who had done the hardest things in the stewardship of the land. The land cradled in the waves, they called it, until the white men gave it a prince's name, and claimed it forevermore.

But the trees had been here longer than any of the men, and the trees closed around her now, keeping the snow from her shoulders as it began to spit from the leaden sky. She drew her Canon F-1 from its bag and began to shoot casually as she walked: the first snowflakes caught on the boughs, the darkening red soil, as everything grew wetter, a skunk footprint crossing a patch of mud through the undergrowth.

There were no longer any moose or caribou here, but she glimpsed antlers through the trees, and followed them. Perhaps they were only branches after all, but they moved as if attached to something living. Her breath caught in her throat as she pursued it, snapping a frame here and there to see what the film might tell her later. It had been a long week, a longer year, and the woods had a way of telling a story even if one hadn't been prepared for such. Her boots sank into the soft ground and she looked down to pull herself free. When she looked up, the antlers had gone.

She kept on, northward of the house, she figured. The snow came and went and came again. It was fitful like her sleep. She paused every few steps to kneel to the ground, to see what she might find. Garlic mustard, glossy buckthorn. Invasive, both, but she photographed them all the same, thinking it would help her case, that this place needed restoration.

In the distance, laughter. She went still at the sound, listening. More than one voice, but all of them male. Deep, happy. She walked slowly onward, closer to the laughter, though she could not see anyone in the trees. Perhaps after all this time it was birds returning to the island, and the idea quickened her pace. The snow increased, blowing down upon her as she rushed past the skeleton of a hemlock. Its branches clawed at her jacket sleeve, but did not slow her. The mud did that, her boot slipping sideways until she was on the ground, hip screaming.

That was when she saw the two figures, walking hand in hand. By their height they were men, but their shoulders were too broad, and their heads too furred, antlers spreading crown-like from the top of each head. One set was broad and flat like that of a moose. The other was more like caribou antler, branching in countless points. Scarlet ribbons twined around the caribou, sparkling with glitter. Caught in a Christmas present, she thought, but the ribbons ended in bows and it all looked intentional. As if someone had decorated him.

The men, if that is what they were, walked away from her, deeper into the trees. They were clad in suits, sepia and black.

One wore a coat of tails, the other a boa of boxwood, dogwood, willow, corn tassels, cone flower seed heads, and lupines. The lupines and dogwood were not in season, but blooming as if they were, bright purple and pale pink.

As the men drew farther away, she remembered her camera. She lifted it, only to find the lens caked with cold, red mud. She dug it free, flung the glob onto the ground, and aimed her camera. Her focus was poor, her grip unsteady, but she shot until the roll was empty, until the men had completely disappeared. There were other houses that way, she knew. Perhaps she had stumbled upon an old winter tradition—though she could not name it.

Turning back for the house, she saw the slate slab emerging from the ground like something of a tombstone. It was marked, though not with a name; the image of a fox had been carved into the stone, its outline weeping with melted snow.

Later that evening, as the prints dried in the windowless bathroom she had converted into a darkroom, she dried her hair by the fire and thought of the fox. She would have to return to photograph it, would want a record of every such thing in the region, to strengthen her case with her boss. The island deserved to be rehabilitated, the forests deserved to grow, after centuries of over clearing.

Her thoughts returned to the men, their hands entwined. If they had been aware of her, they had shown no sign. They had been in their own world, and she the trespasser.

Once dried, the film revealed two mud-blurred figures, shadowed and uncertain. The scarlet ribbon she remembered was a disappointing gray, color only clinging to the woods around the men. Their headdresses appeared clumsy, skewed from the weight of the antlers they had affixed to them. She laughed to look at them now, two young men coming home for holiday break, dressing as the beasts that had once roamed these woods.

She crawled into bed feeling like a fool, for she could not get them out of her head. The follies of youth, maybe, or the warmth of such companionship in the midwinter woods. She had not known either for too long, so naturally the young men felt alien, distant, and kept her mind spinning long after she should have stopped thinking of them. She pictured them entering their home, antlers banging into the door frame, into each other. Each would carefully free the other from the confines of the costume, until they stood laughing at one another still, hair standing on end, eyes wide from being inside the dark headdress. One would pull the remains of the lupins from the other, never once asking how they dared exist in midwinter. It was simply so.

Come morning, she loaded her camera with film, cleaned the lens, and packed more film into the bag alongside a sandwich and thermos of coffee. Notebook and pen completed the supplies alongside the sincere hope she would make progress on her proposal. She went north of the house again, drawn by the memory of the men, perhaps, but the neighboring farmhouse was still but for a curl of chimney smoke, and so were the woods when she set foot into them.

The trees stood in shadow still, though the sky above their crowns was beginning to lighten with the sunrise. Her breath came in gasps of fog, frosted undergrowth brushing glitter onto her jeans as she pushed through them. The woods were good here—diverse and strong—though the farther she walked, the more damage she saw, wide swaths of only dark pines growing where they'd been intentionally seeded.

A hundred years before, much of the land had been cleared for agricultural pursuits, and only now were people realizing the damage done, the birds not only fleeing the creosote-soaked air, but refusing to nest in coniferous stretches. They needed variety, not a thousand pines stretching from shore to shore.

She reached a neglected stretch of asphalt road, at which the trees stood starkly different on either side—pine, oak, ash, and maple to her back, endless pine spreading before her. Stepping from the ground to the asphalt road was like leaving the sea for land; the road was hard, uncompromising. She walked it a while, noting no trace of bird shit, nor any kind of scat from any animal in passing. No fox, no coyote, no raccoon. But there was a shoe, a horseshoe.

She photographed the shoe where it lay, then noticed how narrow it was, surely not for a horse hoof. It was narrow, as if a caribou wore a shoe. The metal was strikingly cold to the touch, as if it had lain there for years without the touch of sunlight. The chill was familiar to her, though the shoe itself called to mind the young men from the night before. Caribou, she had thought.

She left the shoe where it was, and only took a few dozen more steps along the asphalt before diverting back onto the ground. There was a wrongness to the world when she stood on the asphalt, though it had begun to seep into the ground, the dirt, the trees. She tried to put it into words, words that her boss would understand so he would recognize the urgency of her mission, but those words would not come. She walked deeper into the woods, until she found a stone large enough to sit on. She drew out her notebook, her pen, and found herself sketching rather than writing. She drew the trees as she remembered them, and the stone from yesterday with its fox face; she drew the young men, one with a ribbon of scarlet, the other with the end held loosely in his hand.

Hands, but also antlers. The idea stuck like a barb in her throat.

Her boss would not understand anything she wrote or drew; he would be incapable until he came, until he spent time beneath the trees. She closed the notebook and drew the thermos out, to pour a generous cup of coffee. It steamed in the cool morning air the way her breath had, coiling into the air before it vanished. She ate half her sandwich—chicken salad on wheat—and tucked the second half away for later.

She waited for the birds even if she didn't know that was

what she was waiting for at first. She was always straining to hear something that was no longer there. Plovers and blue jays, she thought, and her heart ached to see the paintbrush details on a jay's wing or tail, but none came, the trees only moved by the breeze, or a branch stretching in the warming light. The trunks had begun to steam, frost evaporating as the light pushed deeper into the wood.

The morning and afternoon passed in a rush, coffee and half sandwich consumed in turn. When she returned to the house—not yet home—her bag was light of everything save for film. She spent the evening developing the rolls, hanging prints of local flora and fauna to dry, though she had seen precious little fauna. The horseshoe—the not-horse shoe—stood out among the prints, strange. Unfamiliar as the road it rested on.

She worked until midnight, labeling and categorizing the photographs, remembering childhood on the island, hunters in bright orange vests, stepping into the woods to never be seen by her again. Surely they had come out somewhere, but as she brushed her hair, her mind took a turn toward the outrageous, for what if like those young men, the hunters had donned antlers and furs, and slipped between the trees to live a life no other could imagine. She imagined a crown of antlers upon her own head, antlers the color of her flaxen hair, rubbed to a high shine against the trees, leaf and berry caught in every crook.

Upon waking, she was surprised to find her head so light, not weighed down by an antler crown, though upon her pillow she found the shred of an oak leaf that has escaped her careful brushing. She pressed it into the pages of her notebook, a quick uncertain knock at the front door making itself known. Bundling her robe around her, she went barefoot to the door, finding it was the closest neighbor, an apologetic look upon her face, a casserole dish in her hands.

Time got out of joint, the neighbor said; it was easy to let the days pass in a blur after the loss of a parent, so wouldn't she take this dish, and find some comfort, some fuel, within it. Of course she took the dish, made a fuss of inviting the neighbor in though she knew the invitation would be declined—she'd slept half the day away, was standing there barefooted in her nightgown; the neighbor did her best to not flee instantly.

Alone again, she set the casserole into the fridge and, despite the lateness of the hour, looked toward the waiting woods. The light was bleeding out of the sky, the trees looking as if they'd been drawn upon it by a fine-line marker. Farther down, the marker was saturated, the darkness complete. Nothing pierced the solid line of black until the golden glow of a lantern passed through.

Kids had always loved the woods; her mother often complained about make-out sessions, smoke circles, "wild" parties amid the trees. She had gone there in her own youth, though never to kiss anyone she shouldn't have been kissing. She had gone as she did now, with camera in hand, to see what she could make of the world beyond the tree line.

Nighttime always revealed something different, though it was the wee small hours when that something did finally emerge from the boughs.

The young men were not young men; the sputtering lantern light revealed the truth of them, which she had only guessed before. They were human, and yet not, two spirits seemingly bound into one flesh. Male bodies, showing skin and fur, but no clothing. Their antlers were no headdress at all. There was no delineating mark between flesh and fur, it was all one and the same. One moose, one caribou, the caribou's antlers bedecked in scarlet ribbon. The tails of the ribbons loosely held within the moose's broad hand as the caribou carried the lantern. The scent of lupines out of season.

She was small within their fathomless, black eyes and felt as though she could not move, even as she was also aware of the frantic flutter of her finger against her camera.

The photographs would be overblown, every detail lost in the nearness of the lantern light, but there would still be something, a memory perhaps, a memory of a scent, of a touch—chilled fingers against her cheek—of a sound—an iron-shod hoof crushing a branch—and the impossible awareness of the way they had drawn her through the low snow-decked boughs, the snow melting against her bare arms, the cold mud squelching between her bare toes, and shown her what existed beyond: A place no human could remember, for they had never traveled there in their human skins, could not travel in that manner. A price was required, necessary, and they could not explain that price with words, but she felt the truth of it—it was not her heart, but its beat; it was not her lung, but its breath. And she said yes and yes once more before they set her into the undergrowth where they had found her. You will not remember, they told her.

In her makeshift darkroom, she crumpled the photographs in her hands, feeling again the heat of the lantern, the willow-exhale of the moose, the cool caribou nose. The Mi'kmaq had carved animal images into the rock of the island, but whether it was to mark the passages or their presence, she could not say. By some miracle—being a part of the island itself—the eras of agriculture had not erased these places, but had only more deeply embedded them, until they could never be removed, nor could they be easily accessed. Not without a price.

Like the underworld, she thought, grasping at thoughts of her mother, walking blind into some fictional light (a lantern, why not). She lay dreaming, though wide awake, the scent of crushed willow pervading even her sheets. You will not remember, they told her, but she remembered. She rose remembering, and dressed remembering, and went once more into the trees, remembering.

She could not find it. Where rocks had once jutted, now ferns rose, green against the midwinter chill. She tore them between her hands, but the ferns revealed nothing, as if sworn to an ancient pact. She dug her fingers into the cold red mud until her nails cracked, until she bled, but the ground gave her nothing. She beat her fists against the trees, until blood flecked the air, but the woods did not relent. The way had been shut, and she returned to the house, remembering. The clarity of light, the flaxen antlers emerging unbroken from her skull, the scarlet ribbons trailing like veins from one hand.

The food in the house rotted; the chemicals in the film degraded to uselessness; everywhere she walked, dust stirred into the air. And she remembered: the softness of the fur, the warmth of the stones beneath her bare hooves, the impossibility of lupines.

When her boss called, the ringing of the telephone was something she could not place. It was part of another life, another place, but she found the words easily when he asked what she had found—she could not speak of the young men, her throat tightened when she tried—but she could talk at length about the woods, the ruin of trees, the poisonous line of abandoned railroad that wound itself like a chain around a throat. Tear it out, she whispered; we can tear it out and let this world breathe again. And he said yes and yes once more, and the work began, and she bloodied her hands every day upon the island's dirt and stone. She hauled the used rails from the woods with crane and her very hands; she guided the men to tear it out, tear it all out, and when the hot-rolled steel rails rose into the sky, she felt the air return. It was slow and cautious, as if after a long time of not breathing.

She also breathed. She walked barefoot into the woods once more, and could feel the absence of the steel. She felt the green like a great rushing tide, through the dirt and the roots and the leaves that reached for the sun. She reached too, her flaxen hair gone silver under the warm light, so many years had passed. She had become her mother, inhabiting the woods as if they were a house. She lay among the ferns, and stretched her body into the mud, and prayed a prayer she did not know. She looked every day for a rock, for a sign, but it did not come. She hoped every day for a direction, and when it did not come, she carried on, lifting what she could, mending what others had torn. She guided her people to do the same, and watched in wonder as they did.

In the nights when she brushed her hair, she felt the smallest rise of a bump along her right temple—and its twin along her left. Her calloused fingers did not linger and she dared not look, could only trust in the promise that once her heart's beat and her lung's breath had been given, she would know the way by the curve of a flaxen antler.

ONE WITH THE GROUND

GUILLERMO G. MENDOZA

Originally published by *Reckoning Magazine*

Guillermo G. Mendoza is a Mexican writer from Orizaba, Mexico, though he currently lives in San Andrés Cholula. He's also both a creative writing teacher and a literary researcher. His short fiction has been published in *Bioluminescent: A Lunarpunk Anthology* and *Reckoning 8,* as well as in Mexican anthologies.

I PRAYED A MANDA, YOU KNOW? BEFORE THE NECKLACE, before everything. I asked la Virgencita for help with Abuelito's land, and I offered to act as her in the Via Crucis procession. But I got to be Jesus. Kinda.

That day Mamá didn't wanna leave me alone with the company's trocas roaming town. Not after the threat. She thought of calling her boss at the maquila and asking for a couple days off, but she went in the end. "I'll be fine, Mami, don't worry," I told her at the bus stop, pale sunrise above us. We kissed each other goodbye like any other day. No idea we'd never meet again. At least not in person, because next Sunday she didn't come back.

They asked her to work extra over the weekend. She returned after it was all over.

I drank a couple cups of coffee for breakfast. I needed them. The trucks rattled over the dirt track around the house all night long. They did that on purpose, to snatch away our sleep. To wear us down so we'd sell them Abuelito's land. But we wouldn't. Soon they left anyway, so I put on your Cruz Azul hoodie and got to work. I'd used it since you left. It reminded me you were in el norte, looking after us. It smelled of you at first, but that soon faded off. Still, I wore it to feel you close, and that day I needed you with me.

I cleaned Abuelito's room, and that's when I found it. I'd put it off for weeks because I always wept as soon as I walked in. Couldn't take he was gone. But you were about to come back to help us with the lawsuit, and where would you and Norma and Juanito sleep? So I cleaned the mess up and swept and mopped, flooded in tears. Every sway chlorinated my heart, washed away my grief. I took his things one by one, caressed them. And I found it, below a pile of crumbing pics: Abuela Tonantzin's necklace, a small Tree of Life shaped out of clay. You must remember it: She wears it in every photo, around her neck. I held it, palm open. Its weight was like a mountain. It kinda felt alive in my hand, like I held a lizard or something. Took a pic of it and texted Ma: "Look what sprung up!" I expected a voicemail, an old anecdote for an answer, but you know . . . . They don't want her on the phone while at work. She texted back next day: "Mamá Tona's necklace . . . . It's an amulet, mija. Keep it. It will protect you." And I did. Everything else we gave away to the parish.

I WENT BACK to church after school. The parish managed to get a drama teacher to come from the city in the afternoons, to help the youth group mount the Via Crucis' procession. I'd signed up, so I walked through the atrium, past the teocotes' dancing shade, all the way to the utility room in the back. I could see them through the window warming up already, so I hurried.

The teacher set a new challenge: to improvise a scene with stuff we had in our pocket. No dialogue, no partner, just me and whatever I carried. And all I had was the necklace. So when my turn came I stepped forward. The teacher applauded: my time was on. I held the Tree of Life in my hands as if it was a wounded bird. She clapped again, and the drama crew too. The bird became a baby—your son Juanito, my little nephew. I cuddled him, took him to my breast and sang a lullaby. Another round of applause. I found myself swaying Abuelito's ashes, eyes wet. They cheered one last time. His ashes became a ceiba seed. I kneeled and planted it on the ground. I watered it with my tears. Then I rose with closed eyes, unfolding my arms towards the ceiling, and pictured in my mind a tree rushing out of the seed.

And it did. The ceiba snapped into the room. Like a dream, only it wasn't. The teacher and the drama crew saw it too. The world stilled, a silence. Then flickers of awe. A few went to their knees and prayed. Word spread right away.

All night I looked for an explanation. I even went back next morning before school, to see if all that about a tree sprouting out of my imagination was real. Guess what? It was still there, tiles broken by the roots, branches so high they reached the ceiling, surrounded by a crowd of rezanderas who murmured and counted beads in their rosaries. It was fully grown, bark like a lizard's skin roughed and thorned, branches hanging low like arms extended towards the praying women. And hanging in one of the lower branches, as if the ceiba lifted it from the ground,

Abuela Tonantzin's necklace. With all the rush, I'd left it behind the day before. I wonder how no one else found it. Anyway, I took it back.

"CIPACTLI, what are your thoughts on this?"

It was the Social Studies teacher, the same one you took class with. You know him: Che Guevara shirts every single day, zapatista cap he never takes off. I snapped out of my daydream.

"Que qué, teacher?"

"What do you think about the ejidos expropriation in 1990? San Miguel Ototipac lost half its common land so the state government could build the capital's beltway. I was just talking about it."

The teacher always liked talking politics with tangled words. And I knew the kind of answers he liked to hear. You know I was always good with words. Always the one asked to recite poems on Mother's Day, to pledge allegiance to the flag out loud for the whole school to follow. But that morning I couldn't deliver. My tongue knit into a hank and all I could do was stare out the window, beyond the soccer court and the cornfields, towards Abuelo Juan's plot.

The teacher waited.

I spat out: "That it sucked."

I don't know why I then took my hand to Abuela Tonantzin's necklace and knew what to do.

I WENT STRAIGHT to don Ramiro's wasteland when class was over. It was dry from years of chemical fertilizers. It was the perfect place to try. I set the necklace on the ground, closed my eyes, and imagined a garden growing. When I opened them it was like one of those documentaries the biology teacher used to play, remember? Like one of those scenes where you can see months go by in few seconds. A grove sprouted in the dead land. And when I picked the necklace up, it didn't vanish either.

Don Ramiro went crazy. He went to church to thank la Virgencita for the miracle, he even turned down his land's sale. The company even sent its 'security personnel' after him, to 'negotiate.' But by then the ceiba was the hottest news, and when the news broke about his wasteland turned to grove overnight, the whole town went crazy too. So everyone was at the church, even people from nearby towns. The padre came from the city even though it wasn't Sunday, just to see if what he'd heard on the phone was true. There was such a big crowd in town that nobody feared the company's thugs, despite them showing off their guns. Rumor went around about building a chapel at don Ramiro's and asking the bishop to come declare it holy ground. The miracles of the ceiba and don Ramiro's land were all you could hear.

But in the meanwhile, there was something else going on at Abuelo Juan's: they'd finished the wall and raised a signboard saying, "Gaia's Grove: Your Own Ecological Paradise." They'd already flattened it to build. So I went there that very night. Had to dodge the trucks, but in the end I snuck in.

You would've cried too. Remember the cazahuite tree in the corner, where the swallows nested? And the medlar we climbed as kids? Gone. All of it was. El tecorral where the lizards sunbathed, the knoll the mushrooms crawled over after it rained, the shack where the cacomixtles hid . . . all gone. An eerie extent of flattened sand was all their ghastly lamps displayed. And the concrete wall, all around. Abuelo Juan's beloved terreno split up into lots, ready to be built upon.

I looked towards the guard's cabin: the window flashed blue. He had the TV on. I walked to the middle of the plot, put the necklace on the ground, and let my imagination fly.

Saplings came out of the ground.

WE DIDN'T MEET Abuelita Tonantzin, you and I. We just had family pics to know her by. So I always asked Abuelo Juan about her. "Abuelito, how was she like?"

"She was a very wise woman, mijita, very good with plants," he'd say first, and then carry on about her life. That's how I know who she was, what she did. She helped pretty much everyone in town when in childbirth. She healed those in need. Just for the sake of helping them, never a charge, all with herbs, stones and prayer, like una curandera from legend.

Abuelito really missed her. I felt it in his voice every time he talked about her. But he never got sad, al revés: joy sprang in him. One day I asked him why. "Es que she's still right here, with me, with us, mija. She never leaves." We were in his terreno, foraging mushrooms, and I thought he meant it as a metaphor or something. Pero no.

THE REAL ESTATE company brought back the machines to clear the copse of trees grown overnight. Meanwhile, people crowded outside the wall; it was the third 'miracle' in less than a week. The night guard swore he'd seen it all: vegetation grew out of nowhere, trees reached heights of decades in seconds, long-gone herbs from the time of our abuelas sprouted por montones, buds exploded into flowers like fireworks made of petals. He told it all, then resigned and left for Juquila in pilgrimage. I still don't know how he didn't see me standing there in the middle of everything. But only the guys from drama knew who did the magic, the miracle or whatever. Oh, some of them talked all right. About the girl with the Tree of Life amulet. But nobody heard them. I guess people chose to believe in la Virgencita.

Didn't matter at first. The company flattened it all again. They were eager to build, because that proved they owned our land already despite the lawsuit. But I would use the necklace again. I'd perform its magic, because the land was our abuelitos' and they were trying to take it from us. Like they'd done before with other families, and even with the community ejidos on the slopes of the hill. Back then, not long ago really, they leveraged our poverty and misunderstandings and took advantage of the government's corrupción to change the land use permit. Then they crammed our town with armed men in trocas and also harnessed our fear. And now Abuelo Juan was gone, and they tried to steal his land from us. Su tierra which he cared for all his life. But I wouldn't let them.

So I went back that night. People were camped outside the plot's main gate already, Guadalupanos trying to witness the miracle. I went around them and followed the wall, looking for a spot dark enough to jump out of sight. And I found it, right in a corner. An ahuehuete grew tall next to the creek, and its shade made the wall pitch black. It was like they read my mind, the guys from drama: they were there, waiting for me in the dark. With their help, everything was easier, and soon we were inside. The new guard must've been in the toilet or something, because he was nowhere around. So I set the necklace on the land once again, in the middle of the plot, and I imagined something vaster than before.

And a thick wood emerged.

I WAS late for school the next day. One of the real estate company's trocas camped outside our home after sunrise. I thought they wouldn't dare to break in, not with the whole town roused by the miracles. Still, I waited long after they were gone. When I went out, I saw the message scratched over the gate, saying they would fuck me up if I didn't stop. I tried to calm myself down. "They won't do it, Cipactli, they wouldn't," I kept telling myself. But my body shook all the way to school, and any rattle of a wheel over the dirt made me jump out of the road and hide.

I went back anyway. That night and the next and the next. Their threats didn't stop, pero neither did I. I couldn't stop and leave our Abuelito's land for them to snatch. And they already knew it was me, así que I just slept over at the parish for safety. It stood open now twenty-four hours, as pilgrims arrived from neighboring towns for a chance to watch the miracle. The real estate company brought more and more men and guns to keep the crowd outside the wall. Jumping over it got harder, but the drama crew kept showing up, and every time we managed to get in unseen. Each dawn, thick woods covered the plot. And by night it was chopped down again.

I started falling asleep in class. I wouldn't last much longer, but I thought the company had to give up soon, because the bishop declared Abuelo's terreno holy ground a couple days after it all began. Some parishioners were even at the capital, lobbying for the realtor to give it back to the community. They wanted to build a sanctuary for la Virgencita there. But there was also the money: how much had the company spent already? They couldn't rent all those dozers and steamrollers much longer. They had to step back, someday. Those were my thoughts that last time, as I climbed over the wall with the help of a couple guys from drama.

I jumped over and looked at the guard's cabin. He was nowhere to be seen. Outside the wall, no prayers were sung, no murmurs sounded like the nights before. Somehow I didn't find that odd. I walked towards the center of the plot, under the ghastly light of the lamps. I put the necklace on the ground, then heard the shouts from my companions. Warnings. All too late: something pierced my back.

I DIDN'T KNOW where I was. I felt neither cold nor hot. All was dark. Something pressed on me from everywhere, and I couldn't move. Or rather, I had no body to move. It went on like that for who knows how long. Then the whispers came. Like rustling sounds, like the hissing of a snake, they called me: "Cipactli . . . Ci . . . pac . . . tli . . . " And somehow, I recognized them. The whispered voices belonged to the medlar, the cazahuite, the teocotes torn apart by the dozers. They were the mushrooms' underground nerves no longer growing, the gophers and worms and lizards buried alive in their furrows by the steamrollers. "Ci . . . pac . . . tli," they whispered in entangled voices. After a while I recognized the human ones among them: nuestras ancestras, elder women, called me. "Cipactli . . . Ci . . . pac . . . tli."

THE OTHER GUYS from drama managed to escape. Me, they left right here in the ditch. The necklace broke in my fist, but I no longer needed it. The voices and I raised the forest night after night. Every morning, there it was: enorme, frondoso. The men running the real estate company chopped it down every time, until we won. They never could understand what happened. Just like they couldn't explain what my remains were doing in the plot.

The drama crew told the convenient version of the story, made it true by repetition: we broke into the plot to watch the miracle. The armed men were there. They grabbed the guys, molested me. I defended myself and got beaten down. My friends struggled to protect me. Shots got fired. They managed to escape; I didn't. And no one saw me again. The company couldn't prove its innocence. What were they gonna say? That a bruja grew a forest over their stolen plot every night?

El pueblo went mad. The whole town camped around the terreno and painted slogans on the wall. They occupied the city hall and closed down the highways. They marched to the capital and took over the office of the real estate company's CEO. It all reached national news, and the federal government had to step in. That's how they found what was left of my human body. But you already saw that, hermano. You were back, and you saw how the company left for good.

The only thing I regret is leaving like that, without saying adiós to Mamá. Identifying my corpse broke her heart. I wish I could tell her I'm not really gone, que estoy aquí. I wish you could hear me whenever you come here, to Abuelo Juan's land. But I know you feel my love in the flowers' scent, in the embracing moisture of the ground and the cool shade of the trees. It is all for you. I like it when you play above me with Juanito, mi sobrinito. I like to hear you all laugh. Still, I wish you could hear me, hermano, like you did when we were kids and I told you bedtime stories. I wish I had my voice again, to speak with human words, to whisper in your ear, "Oye, I'm not gone, they didn't kill me, hermanito, not really." To tell you I live in every patch of this land Abuelo Juan tilled with so much love. To tell you that, like Abuela Tonantzin and the women before her, I became one with the ground.

WE THE PEOPLE EXCLUDING I

OSAHON IZE-IYAMU

Originally published by *Lightspeed Magazine*

Osahon Ize-Iyamu is a Nigerian writer whose work explores the intersection of fear, faith, and the fantastical. He is an alumnus of the Alpha Young Writers workshop, and the Clarion Writer's Workshop. His work has published in magazines such as *The Rumpus, Strange Horizons, Clarkesworld, Reckoning*, and *Lightspeed Magazine.* He is the recipient of a MacDowell fellowship and has spoken about his work at AWP, Story Hour, and Berlin's Climate Culture Festival. You can find him online @osahon4545.

We were in the mines when the world was falling apart. I remember, the earth was cracking and the plants were going limp and the world looked dark blue, less full of life. Everyone tried to group together—Nan, Chim, even old Robert who mostly kept to himself—but even staying as one didn't do much. We were in each other's company, and that was something, but we weren't safe. We needed to be free, out of danger once again so we could laugh again and cry and not feel that endless everlasting tension. The one that sticks to your back and crawls up your breath so that even the ins and out of your stomach, the sighs of your mouth, feel weighted. That one that feels like a nightmare—to end that.

The world wouldn't stop shaking. Down in our mines, babies burst into tears and nobody could do anything to ease their worries. We weren't sure we would survive, so how could we be sure that everything would be okay? That we would return back to normal?

Our leader had a solution.

"This doesn't have to be our lives," he said, and we all looked up, desperate. Our leader sure knew how to pick a crowd, and he did, luring us in with the promise of hope. "This nightmare in front of us—it can go away. It can."

"How?" a woman in the front asked, and her baby burst into a fresh set of tears.

Our leader smiled so bright that the darkness of the collapsing world faded behind the shine of his teeth, the cunning of his sharp whites that were as predatory as a fox's.

"One of us has to disappear."

The crowd broke into whispers of confusion. Disappear? What did it mean to disappear in a world where everyone knew each other—our world so collectivist and grouped together, so interconnected? I could walk down to the ends of the earth and still see my mother, and still see my fathers. They're not bound to one person—they're a fluid group of roles and assignments, constantly changing over time as I grow. What does disappear mean, we the people had to ask.

Our leader had an answer.

He said, "See it like this. Every good solution has a sacrifice. This isn't the end of the world, just a stumble, a gash in the way of a beautiful, peaceful world. But it requires a ritual. I've consulted with the oracles, and one of you has to disappear forever in order to bring this world back to balance. Once that person is separated and isolated from this community, never to be found by anyone from our society again, then the world can be restored."

"So they should die?" someone else inquired, and the world fell back into murmurs.

"No, no," our leader clarified, almost breaking out into half-laugh. We the people were afraid, but he was calm, still as a rock. Everything he said, it was as if he'd prepared for this, had grown confident in the words he'd use to appease us.

"No one has to die. But the person has to vanish, never to be seen again. That is what must be done."

There were disagreements amongst the crowd, but all I could hear was the babies crying. They wailed and cried as we heard a meteor tumble overhead us, breaking up all land on the earth. They yelled as up above, animals limped and bled. The babies continued, and their wailings were nothing but an echo chamber for their pain. Everything was dying but the world could still be new. It could still be pure, for the babies. A world to last longer than their lives. One of us just had to do that.

"It has to be forever?" I asked, and we the people looked at me. All my mothers, all my elders. The murmurs fell to silence. Our leader smiled wild and bright, then draped his hand over me. It was supposed to feel like a gesture, comfort, but I just felt pricked all over.

"Yes. Forever and ever. You can't come back."

The whole crowd looked at me, silent.

So, I thought: for the babies. For the aged soil on which my elders and my family, my long expansive family, used to walk on. For centuries more and more. For earth.

"Alright," I said, and our leader drew me into a hug. His fist dug into my spine. The world raged on, but for a minute, I could hear a baby stop crying.

They took me into a chamber in the mines and grabbed all

the food they could find. Stored rice, pickled meat, fruits. Several aunties—Chika, Esie, Sase—came and brought me a bag full of dongoyaro leaves and black soaps, all the medicine I could need. All I really wanted was the memories. Paintings and smiles with people that I could never see again, not for a lifetime, but when the world is dying the goodbyes have to be quick. Our leader made sure I had my things, and he threw me into one final hug, which felt like fire against my skin.

"I hope you hide well," he spat at me in a forced whisper. "The world depends on it."

I didn't think about him. He didn't feel like warmth or even a factor in this decision, but we the people made a decision, and he was a decision too. He was family, though I had barely seen him in the community until election season, where he was flashing big teeth. Bright teeth. I didn't want to think about him as I walked away from the wreckage. From the burning and screaming and the rage. For the world to be new, I couldn't think. We the people had to survive, had to go on and live and thrive, so I had to be the casualty. I had to be forgotten. I went south.

I RAN past a desert plagued with falling meteors and crawled through six burning cities just to be forgotten. I trekked through a river full of drought and fought thorny bushes to ensure that my name was never said, to keep the future of our world. I thought of my elders and home with each place I ventured, how none of these places could replicate the playfulness of children or the tastiness of food that was cooked over a spit. Nothing would be the same and nothing would ever make me feel that happiness, that love that home builds. But the babies would, so I remembered, and then I continued on.

I never was happy in my forgotten state, but I made peace

with this new existence. The world, though temperamental still, had started to rage less, which meant my sacrifices were working. The cities had fewer meteors. The animals could walk without being killed. The forests no longer burned so brightly, although the grounds still screamed; but I could eventually settle in the low woods and make camp. And I knew how to hunt. With time, I had made spears and bear traps that were so lethal that predators wouldn't dare come close to me, so I was content.

But this didn't last for long. Our leader found me in a thicket one night when I was preparing my camp for rest. He came sly and smooth, out of the bushes.

"I see you've made a home for yourself," he said, smiling so wide I felt his gaze gut my chest. I felt *exposed*; I thought I was doing the best to hide my existence.

"How did you—?" I demanded, but I choked on my words.

"It was quite easy, let me tell you. Or did you think it would be difficult?" Our leader laughed. He masked being nice, but all I could truly feel was his cold stare, piercing me till I broke. "You leave trails everywhere you go. There's a path of your scent and your demolished homes in every place you move from. The people could easily notice you if they eventually leave the mines, and they shouldn't be able to, should they?" He shook his head, as though he was disappointed.

I didn't know what to say, so I just shook and stuttered, before I fell to the ground.

"I'm really trying," I screamed. "I'm doing the best that I can. But this is so difficult, and I can't live my life hiding my paths, covering my—"

He cut me off. "But is that not what you agreed to?"

Our leader grabbed my chin and pressed my face into the dirt. He suffocated me in the boiling hot ground, and all I could taste was *death death death*, the bodies of the people who had lived on this world before. I saw it clearly, what had happened to them, how the world's destruction had torn them to pieces, what *he* had done to them. When he raised me out of the ground, I screamed. My face felt half burnt. I could see the daggers on his fingernails and a fox-skull in place of his face.

He smiled again, but this time there was no loving kindness, only pure disgust. "I did say hide well. Consider this a warning. The next time I tell you to disappear and I find you, you will join the leagues of those buried once before."

I got up from the forest floor, shaken. Then he growled at me and I scrambled away as fast I could, taking none of my goods. I ran as fast as the empty oceans, as fast as my ancestors, as fast as all the embarrassment that was rushing through my veins. I ran past my anger and past my shame, my shame that I had been taken away from home, my shame that I had been deceived into not existing. I ran so long that there was nothing left but that misery, that guilt. And fear, haunting me, threatening to never let me go.

I DIDN'T KNOW what the Fox Man had done to the earth or those bodies that were underneath the soil, but I had to keep on running. I had to keep going, to live life away from him his evil. So I trekked till I was out of the forest and I entered into the South of earth, all the way into the giant's world. Everything in the giant's world was many times larger than the world of the North, so the river drew down like a flood and the trees went up to the sky like an infinite ladder. The giants didn't believe in staying underground when the world was rocky, so they made houses out of hard slabs that were meant to persist the tempered nature of the sky. Their world was strange, dreary compared to the little trees and life my family was comfortable with, but the discomfort made me more relaxed. Maybe here, I thought, nobody would find me. Maybe here, I believed, I could exist in peace.

But it wasn't that easy. The Fox's face was plastered on all of the stone in of the giant's world, captured with a sense of admiration. He was a big man here, I learned, the further I went, and he was campaigning for an election, just like he did in our world. He looked different than how he'd presented in our mines: more intimidating. His height matched the length of the giants, but his stare was still the same. The wide eyes, the angular nose, those sharp, bright teeth, they screamed at me. It was him. I felt it in my chest like an arrow shot with warning.

The Fox Man, I decided, was a shapeshifter who could move into any world and pretend to be a native. How else could he slip between communities without any kind of questioning? He was playing a long game, trying to take over community, but I still didn't know what he was. Was he death, some ancient spirit? How did he know what the oracles required to stop the world from ending? Why did someone have to be sacrificed? Who was Mr. Fox but a great deceiver, a trickster? What exactly did he want from us?

All I knew was that every fox needs cunning, their precious silver to chase, and so I ran as fast I could until each day went dark.

Eventually, I started moving with a small team of nomad giants who trekked across the endless world day and night. They were quiet and humble people, and they walked the land without a word or a story to tell. I followed them past deserts and shriveled bushes, past ancient disasters, lamenting to them of how I got here, and they listened to me. They became my new family, my fluid group of people. The only requirement they had was that I did not bring them stress, so I tried to be as little of a burden as possible.

We set up camp in a low forest one night while it was getting dark. We were halfway out of the giant's land, approaching a city that had been submerged in water since the disasters, and it was the first time since we started walking that the giants had taken a rest. I was anxious, paranoid, as the last time I had made roots on the soil the Fox Man had found me. I turned in my bed, restless and unsure.

My dreams were fitful. He was at my tail again, and this time he was faster. I ran quicker than lightening, swifter than hands open wide, but the Fox Man was still faster than all those expected. He grabbed me from where I stood and opened his jaw so wide it devoured me. All I could see after that was his teeth, flashing bright, reflecting the image of my corpse.

I woke up screaming. The giants rustled in their tents at the sound of my voice, clearly disturbed, but only one woke up and faced me with a furrowed brow. It was Alek, who I talked to the most when we travelled, whose curly beard and round face gave me a certain kind of longing. I wanted to be him: strong, above all the world's problems. I wanted to be more intimidating than anything that could destroy me.

I bowed in apology: I knew my presence was already causing them stress. I didn't want to be a burden, but my trauma was so predatory it enveloped the entirety of my being. I was not functioning as a human being anymore; I was the remnants and the leftovers. I could feel the Fox's marks in my skin slowly removing me from this earth.

"Come close," Alek said, and I flinched in surprise at the words spoken. He was being kind to me after I broke one of their sacred rules, so I didn't know what to say. I sat by his side, facing his hairy stature. Alex looked straight into the moon that lit up the blue sky. "You know, we knew your story before you started journeying with us," he said.

I stopped thinking. I scrunched up my face, not knowing what to say, but he prevented me from attempting to speak. "We always notice the pain on someone's face when they've been running. We've seen it before. I'm sure by now you should know that the running is endless, but what you may not know is that you are not the first to walk this path, and there have been many before you. Many who tried to walk with us. Who followed this same direction. He still caught them."

My trauma returned in instinct. I wanted to pack my things, *run*, but Alek stilled me. His furrowed brows softened in the moonlight.

"Let me tell you, there have been some clever ones. There have been ones who made him search for years, who'd resisted him at every step. There have been ones who remolded their identity just to escape. There was even one who he never found, who we thought had escaped him for all eternity. I hoped so badly that she would make it, that she would send us a post bird one day saying she was somewhere safe. But she also never stopped running, and the last note she received to us was the final letter."

I choked on my words. "You don't mean—"

The giant looked away. "She ended it. She couldn't stop, couldn't pause for one minute because he was always one step ahead of her, ready to grab her. The only option was to prevent him from getting her first, stop his attack. She sent us well wishes, but that made me realize that there's no point in all this. He is going to get you. And he will not stop until he does."

I thought of the babies, their crying in the underground mines. I thought of the wails, how I just wanted a future for generations below me, the ones younger than me. I remembered the reason then for my sacrifice, but was it enough?

"But he told me that if I don't leave our land, the whole world would continue to be destroyed. I've been running because I want to protect my family, protect this beautiful world that I've seen. But I don't know what he might have said to the ones before to make them run, or if any of his words are true at this point."

Alek thought to himself for moments upon moments. Then he put his head into his hands. "I wish I knew. I'm lost as well. It seems like he gives different stories to all those who he makes run, tales that vary by incident. Everyone who journeyed with us was running because they were trying to avoid a tragic fate or a curse that he promised would occur if they didn't disappear. And it is true that the world is better these days than it was before, so I cannot say for sure that the world will end if you return to your family, if you resist. But what I can tell you after all these people is that the running does not work. I can't stand to see it anymore. Sometimes the bravest thing you can do is to fight exclusion. And sometimes you have to realize when it's best to go back, to avoid sacrifice. Because it is only when we are alone that we are overpowered. The isolation makes it harder to fight."

The words slapped into the essence of my soul like a hard weight. I never wanted to live this way, lost and traumatized, and I had been unknowingly forced into this suffering. But I had made this pain, this endless running from place to place with no roots my life, and I didn't want it anymore. I nodded and held the giant's arms, trembling, on the edge of tears. He held me the whole time, comforting me like a father.

"Can I ask you something?" I responded after I had gathered myself. I didn't wait for my new father to nod. "If you knew about what the Fox Man was doing to us, why didn't you expose him all the other times people told you about him? Why didn't you stop him? We can't let this go on."

Alek sighed again. "You cannot do much to someone who constantly changes, whose appearance is temporary and limited. We did try to expose him for all he was doing once, but that didn't do anything—he just shifts and everytime he does, we forget who he was. The people who seem to remember his true face are the ones he chases."

I nodded slowly, accepting this information. My giant fell asleep soon after, but he kept watch over me—I could tell he did not sleep in full. I savored the kindness, his protection, but I never wanted to be a burden. Come morning I was off again and far away from his comfort, back into the world unknown.

If a Fox is as fast as his cunning, I had to be his trickster.

I had to work quickly to strategize around his pattern. I ran every day, fast through the South and its giant world. I left my marks in the screaming soil, going past all of the giants' districts in my effort to flee. I had to move away from him, but if I wanted to get anywhere before the Fox, I could no longer take the main roads—I went West.

A trickster Fox is nothing if not sly, so I had to get him off my scent. I didn't sleep in any place for long, but when I did, it was to leave false clues that I was there, to ruin him.

But I knew that was just a temporary fix. I had grown to know the smell of burning bodies that signified he was close, so I knew he was drawing near. His bright teeth flashed closer to me in my dreams, predatory, ready for the final devouring. I created a spear from two sticks from the tallest trees and prepared myself for his attack.

He came one night out of the bushes, unexpected, as I was about to reach the submerged city and move on to my next destination. I had hoped that the rising sea levels of the Western world would slow down the Fox Man, as I knew his animal hated the water, but he still moved as quick as always, only with more agitation. He approached me with that nasty grin, his bright smile so delighted at the thought of reaching his final catch.

"Well, isn't this disappointing," he said. He savored every moment, shaking his head and tutting in fake disheartenment. I could see the edges of his bright teeth, jaws open wide, letting me into the darkness of his inner mouth. I had to act fast. I was still shaken, but I couldn't be ashamed.

I lunged for him with my spear and aimed for his throat.

The Fox Man was faster than me, and so he dodged my parry as if it were effortless. He circled behind me and reached for my spear like I was a messy baby. I made several attempts to grab it back from him, to best him, but he blocked my movements and hit me at every turn. I angled myself away from him, seeking an exit, but before I could run the Fox swiped me with his dagger claws and I fell to the ground.

I could hear the rustling underneath the ground, the chaos. My head felt hot, and I was already imagining flames spreading across my face. The Fox looked down and pressed his mouth close to me, speaking so low it was a whisper.

"I did warn you, didn't I? But you simply weren't good enough. Nobody's ever good enough, and that's the sad part. You should know, though: I like my meals burnt and blackened, but don't worry. I'll leave your bones for the soil so perhaps someone can know where you went."

The Fox Man pressed my eyes into the soil, and the burning immediately overtook me. I could hear the ground in all its char, the cold that existed inside a burn, the delirium that existed long after the pain. Death was in every part of me now, in the deep roots of my flesh, calling. His giant Fox head and dagger mouth appeared for the final time, through the soil, teeth wide and ready to devour. He opened his mouth, and in his tongue I could see the spirits of *death death death*, the souls of those who had long passed before him.

But it didn't look like they were finished.

I could see them in my hazed state, buzzing underneath the ground, rumbling, wailing, demanding. Their bones were shaking, aching for some kind of tempest. They wanted reckoning. They wanted justice. Their souls were still running, running like *me*, but this time it was not away from the Fox. They wanted to run *to* him, to come against him, to finally stop the fleeing. The escaping.

I felt it in my spirit—a sort of ancestral kinship with them, that thread of familial connection. Like my mothers, like my giant family. But the spirits were different. These were people who understood the pressure of a life lived in the sacrifice of preserving everyone else, and what does that to you, and how that harms you. So they floated around me in the burnt soil, and I held space with them, breathing in their consciousness.

I took in their rage, and *lived.* I lived.

I reached out to the spirits and called them from the ground, one by one. The ones who couldn't fight, who got caught immediately. The ones who believed him, who thought he was their leader, their friend. The ones who made him search for years, who resisted him at every step. The ones who remolded their identity, who rebuilt their lives, just to escape. The one who almost escaped him, who did everything she could to survive. They rose with me out of the soil, past the burning, and we stood up to face our adversary. The Fox Man eyed us from all angles, eyes wide with surprise, smile gone. His teeth curved into a snarl.

"What do you think you're doing? You're supposed to be dead. You're meant to

be gone."

The spirits and I stood. "It's enough. It's over."

The Fox Man stared at us before he went back to laughing. His bright teeth flashed once more, and he looked at us as though we were foolish.

"You think it's wise to stop this? Go ahead! Don't you remember that the world was in chaos before I sent you all to run—there is trouble like you couldn't believe. I am a necessary, ancient force, and I am meant to lead, but you all are casualties. So if you want to help everyone and save the world like you promised, then you'll stay dead. You'll stop. Or you'll ruin everything that you've ran for."

The spirits murmured, clearly distressed, and we all felt speechless. The Fox Man had put doubt into us, shame, and so we were full of endless tension. But I thought of the babies again, of how inconsolably they cried in the village mines, of how terrified they were. I thought of my family, of how I wanted to keep them safe and happy, of how hard I tried to preserve everyone that existed in all corners of the world. But I needed to breathe. I needed to be safe.

I thought of myself, ourselves, the spirits, and realized that this wasn't enough.

The sacrifices weren't working, and they never would.

"There's no point," I finally spoke up. I looked at the spirits, and then I stood against the Fox. "Whatever we do, no matter how much we run, it's not going to prevent the world from happening. It's always temporary, a fix, so we'll never be enough. Isn't that the point?"

The Fox's face cracked, growing purple. He tried to protest, argue, but there was no point in believing him. He could not put doubt into our spirits. We didn't let him. We gathered, a united front, bound by unshakeable surety, our existence past the pain, and faced him. No more running, no escaping, no hiding to sacrifice ourselves.

"It's over," we said.

We pressed the Fox's head into the soil and listened as his screams faded into nothing.

THE WORLD WAS FALLING APART AGAIN.

The earth was turning grey and the plants were ashy and the sky, a deep dark blue at midday, turned red at night. The Fox had died, and the world had grown temperamental, into a state ever not still. But it didn't mean that the world had to be chaos. Me and my spirit siblings ran through each land with a bag of supplies, a heart of intention, a hand to help. Two moons ago, we had visited the giant's land and helped them reinforce their huts, keep them stable with new slabs for the windy seasons. We were determined to offset the damage of this world, make it livable, make it last for as long as it could.

Before we embarked on our journey, I had gone back to the village mines to see my old family. They were all still there—Nam, Chim, even old Robert—chatting and cooking food over a spit. Overhead, the world was full with tension, but they were making do, attempting to thrive. To live past the turbulence. I sat with them and shared with them some of my memories, the hard parts of my journey, and we laughed and cried together, felt the hurt over it. But we recovered at the end, grew stronger. That was the necessary part of living.

I remember, I heard the babies wailing again. They burst into tears when they heard the screaming up above, the noise of some disaster so loud it could only mean trouble. And this time I held them in my arms for hours that seemed like infinity, rocking them quietly till they fell asleep. I felt then that the world could still be new for them. The world could last as long as their lives. I could run for them, I could work, I would run to the very ends of the earth just to provide that, but I would not, would not, die.

FATHER TIME DARES YOU TO DREAM

TRAE HAWKINS

Originally published in *New Year, New You: A Speculative Anthology of Reinvention*, edited by Chris Campbell

Trae Hawkins is a writer and dreamer. An editor for *Anathema Magazine* and an alum of Viable Paradise, his fiction has appeared in *Augur Magazine,* the acclaimed *New Year, New You: a Speculative Anthology of Reinvention,* and is upcoming in *Beneath Ceaseless Skies.* He recently graduated with an MFA in creative writing, and in his free time, he enjoys birding, playing video games, or obsessing over mythology. Trae can be found on Instagram @onwa-trae and Bluesky @traewrites.bsky.social.

WELCOME, FRIEND, AND LISTEN CLOSELY! LISTEN WITH AN open heart, for this is the tale of a town, of a boy, of history remade and reimagined. Dream with me, will you? Watch, and allow hope to enfold you.

Here stands the town of New Cairo in all its glory: the descendants of a people forgotten, rebirthed and rebuilt through perseverance. Sitting snugly at the confluence of two great rivers, it is a beacon amongst the wintry land that was Southern Illinois, radiating unique warmth with blazing wooden pillars sprinkled within its fortified walls! Its houses, too, stand strong, their dozens of inhabitants forever intertwined, be it by blood or societal kinship.

Observe—as I have, with roots reaching far into the ground, branches brushing the chilly air—New Cairo as the answer to a humanity-spanning question: *can we exist in peace?* To such a question, the residents of New Cairo might scoff, or perhaps laugh in incredulity, for what form of existence can there be besides peace? Indeed, to consider another way of living... well, doing so would be a great task for the average New Cairene. Understand, friend, that New Cairo has not experienced chaos. A bold claim, one might profess, but a true one, nonetheless.

Perhaps context might shed additional light on New Cairo, beginning with its past, and ending with what may be a luminous, iridescent future.

There stood Cairo, a ghost of a town. Poor and ignored, its population under two thousand and declining every year. Its people were mostly dark of skin—a thing that mattered, before, and determined its inherent value. Enter world wars, nuclear violence, climate emergencies too grand to ignore, and emergency bunkers issued to those deemed worthy of surviving the end of the world. Yes, it was a horrible time, and the people of Cairo—desperate, defeated—dug into the earth and holed up in a makeshift bunker.

And as the world around that tiny town burned and froze, flooded and devoured itself, Cairo endured. (Do not despair; the Earth is resilient, if nothing else. Besides, the world may have devoured itself, but New Cairo is not the only surviving settlement. There are others, though their stories are their own, and this is New Cairo's.) When its residents emerged from the ground, freshly formed and full of hope, reborn into a world where dark skin and empty pockets no longer made them *less than*, its leaders made an executive decision: to leave the world as they knew it behind.

So, they did, and when the oldest of its people died, so too did any knowledge of the twisted world before.

Now, New Cairo is hundreds of years old, boasting a population of fifty thousand. Watch with me, please. Do not be shy; my trees have eyes aplenty, their every leaf spectating in anticipatory pleasure. Watch how the New Cairenes prepare for winter, spreading across the snowy ground like little brown beetles, reinforcing their walls, gathering and storing meats, and quadruple-checking their vegetables for edibility. Look how lovingly they tend to crops, how gently they coax seeds into dirt.

Do you see, there, the sallow-skinned man bending and huffing near the town's center, sweat pouring down his dark face? And do you see how readily others relieve him of his duties, usher him into the warmth of his log cabin home? *This* is New Cairo, where one cares for the next in communal greatness.

Survival, however, is not why New Cairenes live. Look closer, now, at the swaths of paint—made by town alchemists—decorating the surface of every building. Bright and vibrant, the murals plastered onto the homes and hospitals and schools are everchanging; each began as a small thing, gradually growing as each New Cairene added to the illustration of whoever painted before them. And look! Oh, how they dance and chant and beam so widely, honey-roasting pecans gathered in the summer. Listen to their songs, to the birds and wolves singing along.

New Cairo was once a bud, and I swell with pride at having witnessed it watered with communion. Swell with me, will you? Swell as they congregate, smile lines etched onto their cheeks.

Today is a special day, you see. Once the festivities have died down, they march toward the bank of the Ohio River. (That's right, *all* fifty thousand have gathered; remember, New Cairenes care for one another. Those who cannot walk, or have lost the will to, have been assisted. No one would willingly miss this day, after all.)

At the Ohio River, they send off their voyagers, who will travel across the remains of a ravaged country in search of information. Magazine pages, tourist pamphlets, photography albums —such things have impressed upon New Cairo only the most beautiful of the world before, from technological advances to what was modern medicine. And so the voyagers set across the frozen river on muscled horses, hoping to find in the ruins of before the secret to rebuilding the world.

Honesty propels me to say this: New Cairo *is* the rebuilding of the world. What they seek is a misguided portrayal of what *was*, and under no circumstances should they—

Oh.

You see them, don't you? Heads bowed, mouths set in determination. You see them, yet you cannot *feel* them, as I do. They are praying, unified in yearning for knowledge of the world before. Within them burns the hope of a life protected from precarity—of winters survived, sicknesses endured, and lives lived for bountiful decades. Inexplicably, such hope has taken root within myself. I, too, wish for their safety. And although I am only an observer, albeit one with more power than you, perhaps, I—

I am compelled to comply.

Understand this is not an easy thing, nor something my kind might advise. Come, as my leaves shake—not from the cold, I assure you—and my grass blades dance, and every animal wearily watching the New Cairenes scurries in unsettled surprise, for I am bending myself against better judgment.

There. He is young, only sixteen years old, though inside him dwells something unplaceable. Something gleaming, ambitious, and, more importantly, virtuous.

At four, he trundled into a burgeoning snowstorm to rescue a neighbor's cat. At nine, he held onto his sister's hand for seven days and nights, until the grief of their parents' deaths loosened its grip on her. Every week, he teaches children how to merge mind and body, to paint and craft and build. Yesterday, he fell into a dirt ditch, and—contusions blooming purple and oblong on his deep brown skin—spent the evening filling the trench so others might avoid the harm he endured. Do you understand, friend? He *is* New Cairo. He is humanity.

And who am I to deny him the knowledge he seeks? The knowledge sought by the tens of thousands crowding the lake's bank? Follow along, please, as I compile myself—empirically—and press my knowledge into a single flake of snow, so tender and soft and insubstantial, and as the young teen pleads with the sky to protect the voyagers, the flake that is me (and you. *Us*, perhaps) touches upon his dark brow.

We shall call him Josiah. As he inherits the knowledge of a world long gone, he falls writhing to the snow, his mind expanding to accommodate the influx of knowledge. The fastest of New Cairo carry him to town, where he quickly recovers and asks to rest for the remainder of the day. And as everything lulls back into a sense of normalcy—the people outside resume their dancing and sharing of food, and kids build snowpeople, and singers sing proudly, their voices ululating through brisk air—Josiah curls into his bed.

I have given him what he wanted, but... well. It's a bit much. He alone now holds immeasurable knowledge: precise medical formulas, cures for diseases, blueprints for inventions he must first conceptualize as possible. There is happiness in his consumption of the past. Colorful cultures, diverse in a myriad of ways from clothing to music to food to speech bring him comfort. So, too, does he feel warmth spread through his core as he beholds the beauty of fashion in all its facets, of horizons with rising suns, of a drink called 'coffee.' The joys of one hundred and eighteen billion people—indeed, our knowledge extends that far, and even farther, should Josiah wish to probe there—reside within his thin body. The politics of animal kingdoms, the lifecycles of generations of plants—he sees it all. And it is euphoric.

But.

I know. I, too, wish there was no *however* to this ingestion of knowledge. One might think Josiah lucky, for he is alone in his ability to behold such vast amounts of beauty. But, but, but. I am no perfect being, and you can certainly sympathize with this lack of sublimity. To share is to share *everything*, lest we risk disinforming those we seek to preserve. Naturally, then, Josiah has inherited the goods of the world before, along with—

Poor, poor Josiah. Things were so ugly before New Cairo, weren't they?

Although the word 'war' did not exist to him, it makes sense as he chews on its jagged edges. New Cairo is not immune to disagreements, and he has witnessed arguments turn violent. War, to him, is not an inherently evil concept. It is the events that happen during war—lines crossed from reactionary violence to sadistic, psychological, and physical brutality—that open his mind to the concept of *evil*.

Imagine, if you will, Josiah's world held tautly together by threads of logic. Now, watch as our knowledge affects him so. Watch as the horrors of human trafficking, heartless poaching, and greed-driven deforestation unravel those threads of logic. Overwhelming accounts of evil, from the conception of human life to the death of the world as we knew it, break him down, bit by bit. It happens chronologically, though he withstands it all, pushing back against despair, his heart fleeting about, his breaths ragged and piercing. Chattel slavery nearly unmakes him, yet still he holds tight.

It is when he has consumed the knowledge of a small town called Cairo, Illinois—the place that became New Cairo, once bustling with potential, then broken down by lynching militias and prejudiced police—that he truly disappears into himself, made unwhole by it, his world having lost all sense of coherence.

In an attempt to remedy the nausea twisting his stomach, he considers the possibility of hallucination: perhaps he is simply daydreaming about events that never happened! Yet he feels, and therefore knows, that what he has consumed is *history*.

Between bouts of poignant disillusion, however, Josiah determines with relief that none of the evils that governed the past currently affect his home. I have told you, before, that New Cairo has never experienced chaos. This much is true; violence directed toward others for arbitrary traits, mistreatment of animals, lands being stolen and forced from under the feet of those who nourished it into vibrancy... Such concepts do not exist here. Evil does not exist, in New Cairo.

Josiah understands this. But the potential for evil? Surely, it is here, waiting to sink its teeth into every corruptible human. As this thought settles into him, Josiah becomes fearful. Fearful that the evils of the past might soil his mind—if they have not begun doing so, already.

(Worry not. This is not *that* kind of story.)

Let us leave Josiah, for a moment, to wrestle his world back into coherence. Come, and observe New Cairo once more. I fear I may have presented you with a false picture of the bright, bright land. But you see them, don't you? With winter falling over the town, the New Cairenes' work is twofold. See their strained expressions of working toward a goal that not everyone may realize. New Cairenes are a hopeful people—indeed, they understand hope as undergirding all else—but even hope cannot combat the objective truth that no winter passes without death.

Watch them swing axes at trees for firewood. (Please, do not fret! Trees may be my eyes—as are leaves and wind and hail and air itself—but I willingly and painlessly give myself to those in need.) Watch the town alchemists stuff jar after jar with medicinal herbs, knowing their supplies won't make it to spring.

Watch butchers gather to discuss meat stocks, farmers frowning at rotten vegetables. New Cairo exists in perpetual danger. Such danger has pooled their hope into the voyagers, who travel eastward. (I regret to inform you that they will return empty-handed; what was the East Coast is now underwater.)

Yet the New Cairenes hope. See, how thousands of them gather in that tall building? They are praying to the Earth, for they worship Her. She is not me, of course, though She allows me to make use of Her limbs. Time and Earth—our bond is storied and everlasting. My leaves rattle in appreciation.

And—there! Josiah has risen from bed and is now standing outside the building, listening to the humming and thrumming of voices in soft prayer. And he becomes aware of what he can do. It would be simple, to share his knowledge—our knowledge—with his fellow New Cairenes. Not verbally; the information is too vast for simple speech to convey with any sort of sufficiency. But share he can, just by willing his thoughts into the minds of others. That is what I have given him: the power to share.

Silently, though, he trudges from the building and into the forest, where he plants his hands on a tree and attempts to empty himself of what he has learned. You see, he has determined that history is doomed to repeat should he share the past. Every injustice that made the past the chaotic, evil thing it was... Josiah thinks New Cairo is better off without any of that. After all, how might one repeat something they don't know exists?

Unfortunately, the plan fails. Josiah has infused the tree with our knowledge, but it did not transfer out of him, as he'd hoped. (It appears he does not comprehend the specifics of monodimensional fields of space-time omniscience. Curious.) He stumbles away, slouching into a nearby bush. Observe as he scratches at his scalp, at odds with himself. His seeds of knowledge may save New Cairo from the winter-born deaths that occur every year. Yet monstrous weeds may emerge from such seeds, destroying his home with violence and injustices that have not yet affected his community.

A rustle of leaves wakes Josiah from his despair. A girl—a friend's aunt's babysitter's sister, though family, through and through—emerges from the underbrush, chasing a butterfly. Do you see the horror dawning on Josiah's face? The butterfly has landed on the tree he infused with our knowledge, sucking sap from its sticky, dark bark. Josiah considers redirecting the girl. Should she touch the tree, she, too, will be inflicted with the past.

She will become a monster, meticulously crafted by knowledge of the evils of before. How long will it take for her to begin believing in inherent differences between people? How long before she views her values as absolute? She will—

The girl stops before the tree, holding out a hand. The butterfly detaches from the bark and lands on her palm. She coos softly, bending to place it inside a dry log, where it might survive the cold. (It *will* survive—laying hundreds of eggs in that log, many of which will eventually become as beautiful as their mother.)

And despite himself, Josiah laughs.

Yes, he thinks himself ridiculous! He knows New Cairo. It is within him. It *is* him. Oh, how silly he has been. Watch, now, as he approaches the girl, who is startled by his laughter. Watch him guide her to the tree and explain its dangers. He does not hold back; he tells her the great things he has become aware of—holiday celebrations, organizations created to connect those with similar interests, cat cafes! And he tells her the bad—eugenics, land disputes, police brutality.

Yet she is not fazed. See how she places her palm against the tree's rough surface. Listen, as the girl yelps out, elated at the beauty of before, then falls to her knees at the horrors. But look closer! I assure you, you have never seen such a small child wear such fierce determination.

It is with this determination that she and Josiah spend the next several hours weighing their choices, their primary concern to protect the community they have cultivated. They laugh and envision New Cairo's future, so large and glowing and full of joy. And the future Josiah feared—corrupted by evil—seems so small, so unlikely.

When Josiah and the girl return to New Cairo, it is with smiles across their faces. And as they lead all fifty-thousand people into the forest, toward the tree that will be their salvation, they rely not on fear of what may be, but hope of what is to come.

As long as the people of New Cairo—born from the ashes of a crumbling, evil world—understand where they come from and what they stand for, they will fight against devolving into the world of before. They know—as you do, now—that all they need is faith in their ability to reject the cultures that undermined their humanity in the past. Luckily for them, that faith has existed since New Cairo's birth.

Oh, how kind and welcoming their footsteps feel as they march through underbrush and approach the tree! How sweet the chorus sounds as they laugh with nervous optimism! How enthused the animals are, spectating from behind tree trunks or perching in the canopy above! And how proudly I watch, my leaves and branches shaking!

Hold your breath, will you? Just for a moment, while Josiah guides yet another hand onto the tree, tears falling down his cheeks. Hold your breath, as he does, and do not panic. New Cairo has been untouched by chaos, and I suspect that will not change.

There. You may exhale now, with hope tickling your core. Good.

We have hoped, and so it shall be.

BIRDSEED

MATTHEW FREEMAN

Originally published in *Through the Portal: Tales from a Hopeful Dystopia*, eds. Lynne Hutchinson Lee and Nina Munteanu (Exile Editions)

Matt Freeman is a writer, musician, and dog trainer from Idaho, now living on the traditional territories of the hən̓q̓əmin̓əm̓ (Hunquminum) and Sḵwx̱wú7mesh (Squamish) speaking peoples, colonially known as Burnaby, British Columbia. He is working on a collection of stories focused on uncanny interactions between human and nonhuman subjects, attempting to access the haunted, spectral experience of ecological breakdown and the alien regard of the "natural" world. The author encourages absolutely anyone to reach out to him via mtthwfreeman@gmail.com.

NEAR THE END, I BEGAN TO DEVOTE THE BULK OF MY TIME TO what I believed to be a gregarious individual of the species *Corvus brachyrhynchos*—the American Crow. By then a chemical scythe had begun to carve up the clouds hanging over the lands of "Vancouver" in a psychedelic frenzy, and the shocked blue skyline often bled in shades of lime.

Sal, my partner of three decades, worried. About the fervor in which I spent my time, at least. So committed was she to daily life that I'm less certain of her attitude toward the unmaking of the landscape as it happened around us.

"Felicia," she would say to me in her Swedish accent—a voice both sweetly seductive and occasionally comical. "Let us leave the bird alone or it will make a nest of your hair. Come now, come in the bed."

Our home was an extra-large Vancouver Special situated alongside rows upon rows of other neat, plain, suburban domiciles huddled atop a steeply sloping hill. Our orientation afforded a view of the jagged sprawl of the city as it unfolded in all directions, punctuated everywhere with sprigs of strategically planted, non-native greenery.

An empty lot sat at the end of our street, overgrown with yellowing knives of spiky grass. It was assumed that coyotes lived there, though I never saw them.

Initially, I called the crow Angela, plucked from a list of the female names most often chosen by parents in my birth year, 1971. It didn't take me long though, as I got to "know" the bird better, to abandon the name, which felt increasingly patronizing.

It's a psychotic human habit, this naming. A dog will turn its head when you call it, but without even the ability to recognize itself in the mirror, does it regard itself by this same name? Does it regard itself at all? I do not think so.

Instead, as the crow glided down with a whisper to land on

the balustrade, I would simply coo hello, murmur nonsense, or, occasionally, try out a throaty vocalization myself.

I am certain the neighbours loved this, though they never approached me about it.

STILL, even after my epiphany about names, I couldn't abandon the name of my beloved borzoi Talia. I would keep her in the house behind the glass door each time I tried to communicate with the crow from the balcony of my apartment. Shaggy and ancient-looking, Talia watched our conversations from inside with her long snout perched on her paws.

FROM WHERE I waited on the balcony, Sal sometimes had an angle on me from the kitchen window. Occasionally, I could feel her eyes on my shoulders, and I would turn to see her smiling. There was concern behind it, but I think she suspected I had latched onto a new project with what she called my "characteristic intensity." She'd give me a little wave, and I'd wave back and turn my eyes again toward the horizon.

AT FIRST THE bird would stop for a few unsalted peanuts or some mashed scrambled egg on its nightly migrations to Still Creek. Later, as the blanket of black birds papering the evening grew thinner, it came more often.

During our interactions, I became immersed in the bird's regard. I was fascinated with the way it cocked its head. I'd read that the motion gave the bird depth perception with every twitch. Sometimes it would sit with me for over an hour, eating birdseed from my pinched fingers, backdropped by the hiss of the distant streets and the overwrought glass skyline.

One rare sunny spring afternoon, I watched from my perch on the balcony as Sal trimmed the Yoshino cherry. Akebono cherry blossoms clung to the hood of her electric sedan below as she pruned away the sprigs that had failed to bloom.

She looked sturdy and determined on the ladder, her grey, sable hair falling down the curve of her exposed shoulder. She hummed something from Stravinsky.

But as I stared at her, surrounded by imported shrubs with lanky Talia lounging in the ryegrass, I was overcome by a profound sense of estrangement.

I no longer wanted to participate, to be a person. I did not want to move or to look at the yard, so I went inside and sat on the sofa. I could hear the shrill chattering of house sparrows through the windows.

The next day a rain fell that smelled of gasoline, stripping the Akebono's branches of its bruised remaining buds.

Out on the balcony, as I waited nightly for the bird to appear, it grew easy to believe that we would inevitably lose. Or rather, that we, humankind, would win the war we were waging against life. That the Fraser River would shrink and gutter with sludge; that all the corals of the world would expel their life-giving algae and crumble to white sand; that what we thought of as the most noble aspects of our human communities would become further and further diminished, until finally becoming as unrecognizable as the stricken, peeled land.

By then, I hoped, the plants and animals would have changed so that they could finally thrive amid the damage. Sometimes I doubted it.

I won't bore you with how it all came apart. We have had enough exhausted chronicles of the dissolution.

I CANNOT EXPLAIN why I found my interactions with the bird so compelling, other than perhaps that it offered me a space outside my cage of human behavior.

Every day, as the air smelled further of astringent plastics and effluvium and the thick, heavy sky pressed down harder as if to seal me in, my life, to me, grew more fictional. My work-from-home career was relatively stress-free, but ultimately pointless—numbers resettling from one spreadsheet to the next—and the rotating tread of entertainment, online purchases, geopolitical cataclysms, and subsuming panic wore a groove in my mind. Everything seemed to happen elsewhere, in digital space, in echoey department stores and other non-places. The crow's talons clinging steadfast to my knee were more solid in comparison, even when its pale, nictitating membrane peeled back to reveal a remote, black-eyed gaze.

And then, of course, there were the things it said to me.

CORVIDAE CAN PARROT human language using their avian syrinx to mimic sounds they hear. However, these fall far short of the declarations this particular crow made to me. Rarely threatening, but never comforting either, they were complex, and probably a delusional mirroring of my own thoughts. It does not, ultimately, matter.

The crows' words appeared unbidden and vibrated like physical sound passing through the air. Its speech carried the cadence of dreams. It once told me that even after the remaining pockets of bird life had been extinguished, the crows would abide. That they would scrape their talons through the cracked sky, perhaps transformed by adaptations, perhaps the same as ever. That they would roost in halls festering with human skulls.

It told me all this with a wavering voice, pausing to preen its inky wings. And then it nipped its unsalted peanut from my hand and floated away.

SOMETIMES I SUSPECTED that Sal believed me to be "protecting" myself from the surrounding circumstances, insulating myself from the world out there from my spot overlooking the neighborhood.

I found it impossible to explain that I was never at rest there, feeling always that I might attune myself to a more substantial mode of being.

READING everything I could about the American crow did nothing to reveal the specific nature of the creature. It felt the same as walking the flooded banks of Brohm Lake and learning the names of different plant and animal species.

No matter what you do, it's impossible to feel enmeshed with anything you pretend is wild. You walk along the trail. You note the sculpted blade of a leaf, the mud in which the plant grows. You look at the marmorated stink bug gnawing at its trunk. You can even lie down and let the muck seep into your skirt for as long as you like. None of this will make you feel like you're actually a part of that place.

This may be why, late in my attempted communications with

the bird, I mostly stopped leaving the house except to acquire the essentials.

I AM certain Sal's worry must have escalated, but she trusted me. Her fierce ethic of self-sufficiency allowed me the freedom to do as I wished.

Which was, truth be told, not much of anything.

SHE LET me slip away from everything but her.

"I've been reading," I said to her once over a pair of fried eggs on multigrain toast. "Ecologists love scrubbing out the line between humans and what we call 'nature.' But you can't, can you? Can you really commune with the quiet it throws at you?"

"Well," she said, plunging her fork into the arugula, "maybe try communing with your beautiful, aged wife once in one while, then." She smiled at me and stood to leave for the office. But I can tell you, she was trying to understand.

AS THE EVERYDAY wound down and the hours at her work dwindled, she once left early to join me out on the balcony with half a hard-boiled egg.

I taught her to be patient, to wait with the egg white pinched between her thumb and forefinger and her arm leaning on the banister. Our skin was pimpled with goosebumps, both of us underdressed for the uncharacteristically chill evenings of that early summer.

The bird came like always, without hesitation. It snatched

the egg white from Sal's hand as she stifled a squeal of revulsion and delight.

The bead of its eye fixed me with a silent inquiry.

Sal pointed at the bird, clinging there, jittering its head about. "He looks like you," she said, chuckling. "What was his name, again?"

IT NEVER SPOKE in Sal's presence, and I certainly never told her of the visions it shared: the flowering hills absent of human trace, or the swarms of what had once been birds, scattered like stars over the husked city.

AND IF I have reluctantly recounted examples of what the bird told *me*, then what did I tell the bird? I asked questions here and there, but mainly I found myself speaking about my own alienation.

I told it that before I mostly stopped leaving the house, and more specifically the balcony, I liked to take walks around the neighborhood with Talia. We would sit on the bench in the nearby park and stare at the grass dotted with dandelions, and at the clutches of bigleaf maple planted there by who-knows a generation ago.

The maple leaves would shiver in the wind—fresh, but tinged with shifting, pungent odours—and I would begin to shiver, too. Sometimes it would get so I felt I was in a wind tunnel, with the sharp flush of air slicing my sides.

The sensation would inch inward toward my heart until it became so unbearable that I was forced to stand and walk away. My hand gripping Talia's leash would tremble. The skein of grass on either side of the gravel path began to feel like a ghost laid over the Earth.

"But I always ended up thinking," I told the crow, "despite it all: you know my face."

It never indicated even a sliver of surprise.

AFTER I TOLD Sal about these feelings, and of the physical pain I felt when I left our home, she became Talia's primary caregiver. I regretted it, of course, but welcomed the comfort. I wanted nothing more than to hold out a nut or bit of birdseed for the crow.

LYING across from me in bed, Sal would tell me what the city was like now, with its spare storefronts painted over with slurs or clusters of fading flowers; with the tent cities that proliferated along the streets.

"Even with all these people out there now, it is so much quieter than before," Sal said. "With all this stillness, the overgrowth keeps stitching stuff together. It looks wild, like a set from a TV show." She touched my cheek. "But it also smells like a stove with the knob cranked up all of the time."

I nodded.

"What did you do today?" she asked.

I looked at her face, her bone structure, her flickering, green irises, and thought: how lucky I am to share a species with this woman.

"Birdseed," she said when I didn't answer, brushing her fingers through my hair. "Little birdseed."

I hoped she would not cry.

THEN ONE NIGHT, the crow did not arrive.

Traffic, by then, had declined considerably. It seemed no one had anywhere to go.

That first night without the bird, I sat for a long time in the acid breeze. Sal was washing the dishes, and through the kitchen window I could smell the detergent.

I AM certain that by now the bird has died, another victim of the cyanobacteria riding the blooms of teal algae in the cooked waters of the creek.

I am trying not to be sentimental about it, but I am sure you understand that it is difficult.

AFTER SITTING for hours over several evenings without an appearance of the bird I'd foolishly grown to think of as *my companion*, I went inside and closed the balcony door. Feeling hemmed in by every mass-produced thing in our den and eager to get another look at the crescent moon rising in the purple air, I left through the front door without a word to Sal and shuffled down to the empty lot. I found a spot beneath a dead, overgrown ball of cotton lavender and lay down out of view from the road.

I pressed my head into the dirt and breathed in mildew and dust. I closed my eyes and listened to the stalks as they clacked together. I even imagined that I could hear insects skittering across the soil.

When I woke up, Sal was lying there beside me in her pajamas. The night was deep, close, and heated. I could not see a single star in the sky, but I had the distinct sense of them hurtling far above.

I felt Sal looking right at me. “The power went out again,” she said. “Longer this time. I watched you come out here, you know.”

I did not know what to say, so I sat up. I put my hand on her shoulder. It was warm. There came the single yip of a coyote from the far-off road, then silence. I felt hypersensitized, but blind.

I tasted isopropyl on the air. I cocked my head like a crow I once knew: to look, to listen.

I still couldn’t see anything.

THE COLONISTS

JENNIFER HUDAK

Originally published by *Trollbreath Magazine*

Jennifer Hudak is a speculative fiction writer fueled mostly by tea. Her work can be found or is forthcoming in venues such as *The Best American Science Fiction and Fantasy, Strange Horizons, The Sunday Morning Transport,* and *Lady Churchill's Rosebud Wristlet.* She is a Nebula Finalist and a graduate of the Viable Paradise writer's workshop. Originally from Boston, she now lives with her family in Upstate New York where she teaches yoga, knits pocket-sized animals, and misses the ocean.

I've got a story for you. And I'll let you know right now, it's the absolute truth. You're probably gonna think I'm shitting you, but that's okay. I'll tell you anyway, and after you've heard it, maybe you'll change your mind.

It happened last night. I was sitting here, on this very same stool, and down at the end of the bar was the Engineer from Colony Eight.

I didn't believe it either, at first. I figured someone who survived Colony Eight would have had better things to do than toss back shots alone at the station bar. But maybe not. The Inquiry is over, the press have moved on to the next story. Anyone she might have shared a drink with died down there on the planet. And the way she was sitting there—hunched over her glass, staring at nothing, heel kicking against her stool—she looked like someone who's seen some serious shit.

So I bought her a drink. She deserved that much, right? No one from Colony Eight should be drinking alone. I loosened her up with a little small talk until her shoulders relaxed and her mouth softened. And then, once she was several rounds in, I brought it up.

"So. Colony Eight, huh?"

Right away, she hardened again. "I'm not supposed to talk about it."

"So you *were* there." She didn't answer. I slid my chair closer to her, close enough that I could see the tattoos snaking their way out from beneath her sleeves and under her collar. Her type doesn't usually go for that sort of thing, so it surprised me. More to this one than met the eye, is what I'm saying. "Were you friends with that guy, then—what was his name? The one who ended up killing the colony."

"His name was Etan, and he didn't kill the colony." She said it louder than she meant to, and she looked around the bar before whispering, "It wasn't like that. It wasn't his fault."

"Well, that's what they're saying on the feeds."

"The feeds," she said bitterly. "They're just looking for clicks; you know that, right? The truth is, it was a *tragedy*. A tragedy for the colony, yeah, but also for Etan, and for..." She cut off, and started kicking her heel against her stool again, harder this time.

"But you know what? It doesn't matter. People are going to believe what they want to believe. They make up their minds and nothing's going to change them. They don't care about the other side of the story."

I set down my drink—slowly, like I was dealing with a skittish animal. "*I* care," I said. Then I placed my hand on top of hers. She twitched, but she didn't pull away, and that's when I knew I had her.

And sure enough, once she started talking, it was like she'd been waiting her whole life to get this story off her chest.

You have to understand, there was nothing on that planet when we arrived. Nothing. Anything we wanted, we had to build for ourselves. None of it came easy, and the stress could just about kill you if you let it. We all did what we needed to find respite. For Etan, that was Silver.

That's what he called her—Silver—because she didn't have a name, and because it suited her. Like the rest of the Champignon, she sprouted from the ground like a mushroom, delicate and smooth. They start out so small, just soft little caps, gray and brown. So fragile; so easily broken. Even when they're fully grown—nearly human-sized—their flesh tears like tissue. Our ships crushed thousands when we touched down, and thousands more when we started cultivating the land. We didn't know. How could we have known? People step on plants all the time without crying about it.

It wasn't until the Champignon started migrating away from the settlement that we began to suspect they were sentient. There'd be plans to clear-cut a particular area of forest, and before we could uproot a single tree all the Champignon in the vicinity would have already withered to husks, as if they'd anticipated the settlement's expansion. It was beautiful to watch, if you caught it at the right time. Particularly at night, when they all glowed in varying shades of orange and green and blue, and their spores drifted like smoke away from the colony.

Only Etan insisted that the Champignon could actually speak. Only he claimed to understand them. And even he really only talked to Silver.

"It's a mistake to see me as an individual," she told Etan. She didn't speak out loud. It was more like she sent the words up from the soil, into Etan's nerves. But he heard them all the same.

He gazed at her, at the way her skin bioluminesced in the moonlight, and said, "Of course you're an individual. You're my Silver."

She looked back at him without responding. Etan didn't mind her silence. He knew he was right. Silver was unique; how else could he recognize her out of all the Champignon on the planet? The slope of her cap, the precise ecru shade of her flesh. The delicate, almost erotic flutter of her gills.

He trekked out to see her whenever he had a chance. Her cluster grew in virgin land, where the Champignon still covered the ground, and Etan walked carefully to avoid stepping on the young ones. Once he reached Silver's cluster, he'd sit himself down and tell her about the malfunctioning distiller; the infection that had claimed a colonist's left index finger; the dense, wet, root-bound soil that made it so difficult to grow crops. Sometimes a man just needs someone who'll listen to him, and Silver did so—patiently, quietly. It soothed and bolstered him, and afterward, he'd return to the settlement refreshed and eager.

Silver, too, looked forward to their meetings. When Etan was gone, she and her sisters murmured to each other beneath the soil. They were intrigued by the colonists, these beings who were alone and separate from the rest of their kind. Separate, too, from one another, communicating using vocalizations, like the flying and skittering creatures who are born and die too quickly for the Champignon to know.

"How lonely," they agreed, "to be trapped inside one's own membrane. How frightening, to know only what is there in front of you."

Did you catch that?

That's the problem with stories like these, isn't it? Sometimes you forget that you're listening to a teller. That there's a lot they couldn't possibly have seen, that there's no way they could have dipped into all of these heads. And when *you're* the teller, sometimes you even forget whose story it is—I've spun my share of yarns, so I know. But I was drunk, and it niggled at me, and I couldn't let it go. So I asked the Engineer, "How'd you know all that?"

"How did I know what?" she said.

I blinked and tried to focus my thoughts. "What the Champ-whatever-you-call-it were saying to each other? You said only Etan could hear them, and he'd already left. So...?"

She just signaled the bartender to give us another pour. "Do you want to hear the story or not?"

And I did. I wanted to hear the story. Don't you?

So listen.

Etan knew the rest of us thought he was delusional, that the pressure of building a life here on this planet had finally crushed him. We all agreed that the Champignon were sentient, but few of us believed they were *intelligent*. But even beyond that, the Champignon were just...uncanny. The way they grew, for instance. They popped up overnight, you understand. Sometimes it seemed like they emerged behind our backs when we were looking in another direction. They blanketed the ground anywhere there was a bit of moisture.

They even grew out of the bodies of their planet's insects and mammals. You didn't see that part on the feeds, did you? Intellectually, we understood that this was the way the ecosystem worked, but even Etan was taken aback the first time he saw an animal decomposing on the forest floor with Champignon bursting from its head, thin stalks like antennae poking out all over.

"I'm glad I didn't find you in a place like that," Etan told Silver, gesturing at a fungus-prickly corpse. As if his pure, beautiful, soft Silver could ever have emerged from such grotesque ground.

"My cluster has adapted to grow right here, by this tree," Silver responded.

Etan swallowed. "Only this tree?"

"This is where we grow."

Etan, troubled, uncharacteristically lapsed into silence. The colony was expanding rapidly, and Silver's cluster wasn't far enough from the settlement to remain untouched. The land was too valuable; they'd eventually need to clear this tree—all these trees—for crops or shelters or something else. Silver and her sisters would need to move.

That sounds heartless, I know, but really, it wasn't a huge ask. The planet was big enough for all of us, with plenty of resources to go around. And honestly, the Champignon were used to migrating from place to place; that's how they spread so easily. But Etan was all torn up about it. He couldn't stand the idea of Silver migrating away. He loved her. I told you it was a tragedy, didn't I?

The day before the planned excavation of her grove, with the equipment charged and ready, Etan sat on the damp ground next to Silver and told her what he'd come to say. He hadn't asked the colony for permission. He hadn't shared his idea with anyone else. He knew what they'd tell him, and he didn't care. He didn't even care about the rest of the Champignon—they could all migrate off-planet, as far as he was concerned—but he wasn't going to let Silver go. He couldn't bear it.

"Your sisters are going to have to move a bit further away," he told her. "We're going to be clearing out some more vegetation, building some new housing. Maybe even laying down some roads."

Silver most likely already knew this. The Champignon knew all kinds of things they shouldn't know—when a tree had been felled, when the soil had been overturned, when another ship had landed on the opposite side of the planet. But all she said was, "Why?"

"It's why we're here. It's kind of what people do. Increase and multiply." It was supposed to be a joke, but of course Silver didn't understand. He tried again. "More ships will be landing. And eventually, you know, there'll be babies. Whole generations born right here." He blushed and cleared his throat. "Actually, that's kind of why I came to talk to you."

Silver hummed in thought, or maybe in conversation with her sisters. Then she said, "We'll spread our spores tonight, and migrate our cluster further away."

"What? No!" Etan stumbled to his feet. "That's not...I'm saying I'm going to bring you home with me. That way you won't have to, you know, spread anything. You won't have to migrate. You can stay right here."

"We can stay," Silver said. Or maybe it was a question; it was difficult to make out the inflections of the Champignon's speech.

"*You*." Etan pointed a trembling finger at Silver, beautiful and precious, who alone among the Champignon had captured his heart. "I can't keep everyone. But I'm telling you, Silver, *you* can stay."

Silver and her sisters bowed their heads toward each other in silent conference. If they spoke, Etan couldn't hear it.

"Look, the rest of your sisters can do what they want. But I'm not letting you go. You're my Silver. You understand? It's already decided. I'm coming back tonight, and I'm going to bring you home."

After his speech, Etan held his breath. Finally, Silver tilted her cap toward him.

"Tonight," she agreed.

Before returning to the settlement, Etan let his eyes travel down the length of her stalk, where it coyly disappeared into the soil. He'd always been frustrated that some part of her remained hidden from him. But tonight, he thought, breathing in her earthy scent. Tonight, she'd belong entirely to him.

It was full dark when Etan returned with his shovel. The Champignon glowed in varying shades of green and orange, lighting his way to Silver as if she'd told them to, and perhaps she had. When he finally saw her, she was so beautiful he trembled all over. Her cap, shining orange in the moonlight, swelled like ripe fruit. He inched closer, overcome by a desire to stroke her gills. Still holding the shovel with one hand, he reached for her with the other.

"I'll try to be as gentle as I can," he said. "I know how delicate you are."

A tremor beneath the soil, like laughter.

As soon as his hand brushed her smooth flesh, her cap erupted with a small sigh and released glittering spores into the air. Etan gasped in shock, and felt spores tickling the back of his throat. He stumbled back, dropping the shovel.

"Silver?"

One by one, her sisters' caps burst as well. Their spores settled around him in a fungal cloud, invading his eyes and ears and nostrils. He coughed and retched, rubbing at his eyes and clawing at his throat.

"We won't migrate," Silver said, swaying gently as she

expelled another dusty cloud, her cap deflating as Etan watched. “We can stay right here.”

“No,” he whispered, but already he could feel the spores burrowing deep into his tissue, weaving themselves through his spine, hijacking his nervous system. Already he was walking back to the colony, bristling with fungus.

“THAT’S...DISTURBING,” I said. “Then what?”

We’d ended up in my cabin, of course. I’d planned a whole song and dance about coming here, but she’d followed me without complaint—without comment, even, as if this was where she always knew things were headed.

“That’s it,” she said. “What more do you want?”

“I just, I don’t get it. How did you get away, when everyone else died down there on the planet? And...” My words were slurred with drink, and I was annoyed that I even cared so much about her story. The whole point was to get her here, wasn’t it? In my cabin, on my bed. And now we were here, but I couldn’t let it go. That’s what a good tale will do to you. “And I still don’t understand how you know everything you just told me. How you know exactly what happened.”

She looked different, away from the lights and noise of the bar. Here in the dimness of my cabin, sitting cross-legged on my bed, it looked like she emitted her own kind of light: a soft, blue glow. The tattoo that reached out from beneath her collar was a vivid green, and it looked longer, somehow. Like it had been snaking up her neck while she’d been talking. “Didn’t you listen to the story? We know lots of things we shouldn’t.” I could feel her voice inside me, her words snaking through my arteries like filaments. Like thousands of voices speaking together. She smiled then, for the first time that night. It was the strangest smile, like it had just popped up out of nowhere. Like she’d become a different person when my back was turned. Something was sticking out of her hair, like tiny antennae.

No. Like mushrooms.

I jerked back from her, but it was already too late. The mushrooms burst, expelling their spores, and my cabin was so small I can't help but breathe them in.

YOU'RE AFRAID NOW, aren't you? You think you understand. But you don't. You're still stuck in your own perspective, just like Etan was. Just like all of the colonists, trapped inside their own membranes. You thought you knew how this was going to turn out. But I've been trying to tell you, all along: This wasn't ever my story. It wasn't the Engineer's, either, and it wasn't even Etan's.

It was ours.

Ours.

We've decided to migrate, after all.

And the inside of your body is as dark and damp as the forest floor after a rain.

MANGROVE DAUGHTER

E.M. LINDEN

Originally published by *Kaleidotrope*

E.M. Linden is from Aotearoa New Zealand and likes coffee, books, owls, and the sea. Her work has appeared in *Strange Horizons, The Deadlands, PodCastle, The Dark, Flash Fiction Online*, on the *Locus Recommended Reading List,* and many other places. She is online at emlinden.blog or emlinden.bsky.social.

You always return to the mangroves. Even if what happened had not happened, they would be your homecoming. Your transition point. They are both earth and sea, death and flourishing, strangeness and familiarity. You tell me you love them because they are green and smell of salt, mud, life, decay; because the twisted roots and branches are ugly in a way that you find restful; and because this is where your friends live, now.

All this helps.

This—after a year or years abroad, after days in flight or transit, after hours on the road from the city—this is where you breathe in. First you go to the mangroves, and then you come home to me.

And I say, *tell me about your friends.*

Once, you described Peri by her quickness. Mathematics prizes. Netball shots sunk from anywhere on the court. Smoked before the rest of you ever snuck a cigarette. Told her parents about her girlfriend before her older sister could tell them about *hers*, neatly shuffling the burden of expectations like a card-trick. Suspended for getting a tattoo of a mathematical equation like a bracelet around her wrist. You thought it was beautiful, although you didn't understand it.

Or Kura, who won a snowboarding sponsorship when you'd barely graduated high school, even though the mountains were hours away. Winters training during northern summers, summers competing in northern winters. He was the first vegetarian you knew in your tiny, backwater, nineties town. Persuaded your school principal to play both versions of the national anthem in assembly. Every month he got you in detention by cracking you up in class.

Lily was the only one you'd have described as a water person. Hurtful comments, raised voices, anything she didn't want to listen to slid off her like raindrops; she shook them laughing from her hair. Lily swam lengths in the local pool; she kept tropical fish and wore blues and greens, she had a poster of a dolphin on her bedroom wall when the rest of you had moved onto boys, girls, and bands. She dived from the highest diving board before you could even swim; she rescued a boy from a rip when she was only fourteen.

All of them fearless in their own ways. That's what you might have said before. If you were being honest, you might have added that they were all braver than you.

Don't take that the wrong way. I'm glad of it. I'm glad that you're still here.

Because at the mangroves that last night, you were too afraid to join them. The four of you came back from where you'd scattered after high school—university, work, travel_to converge on Lily's family bach. Homing. Retracing. You drove over the bridge, the drowned pewter landscape. Over the flooded fields, where cows waited at the fence lines like stitches for the patchwork squares of water. The firth. The small-big city with its life-and-death hospital, an hour's drive from where you grew up—an hour, you learned when you were eight and plunged off that wall, that your desperate mother could do in forty minutes. The concrete UFO sculpture, stranded by the picnic table. You'd loved that as a child. Fish and chip wrappers escaping from an overfilled bin.

The coast, finally.

In my memory the plains and the coast never match. The plains are always flooded but the coast is spangled by summer light: an overcast sky but a lapis sea; the pōhutukawa blooming like every month is December. What was it like when you last drove there together?

I imagine a night fuelled by junk food, movies, and beer. Then, just before dawn, "Let's go down to the sea," said Lily. I imagine it was Lily. It could have been any of those three, but not you.

"Let's go down there." She didn't say why. But you all knew.

You've tried to explain it to me, since. It was somewhere between a thread and a song. A tug, *here,* you say, motioning to your gut and chest. You were being called.

"It's only the mangroves," you would have said, unwilling to stir. You liked the beach. You liked knowing exactly what the plan was before you set out. At eighteen, you liked the same things you did at eight: your pet rabbit Neo, being home and sleeping-in, friends you knew well, your mum being proud of you. (I was. I am).

You did not like sharp oyster shells underfoot, and crabs and eels and risk. You did not like the rain. You had not outgrown your childish habit of imagining taniwha and crocodiles lurking under the twisted roots, ready to grab. Had never liked the squish of black mud between your toes, or spattering your new board shorts.

Bad reasons, maybe. Insufficient. But yours.

Did you know? Certainly, you all knew *something* would happen. The song rising from the mangroves told you. You had heard the myths.

And you could see it for yourselves. In the predawn, the mangroves spread for miles along the coast, unbounded by their usual limits of houses and farms and beaches. No town lights were visible. No bridge. No traffic. It was silent except for the gentle sound of water and night-birds. A ruru called from where the road should be, though you didn't cross the tarmac like you usually would, when you walked barefooted down from the bach. Had you gone back in time, or forward? Even the stars were different, faint inland and overhead, but distorted and compelling on the horizon above the mangroves. Magnified. Like fishing lures, you told me later. I found this out, drip by drip, over many years.

And from the mangroves came a kind of breathing, but that in itself wasn't unusual.

Your friends kept walking, and you did not.

Now you have a fist of mud-root-saltwater lodged up under your ribs, dragging you back. But your friends? They have the whole of the mangroves. They changed, while you stood on dry land and waited for them.

They left you behind.

But not entirely.

Each year the mangroves grow, encroaching a little more on the lands around them.

Now, if I say, *tell me about your friends,* you describe Peri not by her cigarettes but the constant shifting smell of the mangroves under her skin. When you lean close you can feel its steamy heat. Her eyes are tidal, drawing you in, pushing you away. Birds live in her hair. Her voice contains the swell and fall of water. Kura, mangrove-rooted, tugged by sea. When he strides out of the black mud to stand under the moon, he is stronger than any bridge or town. His heart is an oyster, purifying the water. His eyes are stars like fishing lures. And Lily, who drowns people; who goes beyond; who has silt in her veins; who eats handfuls of crabs, exoskeleton, pincers and all.

Their families and friends think they've gone. You and I know different.

The blood-warm saltwater washes through the mangroves' atria. The heart beats slow, counting not hours but nightfalls, daybreaks, moon phases, tides, seasons.

It scared me, when I learned the truth. First, I thought what everyone thought: teenagers, beers, an ill-fated midnight swim, a traumatised survivor. Then, even when I finally believed you, I misunderstood. I thought you were telling me that your friends had been devoured, or maybe had become monstrous.

No, you said, patiently. *They've become the mangroves.*

You always teach me what I've missed. They keep the land together, you explained. Protect against storm-surges and pollution. Keep the coast from falling away. They shelter life, like once they sheltered you.

We don't talk much anymore. But whenever you're home, you tell me a little more. And, always, you talk about regret. You wish you'd gone with them: jumped down from the boardwalk, walked out through soft-sharp mud and shoots, hand in hand. Waded out to where the mature trees, over centuries, knit together roots and branches, land and water, shadows and light; walked until you were too far to be seen from shore. You tell me your heart went with them. Your longing fills everything between us so that there is no space for anything else.

If only I'd gone too, you say.

You never notice how much this hurts me. It never occurs to

you that if you'd walked into the mangroves, I would have lost you too.

But that's all right. You're my daughter. Maybe that's how it should be, mangroves or no.

And I never tell you what should be obvious: that you are not the person you once were. The mangroves changed you, too, that night. You're just too filled with regret and longing to see it.

If you hadn't changed, I would not have believed your story. The obvious explanation—your friends drowned; you hide your grief behind layers of myth-making—convinced me. But that was before I saw what you had become. The quicksilver movements behind your eyes. The way your hair haloes your head, as if you're suspended in water. The smell of the sea in your room. Once you picked up a half-crushed dead crab, dropped by a gull. You held it in your cupped hands, breathed once, then let it scuttle alive and whole back into a rockpool. And when we walk down the beach together, we leave one normal set of footprints—mine—and one ribbon of tidemark, tiny shells, mangrove shoots, dancing in your footsteps.

So eventually I believed you.

But when you visit the mangroves, in your head, you're still the same person you were that night. Part of you has waited for ten years for your friends to turn back and take you with them. When they visit, maybe they're just as they were on that last night: laughing, legs flecked with black mud, smelling of salt and oxygen. Taller and braver than you. Or maybe they are vaster and stranger and wiser than that, now, when they stride out of the mangroves to see you. Maybe their hair ripples through the whole sky. Maybe their shadows tug the moon, and stars catch in their teeth.

You think you missed out. Lingering on the boardwalk, too frightened to follow. You think you'll always be left on the boardwalk. But you're wrong.

You know what your heart is now? It's not gone. It's the tiny seed that floats to a new life: a pale shoot, two round green leaves, waxy and protective. The mangrove propagule (I looked it up). Cradled within the dark waters of your body. Across oceans.

I don't mean this in a metaphorical sense, like the way you floated in my womb. What I'm talking about is something far less human.

Why else do you think they still come to you, when no one else has seen them for ten years?

You're one of them.

If someone said *tell me about your daughter,* I'd tell them that fear and courage live side by side. That you have always been worthy of other people's secrets. My mangrove daughter, there's a reason you're the only one who ever saw Lily cry, who knew how homesick Kura was on his trips away. In Year Three you scolded the older boys who bullied Peri for her accent, even though your voice shook. It was you who gathered up the snapping dog that was struck by a car, and rushed it to the vet.

There is power in waiting. There's a reason you were chosen to contain the future.

They need you.

You've always been more like them than you know.

So, you float away and return, but one day you'll put down roots. You'll sustain a web of life, joining Kura's branches, Lily's currents, Peri's birds.

Your body will nourish something huge and breathing. It will fill with rich, black, life-giving mud. It will shelter crabs, frogs, and insects. A sanctuary for birds, a nursery for fish. Cicadas will sing through you.

I know you think your humanity is a small price for this, mangrove daughter. And maybe you're right. More and more, I look at the world, and think maybe you're right.

But I will miss you.

ACKNOWLEDGMENTS

Many wonderful people worked together to bring this anthology into the world. A massive thank you to the *ECO24* associate editors and judges, Rebecca Summerling, Guan Un, and Alana Perrin, who were part of every stage of selecting the finalists; to the cover artist Marcela Bolívar and cover designer Mikio Murakami for their stunning work; and to the Apex Book Company team, publisher Jason Sizemore and managing editor Darian Bianco, who helped bring this project to life. And of course to all the authors and editors who wrote, published, and nominated ecofiction in 2024.

And a personal thank you to my husband David, who built us a cabin in the woods and makes sure my life is always filled with nature. He is the reason that so much of the reading for *ECO24* was done sitting beside a pond, surrounded by bird song, visited now and then by passing otters and beavers, and being yelled at by outraged squirrels.

Last, a thank you to every human being who cares for our natural world. You are not alone.

RECOMMENDED READING

"A Cure for Solastalgia" by Em Starrett (*Strange Horizons*)

"A Descending Arctic Excavation of Us" by Sara S. Messenger (*Diabolical Plots*)

"BLIGHT" by Samir Sirk Morató (*Other Worlds* anthology, A Coup of Owls Press)

"Breathing Constellations" by Rich Larson (*Reactor*)

"Hunting for Rain" by Lyndsey Croal (*Solarpunk Creatures* anthology, edited by Christoph Rupprecht, Deborah Cleland, Rajat Chaudhuri, Sarena Ulibarri, Melissa Ingaruca Moreno, and Norie Tamura)

"Root and Thorn and Broken Heart" by Addison Smith (*Bitter Become the Fields: A Horror Anthology*, edited by Victoria Moore, H.V. Patterson and Jes McCutchen)

"Ruminants" by Kay Chronister (*The Dark Magazine*)*

"Sea Walkers" by Eliane Body (*Solarpunk Magazine*)

"Slipstream" by Ash Huang (*Ecotone*)

"Some Have No Shield At All" by Karter Mycroft (*The Off-Season: An Anthology of Coastal New Weird* edited by Marissa van Uden)

"Sonora's Journey" by Kai Holmwood (*Solarpunk Creatures* anthology, edited by Christoph Rupprecht, Deborah Cleland, Rajat Chaudhuri, Sarena Ulibarri, Melissa Ingaruca Moreno, and Norie Tamura)

"Symphony of the World's Roots" by Damian Neri (*The Deadlands*)

"The City and the Styrofoam Sea" by Mar Vincent (*Apparition Lit*)

"The Ecological Impact of Resurrection: a Field Study" by Corey Farrenkopf (*The Deadlands*)

"The Passing" by Semilore Kaji-Hausa (*Lacuna Magazine*)

"Ruminants" was selected as an *ECO24* Finalist but was unavailable at the time of print.

ABOUT THE EDITORS

SERIES EDITOR

Marissa van Uden is a writer and editor who grew up in Aotearoa New Zealand and now lives in Vermont, in a little cabin in the woods overlooking a beaver pond. She is a lifelong nature lover and friend to small creatures. Her editing credits include the award-winning *The Off-Season: An Anthology of Coastal New Weird* and the *Apex Magazine* Strange Microfiction anthologies (*Strange Libations*, *Strange Machines*, and *Strange Locations*). Her own short stories have appeared in *Vastarian Literary Journal*, *Dark Matter Magazine*, and *Small Wonders*, among others. You can find her at @marissavu.bsky.social or marissavu.com.

ASSOCIATE EDITORS

R.L. Summerling (she/her) is a writer living in London, UK and has a particular fondness for all urban wildlife. She loves stories about decaying environments, the survival of nature in unlikely places and unflinching writing that deals with climate catastrophe. Rebecca is the assistant editor at *Seize the Press Magazine* and has fiction in places such as *The Dark*, *ergot.*, *Interzone* and *Year's Best Dark Fantasy and Horror* Volume 5.

Guan Un is an Australian-Chinese writer of speculative fiction based in Sydney. His work has been featured in *LeVar Burton Reads*, *Year's Best Fantasy* Vol 2, *Strange Horizons* and more. He works as a freelance editor and has now read so much ecofic, his eyeballs are growing slightly mossy. You can find him at @thisisguan.bsky.social or guanun.com.

Alana Perrin is originally from Los Angeles but now drifts from city to city across the US, somewhat like a haint. You can find her hiking with her dog or reading with her cat. She is a slush reader for *Apex Magazine*.

CONTENT WARNINGS

"In the Field" by Shelly Jones
death, dying

"The Water Runner" by Eugen Bacon
death of a child, systemic abuse, domestic abuse, mention of suicide

"Ama's Jungle" by K-Ming Chang
mention of domestic abuse, oppression of women

"A Seder in Siberia" by Louis Evans
systemic abuse, mention of violence towards refugees, cancer

"Love, Scotland" by E.M. Faulds
death, violence towards refugees, systemic abuse, racism, homophobic violence, genocide

"Our Best Selves" by Hiron Ennes
body horror, death of an animal

"The Ghost Tenders of Chornobyl" by Nika Murphy
violent death, war, parental rejection (gender identity)

"Swarm X1048 - Ethological Field Report: Canis Lupus Familiaris, '6'" by F.E. Choe
species loss, death of an animal

"Thirteen Ways of Looking at a Blackened Husk of a Planet" by Adeline Wong
species loss, climate grief, mass death

"The Last Library" by Joshua Jones Lofflin
death

"Bodies" by Cat McMahan
industrial abuse of animals, bigotry, death

"Pig House" by Kay Vaindal
violent death, references to abortion, reference to domestic abuse, reference to sexual exploitation of minors, species loss

"The Plasticity of Being" by Renan Bernardo
systemic abuse, effects of famine

"Batter and Pearl" by Steph Kwiatkowski
none

"Parasite's Grief" by Katharine Tyndall
death

"Skittering Within" by Kelsea Yu
pregnancy, childbirth, animal suffering

"To Drive the Cold Winter Away" by E. Catherine Tobler

death of a parent, colonialism

"One with the Ground" by Guillermo G. Mendoza
corporate exploitation, death

"We the People Excluding I" by Osahon Ize-Iyamu
death, violence

"Father Time Dares You to Dream" by Trae Hawkins
none

"Birdseed" by Matthew Freeman
species loss, mention of animal death

"The Colonists" by Jennifer Hudak
colonial violence, body horror

"Mangrove Daughter" by E.M. Linden
none

ABOUT VIOLET LICHEN

Founded in 2024, Violet Lichen Books is the sister imprint of Apex Book Company. Violent Lichen was created by Marissa van Uden to give a home to those dark, literary, weird books that might be a little outside of the norm. The imprint focuses on speculative ecofiction, Weird and New Weird, and moody science fiction with uniquely memorable characters.

Find out more at www.violetlichen.com.